Praise for
TARA TAYLOR QUINN

"One of the skills that has served Quinn best...
has been her ability to explore edgier subjects."
—*Publishers Weekly*

"Tara Taylor Quinn's deeply felt stories
of romance and family will warm your heart."
—*New York Times* bestselling author Jennifer Crusie

Praise for
KAREN ROSE SMITH

"Powerful characterization, balanced emotional moments
and a tense, compelling story line."
—*Romantic Times BOOKclub*

"Karen Rose Smith writes her books with heart, flooding
her words with emotion and demanding a reaction from the
reader. Ms. Smith is a shining star in the romance world."
—*WritersUnlimited.com*

Praise for
INGLATH COOPER

"I most definitely highly recommend *John Riley's Girl* and
award it *RRT*'s highest honor, a Perfect 10. May Ms. Cooper
keep bringing us more of the same caliber."
—*Romance Reviews Today*

"*The Lost Daughter of Pigeon Hollow* by talented
Inglath Cooper is a feel-good book that you will
want to read again and again."
—*CataRomance.com*

Dear Reader,

Spring is on the way, and the Signature Select program offers lots of variety in the reading treats you've come to expect from some of your favorite Harlequin and Silhouette authors.

The second quarter of the year continues the excitement we began in January with a can't-miss drama from Vicki Hinze: *Her Perfect Life*. In it, a female military prisoner regains her freedom only to find that the life she left behind no longer exists. Myrna Mackenzie's *Angel Eyes* gives us the tale of a woman with an unnatural ability to find lost objects and people, and *Confessions of a Party Crasher,* by Holly Jacobs, is a humorous novel about finding happiness—even as an uninvited guest!

Our collections for April, May and June are themed around Mother's Day, matchmaking and time travel. Mothers and daughters are a focus in *From Here to Maternity*, by Tara Taylor Quinn, Karen Rose Smith and Inglath Cooper. You're in for a trio of imaginative time-travel stories by Julie Kenner, Nancy Warren and Jo Leigh in *Perfect Timing*. And a matchmaking New York cabbie is a delightful catalyst to romance in the three stories in *A Fare To Remember* by Vicki Lewis Thompson, Julie Elizabeth Leto and Kate Hoffmann.

Spring also brings three more original sagas to the Signature Select program. *Hot Chocolate on a Cold Day* tells the story of a Coast Guard worker in Michigan who finds herself intrigued by her new downstairs neighbor. Jenna Mills's *Killing Me Softly* features a heroine who returns to the scene of her own death, and *You Made Me Love You* by C.J. Carmichael explores the shattering effects of the death of a charismatic woman on the friends who adored her.

And don't forget, there is original bonus material in every single Signature Select book to give you the inside scoop on the creative process of your favorite authors! Happy reading!

Marsha Zinberg

Marsha Zinberg
Executive Editor
The Signature Select Program

Signature Select™

COLLECTION

Tara
Taylor Quinn

Karen
Rose Smith

&

Inglath
Cooper

From
Here to
Maternity

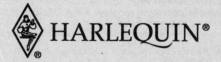

HARLEQUIN®

TORONTO • NEW YORK • LONDON
AMSTERDAM • PARIS • SYDNEY • HAMBURG
STOCKHOLM • ATHENS • TOKYO • MILAN • MADRID
PRAGUE • WARSAW • BUDAPEST • AUCKLAND

ISBN 0-373-83698-8

FROM HERE TO MATERNITY

CONTENTS

Dear Reader,

There are just some stories that are meant to be, and for me, this is one of them.

There are so many special things I could tell you about this story, but there's one that far outshines the rest. *A Second Chance* tells the truth—it's about a new beginning, a meaningful, meant-to-be life that starts after forty. And I don't mean a life of settling for less, but a full, complete life. It's about a love that won't die, a family that should have been—and a new unexpected chance to start that family. Though the characters in this story are fictitious, the experiences are not. Having a baby after forty is highly possible. It's real and it's happening, and happening happily.

And the reason this truth is so special to me is that I was experiencing, through my brother and his wife, the very situation about which I was writing. After giving up hope of having a son, after having surgery to prevent more children, my brother and his wife found themselves expecting a baby at forty-two! I won't forget the morning when my brother phoned to tell me they were on the way to the hospital for one of the recommended prenatal tests. He was so excited; he sounded like he was fourteen instead of over forty. I spent the morning with my character Melanie, waiting for the results. And when I did, I heard, "It's a boy!"

Three weeks after I finished *A Second Chance*, I was sitting in my brother's family room, holding my little nephew, and falling in love again. I changed my first baby-boy diaper—and learned why it's necessary to get the new diaper on before the old one's completely off. I felt alive, energized and hopeful for everything in life waiting ahead, for all of us. And I saw two very happy parents, two people who get up each morning completely aware of how lucky they are, two people who are embracing their second chance.

I wish you all as many chances as you want—for whatever makes you happy.

Tara Taylor Quinn

A SECOND CHANCE
Tara Taylor Quinn

For Scott and Carlene and my dearest baby William. Whatever life holds will be richer because of this new addition to our family. William, you showed us all that miracles are real and happen to everyday people.

CHAPTER ONE

I JUST COULDN'T BELIEVE IT.

Me.

Forty-eight years old. A woman who had gray hair hiding beneath the blond highlights.

A woman whose entire adult life had been shaped, colored and bound by the unplanned pregnancy of my youth, by the giving away of an illegitimate baby girl when I'd been a mere child myself. There I was, looking at not one but three test strips—all delivering the same shocking news.

I was pregnant.

"God, if this is your idea of a joke, your sense of humor needs a serious overhaul," I muttered, sitting at the glass-topped teak desk in my home office, staring at the three slightly wrinkled pregnancy test strips I'd brought in from the bathroom, one a day, for each of the past three days.

The generic music playing from the phone at my ear wasn't affected by my obvious anxiety. Neither was the four-pound toy poodle curled up between me and the arm of my chair.

"This is Dr. Marsh."

"Oh, Lynn, I'm in one hell of a mess."

"Melanie?" My gynecologist of more than twenty years—and sorority sister at the University of Colorado before that—knew it was me on the line because I'd just given my name to her receptionist. I'd practically started to cry, begging her to put the doctor on the phone. "What's wrong? Your hot flashes driving you crazy enough to make you consider hormones?"

I bit back a sharp retort, remembering that this was not Lynn's fault. And that I needed her help.

"I didn't say I *am* a mess, I said I'm *in* a mess."

"Okay, tell me about it. But I've got patients waiting, so make it quick."

Lynn worked longer hours than any doctor I'd ever known. I was lucky she'd taken a minute to speak with me.

"I want to know how a woman who hasn't had a period in months, who's been having hot flashes for over two years, could possibly be pregnant."

"She has unprotected sex with a man when she's ovulating."

All those years of med school and Lynn couldn't come up with anything more original than that? I needed aliens—at the very least.

"How often do test strips lie?"

"About two percent of the time."

"And if there are three of them?"

"There's a pregnancy."

My insides somersaulted and dropped with a thud, leaving me feeling sick and shaky and weak.

"Melanie?" Lynn's voice brought me out of my panicked stupor long enough to focus on those damn test strips again. I was tempted to sweep them off the desk and into the trash. And yet I couldn't. "Did you really do three tests?"

"Yes. One a day for the past three days."

"And they were all positive?"

"Completely," I said sullenly. "Not even a bit of faded color."

"Then we need to get you in here as soon as possible," my doctor said. "You're forty-eight years old, so this won't be easy."

I'd already figured that out.

"How far along do you think you might be?"

"I'm six weeks at ten tonight, give or take half an hour or so for egg and sperm travel time."

I felt dizzy and bowed my head, rubbing it with my hand, hoping that the touch would somehow calm me, reassure me.

If nothing else, it distracted me from my aloneness for a moment.

"You seem pretty certain about that."

"I've had sex once in the past nineteen years." I admitted the sad truth only because, as my gynecologist, Lynn knew I hadn't been sexually active. "I figure that's gotta be the time that did it."

"Okay, well, six weeks gives you a little while to decide what you want to do."

Decide what I want to do? "If there really is a baby, I can't abort it."

"Let's wait and talk about this when I see you," Lynn said briskly. I forgave her because I knew she had other patients to see. "This is the busiest March I've ever had, but I'm going to switch you back to Mary and have her work you in tomorrow. It'll have to be in the morning. I'm in surgery on Thursday afternoons."

I had a quarterly sales meeting in the morning, one that was bringing men and women from all over the country into town. "Okay."

"Melanie." Lynn's voice came over the line just when I was expecting to be driven insane by the background music. "Whatever you decide, it'll be okay."

I wasn't so sure about that. From my perspective, I

couldn't quite see how anything would ever be okay again. At least not for me.

"I'm forty-eight years old, Lynn," I said now, holding tears at bay by sheer force of will, driven by the pride that had carried me through most of my life. "Is it even physically possible for me to go full-term and deliver a healthy baby?"

I had to know.

"Yes." My doctor's pragmatic personality was a blessing at that moment. I actually believed her. "More and more women are waiting until later in life to have children," she continued. "There will be more risks and precautions than if you were twenty, but chances are in your favor."

I nodded, tried to thank her and ended up just hanging on to the phone until Mary came back on the line.

She gave me an appointment for seven-thirty the next morning.

I could still make my sales meeting. Somehow, that made it all a little less frightening.

CHAPTER TWO

"LADIES AND GENTLEMEN, we have a tough act to follow at Vector this next quarter." I walked back and forth in front of the fifty-two regional sales directors seated in the resort-hotel meeting room in Palm Desert, California. "Which is my way of saying you've outdone yourselves. Congratulations!"

Applause resounded throughout the room and I wondered, as I had so many times before, if the dynamic men and women in front of me were genuinely pleased with their production or if the outburst of emotion was really just a manifestation of the relief they felt, knowing their jobs were secure for another three months.

Being in sales was tough. You were only as good as your most recent accomplishment.

Everything looks good. Your blood pressure is perfect, no thyroid concerns and you're healthy.

Yes but I…sag…in places I can see. Am I sagging in…there…too? Will my body be strong enough to hold six pounds of human being in place? Or will the baby hang down to my knees as my breasts are threatening to do?

I suddenly realized I was surrounded by silence—and an uncomfortable sense of expectation. They'd finished applauding and were waiting for me, their leader, to…you know…lead.

"This quarter we signed a three-year windshield

contract with Detroit's biggest manufacturer, a two-year
deal to provide windows to a national builder of custom
homes in upscale retirement resorts and—" my favorite
"—we finally closed a major deal with J. D. Heath…."

Murmurs of approval spread throughout the room. I
paused, making eye contact with as many of my sales
directors as I could. I knew them all personally, had
chosen them all personally. I waited for the goose
bumps, and for that heady feeling of success that accompanied the closure of any big deal. It was the thrill of
the job, the adrenaline rush that kept us all going in a
business that was cutthroat at the very least.

*These next weeks will be critical. I'm not going to kid
you, here, Melanie. Your chances of miscarriage are more
than double what they were the first time you did this.*

Rick Stevens caught my eye and nodded. His hair
was starting to gray, but the color was attractive on him.
Six feet, slim, athletic and with a warm smile that was
as quick as it was sincere, Rick didn't look any older
than the first day I'd met him—just more distinguished.
He'd been the first salesman I'd hired ten years earlier
when I was promoted from Vector's sales force to
manage my own corporate sales team. He and his wife
were two of my favorite people.

"Good work, Melanie," Rick called out.

Yes, well…

I smiled and stepped behind the podium, something
I almost never do, needing to put my hand on my belly.

"It was Rick's account, guys," I said, smiling at the
audience. J. D. Heath built skyscrapers and I'd been
after them for about fifteen years—knowing that Vector
was the best company to supply their millions of pounds
of custom glass walls—and that I could secure another
year of my retirement with that one signature.

I'd worked the deal, put together a package they couldn't refuse, but it had taken Rick's 81 on a par-five championship course right here in Palm Desert to cinch the deal.

Did I mention that I hate golf?

Rick turned around in his chair, one ankle resting on the opposite knee. "All I contributed was a handshake," he told his peers. And that's probably why I liked Rick so much. He was my top producer, gifted at getting people to believe him when he told them he had just what they needed, but he was also honest.

I have to be honest with you. I'd rather you aborted....

No. I shook my head, and stepped out from behind the podium. I wasn't going to listen to those words. Didn't when I was seventeen, and wasn't going to now. No matter how trusted the source of the advice.

"And a year's worth of meetings and phone calls and compromises..." I said to the group. "Which is what I want to talk to you about today. Ladies and gentlemen, we can railroad a lot of people into buying. Once. Maybe twice. But I don't just want food on my table today. I want it there for a lifetime. I want it for each and every one of you. And the way to get that is to sell with what?"

"Integrity," fifty-two voices chorused.

"Right." I stepped down, needing to be among them. I was one of them, nothing more. Always would be. "We need to sell with the customer in mind," I continued, feeling better now that I was in the bosom of my "family." "We need to think about the person, the company— not the wallet. We need to listen to what they *aren't* saying—not for the advantage, not for information we'll use to manipulate them into doing what we want. Not for a sure way to the desired sale. But so we can figure out what they *really* want and need, and find out if there's a way for us to give it to them...."

What do you want, Mel? Do you want to give it up?

I don't know, Denny. No. I don't. At all. This baby is us. Me and you. But how can I keep it? I'm only seventeen. I have another year of high school. So do you. My parents will kick me out. You won't let me near your place with your old man there. We can't raise a baby in a tent. And what about college?

I'll skip college if you want.

I meant for the baby.

"HI, MELANIE, sorry I'm late."

I smiled, astonished, as I was every single time I saw Kylie, that this beautiful, successful, confident brunette with the impeccable skin, stylish clothes and genuine smile was my daughter. Mine and Denny's.

I'd been waiting at the little café on Palm Desert Drive for half an hour. And I didn't care a bit. The Thursday-night crowd had been steady enough to keep me company—and they'd done a lot better job of it than my own thoughts were doing.

"Tough day in court?" I asked. Kylie was an attorney with the county prosecutor's office, chief counsel on juvenile abuse cases.

She nodded, her big brown eyes moist at the corners. "Remember Brian, that five-year-old boy with the cigarette burns?"

My stomach turned over. I wasn't usually queasy, but then, there wasn't anything about me that was usual anymore. Except perhaps that I'd enjoyed the meeting with my sales staff that day. They were all the family I had. Or they had been until a year ago, when I'd been sitting at my home computer one evening winding down with a game of solitaire and heard the familiar ding that announced a new e-mail message. I'd thought it was from one of my newer associates who'd been trying to close his first deal.

Instead, the message was from the daughter I'd given up for adoption thirty-one years before, asking if I would be willing to meet her.

"I remember," I said now.

"The judge gave him back into his mother's custody today."

"You told me when they took Brian from her he had burns all over his legs and hands! How could a judge give him back?"

"The mother claims she had no idea her boyfriend was abusing her kid. She broke up with him."

"Do you believe her?"

Even after only a year, I trusted Kylie's instincts completely.

"He went to school with burns on his extremities," she said now, running a finger lightly along a fold in the white tablecloth. "What kind of mother dresses her five-year-old for school and doesn't see major burns?"

"Maybe she didn't dress him. Maybe she wasn't there."

"Maybe she knew and just didn't do anything about it."

I gazed at this daughter of mine, in awe of what she'd become. "You think she knew?"

"Brian said it wasn't the first time."

"So why would the judge give him back?" It made no sense to me, but then, a year of looking at life from Kylie's perspective had done drastic things to my opinion of the California justice system.

"When I put him on the stand, Brian claimed he'd never said that."

"He wanted to be with his mother."

"Yep." Kylie slipped out of her navy suit jacket, carefully hanging it over the back of her chair. All the other tables in the quaint, eclectically decorated room were filled, yet the atmosphere was intimate, the tables angled to maximize diners' privacy.

I took a sip of water, watching her. Wondering. And then I had to ask. "Do you think being with his mother is better for Brian than being a ward of the state?"

After all, Kylie hadn't had that chance. That choice.

She stopped fidgeting and stared at me, her eyes warm and tender and filled with compassion—reminding me so much of Denny, I ached with memories. "I think the world has many women who are eager to share their love. They're mothers who are capable of loving children who aren't their own, biologically speaking, anyway."

How I hoped so—had spent most of my life hoping so.

"But do you think it's still better for a child to live with disadvantages, if it means he's with his mother?"

"Honestly?"

No. But…I nodded.

"I can't speak for everyone, Melanie. I can only speak for me."

"And?"

"Look at me. I'm thirty-one years old, married to a wonderful man. I have adoptive parents who are as much my parents as any biological parent could have been. My whole life I've felt special, secure, sure I could do anything I set my mind to."

Her words cut into me, hurting horribly. Yet they also soothed my heart, opening it, giving it freedom. Freedom to feel pain.

I'd met her parents shortly after I'd met Kylie and had been invited to their home several times since—I had even spent Christmas Day with them. They were wonderful people and they welcomed me as part of their family. I thanked God every night that my greatest de-sire—to have Kylie safe and happy—had been fulfilled. Still, to know that my daughter hadn't ached for me as I'd ached for her…

"And…" She reached across to cover my hand with hers. "Every day of my life I wondered about you and my father. Every day of my life, a part of me felt incomplete."

Whew. I shriveled up again just a little. But the hurt dissipated enough so that I could pretend I was all right.

"What can I get you two ladies to drink?" The chipper young server finally noticed that my dinner companion had arrived.

I wanted a bottle of wine. Without the glass.

I opted for sparkling water instead.

CHAPTER THREE

WE BOTH ORDERED baked potatoes and house salads with honey mustard dressing. I had no idea whether it was genetics or a crazy coincidence, but my daughter and I had discovered months ago that we had exactly the same taste in food. Out of all my traits she'd got my taste in food—which was boring at best.

Please.... I sent up a silent aside. *With this one still in the barely-a-blip stage, can I put in an order for him or her to have my blue eyes or my athletic body, instead of my penchant for potatoes and crackers?*

I wanted to hear everything that had happened in court in the week since I'd last seen Kylie. I was still in the proud-mama stage—feeling as if every kid she represented was a client of mine, as well. But, hey, while I might have given birth thirty-one years ago, I'd had a child to mother for less than a year.

We were halfway through dinner by the time I was satisfied that I was completely up-to-date. I knew all of Kylie's current clients' stories, the friends she'd had lunch with and I'd heard about the cruise her parents were on. I knew that Sam, Kylie's tall, blond husband of almost ten years, was still encouraged by the early success of his recently launched chiropractic practice.

I told Kylie about my sales meeting.

I couldn't have her thinking her birth mother was a

write-off. She'd feel bad about herself if she thought she came from inferior stock.

Okay, even after a year I was still anxious to have her like me.

My daughter's eyes lit up as I replayed some of today's key scenes—particularly the one during which Rick admitted that the Heath deal was mine.

"An honest salesman," she said, grinning at me with lips that were as generous as her father's. "Who hired that guy?"

"I did." I tried to hold her gaze, but couldn't. Really, hiring Rick had been a fluke more than a brilliant instinct or any great act of knowing. I'd had too much work on my plate, I was due to report to my new boss, and Rick had walked in the door for an interview I'd completely forgotten.

He'd been punctual. He'd been wearing a suit. And he'd been happily married with two young daughters he doted on. Still was happily married. And he still thought the world of his daughters, too, though at thirteen and sixteen they were giving him more stress than laughter these days. Giving him gray hair and high blood pressure.

And he was in his forties, dealing with it all. Younger than I was…

"SAM AND I HAVE DECIDED to try one more time," Kylie's softly spoken words cut through my haze of panic.

"Oh, sweetie." I cringed, as I recognized remnants of my own mother in my reaction—even before the words escaped my mouth. "You said the last time was it."

How can you be pregnant, Melanie? You said you weren't seeing him anymore.

Kylie's dark eyes were wide and sad and the look broke my heart. "I know, but…"

I know, Mom, but I love him....

"Kylie." I leaned forward, moved by my own unrest and by my need to make life right for my child. At least one of my children. "You're still in debt from the last procedure."

What is it about mothers? Even new ones. We can't just offer support. No, we have to jump right in there with judgment and our "greater" wisdom. As if money mattered at such a time.

"When you miscarried, the depression afterward almost killed you." Perhaps not literally, but...

The last failed procedure had brought Kylie looking for me. I've wondered many times since then what would've happened if she hadn't found me.

Did this child of mine have my inner steel? Could she get up every morning for years if that was what it took, put one foot in front of the other in spite of feeling dead inside? Or was she more like my mother, who'd spent her life on medication, then with a bottle when her dissatisfaction persisted—even with help from the strongest antidepressants.

"I'm only thirty-one. We know that with in vitro I can conceive. If I can get through the first trimester... I could still have a whole houseful of kids. Sam's willing to do this and I can't not try."

"You have a thin uterine wall. Which is why your doctor doesn't think you'll ever carry a baby full-term."

"She's human. She could be wrong."

Maybe Kylie wasn't my mother or me. Maybe she was like her father, turning her back whenever life got too tough. Believing in illusions. Or refusing to believe?

I didn't miss the irony in all this. My daughter was risking her sanity because she couldn't have a baby. And I was risking mine because I was.

"I wish you'd think about this for a while." Where did I get such a big, interfering mouth?

"I have thought about it," Kylie said, pushing her plate away. She folded her napkin into a neat square and set it on the table. "Look at you and Shane."

What? What did my ex-husband have to do with *this?*

"You were married for ten years."

"Yes." The irritating tic in my neck was at it again.

"Sam and I have been married that long."

I wasn't following, but okay.

"You never had kids."

We never had sex, but that hadn't come up in any conversation with my daughter. "Right."

"Do you ever think that maybe if you had, you'd still be together?"

Whew. My breath left along with a load of tension. "Kylie," I said, making eye contact with her to ensure she understood the confidence I felt on this point. "Marriage is a relationship between two people and two people alone. Children can add a dimension to that shared life, but not to the marriage itself. If children are the only thing holding a marriage together, it's not really a marriage. It's a partnership, two people in the business of raising children."

"Children bring couples closer, Melanie. I see it all the time."

Yeah. *Shit.* I forgot for a second there that Kylie's business was children—those whose lives had gone astray.

"They might not create the love between you," Kylie continued. "But they're an extension of it. Something that bonds you even more closely."

She was smart, this kid of mine.

"Maybe if you and Shane had had children, you'd have seen that," she said softly.

"Kylie…Shane was gay."

CHAPTER FOUR

AT MY BALD PRONOUNCEMENT, my daughter's jaw dropped—probably not something that happened often to an accomplished prosecutor. I hadn't meant to tell her. Bad enough that she knew I'd been pregnant and unmarried at seventeen. She didn't have to know everything about me.

Kylie stared. And stared. As if she'd asked a question and was prepared to wait and wait and wait for the answer.

I gave in and told her. "Shane was my boss's son." She was going to get it out of me anyway. And at this point, it was probably better for her to hear the rest. I just hoped she would understand and not judge me too harshly.

"I thought your father was your boss at Vector back then." Kylie was frowning.

"Shane's father was my father's boss," I explained. "The two of us spent a lot of time together during college, and a couple of years after graduation he asked me to marry him. Then it seemed like a good idea." Then I was nothing but a face in the mirror, an empty young woman going through the motions of living.

Not that I was going to admit that to my daughter. No matter how good she was at getting information out of people.

"My parents were thrilled. His parents were thrilled. I'd had the love of my life…." I'd already told Kylie that part. About Dennis. About letting him go because I'd known that he could never begin to realize the possibilities life had to offer, or even know such possibilities existed, if he didn't have the freedom to leave his early life behind and discover a world that would recognize and welcome him. "Shane was my best friend. It could've worked."

"So what happened?"

"Actually, it worked for about ten years. We tried to have a sex life that first year…" It was strange talking to my daughter about that—thirty-one or not.

"It didn't do much for either of us," I explained. "But I was okay with that."

"You were content to live the rest of your life without sex?"

Yes, well, I'd thought so. Until about six weeks ago…

Stop it! My head snapped at me. I couldn't think about that night with Denny right now. I couldn't risk having Kylie work out that I was withholding a major secret. More than one, actually. Not until I could figure out how I was going to tell her.

I shrugged off her sex question. "It was nice to have someone to do things with. To share bills and holidays with, to share work and home concerns. It was an okay life for both of us until Shane met Derek. I knew that he'd met his soul mate when Derek got Shane to agree to tell his folks about him."

"Are they still together?"

There was no shock in Kylie's expression. No disapproval. I loved her for that.

"They are," I told her, feeling relieved, even closer to her. "They've been living together longer now than Shane and I did, and they're still wonderfully happy."

"You see them?"

"At least once a month—more when we can swing it."

"I'd like to meet Shane sometime."

Did I mention that I love this kid?

"He'd like to meet you, too." I smiled, as I admitted that part. "He's been after me for six months to bring you over for dinner."

"He knows about me?"

"He's one of my best friends, sweetie," I told her. "He knows pretty much everything about me."

Pretty much.

He didn't know I'd seen Denny again.

Or that I'd repeated history.

I just couldn't figure out a way to tell him that wouldn't make me sound like a forty-eight-year-old idiot.

I paid the bill and walked Kylie to her car. It was a little past eight, but in the desert March nights grew dark early. Lights shone on the boulevard. The smart shops were closing now, but the restaurants would be busy for another few hours at least.

"You got a great spot!" I told my daughter as we reached her dark blue Infiniti just a few steps down the walk. I wasn't ready for her to go—wasn't ready to be alone. Here I was, a woman who'd spent a large part of her life completely solo, feeling needy.

What did I do with that? When no immediate bits of wisdom popped forth in answer to the unspoken question, my stomach tightened with another bout of panic.

"Melanie?" Kylie was standing on the curb, keys in hand, poised to step off and climb into her car.

"Yeah?"

"Did you find him?"

There was no doubt whom she meant. She was bound

to ask eventually. But I still hadn't heard from him. Didn't know if he'd ever agree to see her.

And now things were so much more complicated. Just like me to screw things up for those I loved most.

Which made it a good thing I'd spent so much of my life solo, right?

"Yes, I found him."

I had to tell her. Because she'd asked and I couldn't lie to her.

"And?"

"He's on the road a lot."

"He doesn't want to meet me."

Kylie's expression didn't change a bit. Cool, composed, completely the attorney facing a tough jury. I ached to know what was happening to the little girl behind the facade.

"He didn't say that, sweetie."

Her eyes glinted as she looked at me across the evening shadows.

"What did he say?"

Passersby strolled around us. I could sense their presence, and yet I was oblivious to them at the same time. All I felt was the briefest wish to be any one of them, free of the need to find the words I had to find.

"That I looked good."

Oh Melanie, you'll never make it as a mother. You were right to give this child away and you've got no business thinking about keeping the one coming up.

"You saw him?"

I hadn't said that, had I? Screwup number two, if anyone was counting.

Deciding it was safest to keep my mouth shut until I could get control of it, I nodded.

"How'd he look?"

"Good." A question I knew the answer to. "Older—but good."

She nodded, watching me. Waiting. Making me squirm inside. I wondered if she knew the effect that look of hers had on others and somehow I doubted it. There didn't seem to be a calculating bone in the girl's body.

But I might very well begin to hate that innate talent of hers.

"He…uh…has a place somewhere up north, in wine country."

"You went up north?"

"No. No." I shook my head. "As it happened, he was on his way to Palm Springs when he returned my call. He had some business here."

"He was in town." Still no change in my daughter's expression, but her voice fell. Or perhaps I was just imagining it had.

"Only for one night," I hastily assured her. And what a night it had been….

There I went again, lost in my thoughts. I had to stop. These were critical moments.

"So what did he say?" Kylie swung her key ring around her index finger. "About me?"

"That he wanted some time to think about things."

After I'd told him how badly Kylie needed us. That something in her wouldn't be complete without closing the circle. After I'd told him how meeting her had changed my entire life, giving me a peace and a joy I'd never expected to have.

"Thinking's not a bad thing," Kylie allowed with a tentative smile. "I like to work through situations, too."

Because I wasn't about to tell her at that point that it

had already been six weeks, I couldn't do anything but nod.

Neither did I tell her that her biological father had just sired a biological sibling for her.

CHAPTER FIVE

"WHAT DID YOU DO THAT NIGHT beside talk to Denny about Kylie, Mellie?"

Only Shane could get away with calling me that dreadful name. "I did the second most stupid thing of my life, okay?" I said, pacing in front of Shane and Derek in their blue-and-green living room after dinner the next night. Turning, I stared them both down. "I had sex with Denny." Then, to break the stunned silence, I added, "I'm sorry, I just couldn't help myself."

Shane lifted a hand, let it fall back on his leg. "You don't have to apologize to me."

Right. I knew that.

Plopping down between the two men, who sprawled in identical fashion at either end of the sofa, I looked back and forth between two pairs of understanding eyes.

I almost couldn't bear being here with them. This was so different from any of the other hundreds of times I'd been in that room. I'd chosen these blues and greens fifteen years ago, when I'd been the one sharing this home with Shane. I'd spent weeks searching for the couch on which I now sat.

I'd never expected to be sitting on it pregnant.

Life was filled with ironies.

I noticed I was wringing my hands and clasped them together. "We met at his hotel—you know that resort just off Highway 11 by the lighting place? I insisted that we meet in the restaurant and talk over dinner, like two adults who barely knew each other."

"Good choice," Derek said, and nodded his encouragement.

"I'd only contacted him because I'd promised Kylie I would. We were there to talk about her, period."

With another glance back and forth, I jumped up, rounding the coffee table to face Shane and Derek. "We couldn't talk there," I explained. "There was this little Mexican band playing and they kept coming up to our table to serenade us."

"Ah, must've been a Wednesday night," Derek said, naming the band and telling me they'd been playing there for as long as he could remember. Where'd he been when I'd made my plans?

And if that was a smile he was trying to hide, I was going to—

Shane coughed, attracting my attention. He wasn't smiling at all. In fact, that sweet ex-husband of mine had drawn brows and a look of concern I recognized quite well.

"A busload of senior citizens was arriving in the lobby," I continued. "A couple of families out by the pool."

"You went to his room." Shane's voice was full of empathy.

"It's just that…being with him…it was like nothing had changed, you know?" I needed someone to understand. To tell me I wasn't completely crazy. "More than thirty years had passed and yet when I looked in his eyes, I knew what he was thinking, the doubts and regret, the relief. And the whole mind reading thing wasn't just one-sided. He was dealing with my own confused emotions before I'd even sorted through them. It was as if he looked at me and saw me—the real me, just as he always had."

"You went to his room," Shane repeated softly.

"Yes."

My legs were going to give out on me, so I sat back down between my friends.

"My heart recognized him instantly." I looked at each of them. "Being with him felt so natural, you know?"

"Yeah," they said simultaneously, both nodding.

Folding my hands on my knees, I stared at the floor. "He was so *there*. So alive."

I looked at Shane then. "And for the first time in over thirty years, so was I," I murmured. He more than anyone would understand that.

Shane's eyes darkened and grew warm, as he rubbed my back.

"Of course, afterward I wanted to die." I cringed inside, as I had every single time I relived those moments in Denny's arms.

"My forty-eight-year-old bones are certainly no match for the seventeen-year-old body of his memory."

"Come on, Melanie, you're gorgeous and you know it," Derek said. "The past twenty years on that treadmill of yours have served you well."

Yep, that summed me up. The longest relationship I'd ever had was with a treadmill.

"He fell asleep, but then he woke up while I was getting dressed to leave."

"You didn't stay the night."

And how I regretted that. "I couldn't. I'd started to think, to worry…."

"And?" Derek sat forward.

"He said he needed time to think."

"Understandable," Shane murmured.

"It's been six weeks and I haven't heard a word."

"Some guys are slow thinkers." I looked at Shane as he said that and his grimace was a pretty good indication that even he knew how weak an excuse it was.

"He had the best of me thirty years ago," I said to the floor between my feet. "He probably thinks that sleeping with me now paled in comparison to the memories of his youth—if he remembered me at all."

"Okay, woman, enough of that," Shane said with all the authority of the vice president he was, nudging my shoulder. Did I mention that Shane went from husband and coworker to boss? It never really seems to be an issue with us. He's not my husband anymore. And he doesn't feel like my boss, either. He's Shane. My friend. And we work together.

"Of course he remembered you. And unless he's changed completely from the man you were in love with, he wouldn't have compared your body then and now. Nor would he have slept with you if it hadn't meant anything to him. And you wouldn't have felt the years fade away if he hadn't let them go as well."

See why I love Shane? He always knows just what to say. But what if he was right? Fear came around another corner. Which was something else I'd learned on the bumpy road to happiness—there's always another corner.

So, what if that night in Palm Springs had meant even a smidgen as much to Denny as it had meant to me? What if he called and wanted to see me and then found out that I was pregnant?

"Is he married?" Derek asked, still leaning forward and glancing sideways at me. I had a feeling he was hankering for the beer he'd declined earlier when I'd said I wasn't having anything to drink. I couldn't remember any other time we'd all three sat there during an evening without something to sip on.

"No," I finally answered. Denny had never married. And that fact just won't leave me alone. Sometimes, in the darkest part of the night, it torments me with hope— the hope that Denny, like me, had had the love of his life at seventeen, that no one else could fill the spot. Then, in the reality of daylight, I realize it probably just means Denny's happier alone.

"You used to torture yourself with visions of him happily settled with another woman."

"I wanted that for him," I said, meaning every word. On one hand. "I wanted him to be happy."

"I know you did."

The year I graduated from college Shane had urged me to try to find Denny, if for no other reason than to put the past to rest. To free my heart. I'd been afraid to interfere with whatever life he was making for himself, afraid to impinge on the freedom he'd never had when I'd known him. Heck, I'd just plain been afraid of what I might find.

My heart had been too shattered back then to ask for much. To believe.

Shane had made the suggestion a second time, shortly after our marriage ended. I thought about it, briefly. But I'd made a decent life for myself and I figured Denny had, too. He'd never come looking for me—and I hadn't gone far. Besides, what were the chances of him being in his early thirties and still unattached? And what was the point of dredging up old and painful memories? They'd almost destroyed me the first time around.

"Does he live alone?" Shane asked, bringing me back from my solitude.

"I don't know," I confessed with regret. I'd slept with the man and I had no idea if he'd been with a hundred women in the past two months, or had one special one whose heart would be broken if she found out that he'd slept with me. "He said he wasn't married, but we didn't talk about other relationships. He could have a girl-friend, could be living with her. For all I know he could've been with her for the past thirty years." I gulped. "He could have a houseful of grandkids."

He hadn't said. I hadn't asked.

"Cheer up, Mellie," Shane said, massaging the back of my neck. "You've been laid for the first time in far too many years and you've come back to life. That's a good thing."

"I'm pregnant."

The hand on my neck stilled.

"Damn!" Derek muttered softly.

"I'm not surprised, really," I heard myself saying, although I knew perfectly well I had no idea what I was talking about. "It's just so unjust, how could it *not* have happened?"

"You're pregnant." Shane sounded disbelieving. I didn't know whether to be amused or offended. Perhaps I was a little of both.

"Yep."

"You're forty-eight years old," Derek contributed— as if I didn't already have that handy bit of information.

"Yep. Divorced, too."

The room grew so quiet I began to panic again. "Oh, and let's not forget I'm the mother of a thirty-one-year old." I added, mostly because it was easier to talk than to think.

"You already went through menopause," Shane told me.

"Guys!" They both jumped as I spoke a little too loudly. "I don't have the option of changing my mind here!" What I needed from them was some magical solution that I hadn't thought of yet. Something that would at least slow the spiral of fear that was spinning through me.

"So much for having a grip on anything at all," I said. "I'm nearly fifty years old and I'm going to have a baby. Oh, Shane, what am I going to do?"

And at that moment, I started to sob.

CHAPTER SIX

DEREK THOUGHT I should call Denny immediately to tell him about the baby. Shane told me to wait for Denny to call. But I didn't have another thirty years to do that. According to Lynn Marsh, my baby was due a couple of weeks before Thanksgiving. This year.

A month before my forty-ninth birthday. Thirteen months before my fiftieth.

Great. Now I was counting in months. Only mothers of new babies count in months. Eighteen months. Twenty-four months. Why didn't a year and a half or two years work as well for new mothers as it did for the rest of the world?

Denny's phone had rung four times. Maybe he slept late on Saturday mornings. Maybe he was off for the weekend on some lovers' tryst.

It was possible I was going to throw up. Apparently I hadn't grown out of morning sickness over the years. Six rings.

I paced my kitchen, tennis shoes squeaking against the hardwood floor, phone at my ear, thinking about the long day that loomed—hours and hours to spend battling panic.

Perpetua, my poodle, paced behind me. I'd ask her opinion, but I wasn't ready to deal with her disdain over my stupidity. Or her worries that her utterly spoiled days might be over when my attention was shared by another baby in the house.

Eight rings. Didn't the man have voice mail?

Four framed prints filled the wall between my cupboards and countertop. Each was a different depiction of brightly colored pansies—my whole house was filled with bright colors and floral prints.

I couldn't figure out what I'd been thinking when I'd made those choices. What was wrong with bare white walls? They didn't imply hope or expectation or express individuality of any kind.

Ten rings.

"Yes!" The male voice on the other end of the line was clearly irritated and breathing heavily.

Abruptly I stopped pacing, not sure what to say. Perpetua stopped pacing, too, and stared at me. I hoped she couldn't read my mind.

"Hello?" Denny's voice crackled over the line. "Who's there?"

"Hello." I turned my back on my canine companion.

"Mel?"

"Yeah," I said now completely embarrassed I'd let the phone ring so many times. What had I been thinking?

"Anything wrong?"

"No! Of course not!" I answered too quickly and then had to stop myself from babbling. Denny had figured out thirty-odd years ago that I only babbled if I was hiding something. The day he'd pointed this out was the day I'd fallen in love with him. I'd never known such attentiveness before. I was fifteen at the time.

Perpetua curled up at my feet, apparently bored.

"I just wondered if you were going to be in the desert anytime soon. Maybe we could have a drink…or something." I added the last when I remembered that I wouldn't be drinking.

"I'm heading down today."

And he hadn't called. Now I really felt like a fool. And desperate and alone and frightened and lost and…

I guess the long hours of panic I'd predicted for the day had already begun. I needed to get out. To be among people. Immerse myself in work. I needed to find something that felt good.

I needed to stop shaking.

I paced, Perpetua trotting beside me.

"I make things out of wood—decorations—in my spare time and I have a couple of clients there who carry my stuff."

"You do?" I asked, instantly curious. "Who sells them? I'd love to see them."

I was being way too forward. But then, around Denny, when hadn't I been? Asinine to worry about it now.

"They're no big deal," he said. Of course, he'd said that about his writing in high school, too, and he'd won a state competition with a piece I'd submitted without his knowledge. "I'm small-scale, just me, no production team, and I have no intention of changing that."

"I wasn't asking you to change." I couldn't believe I was grinning. Talking with Denny just felt so right—and I hadn't felt right since I didn't even know when.

"A drink would be fine, Mel, if you're sure that's what you want."

Hell, yes, I wanted it. I just couldn't have it. At least not the alcoholic kind.

"I'm sure," I said, feeling sixteen and excited again. "Why wouldn't I be?"

"I haven't called."

"I know."

"Nothing's changed since we last spoke."

Well, yes, it had. "You still haven't decided about Kylie, you mean."

"Right."

"I understand."

He asked me where I lived and said he'd swing by to get me. I arranged to meet him on Palm Desert Drive, instead. On a Saturday night it would be a place where I could get lost in the crowd, hide from the questions in my head—and maybe even, if the need arose, hide from him.

I thought about telling Denny that I wasn't going to sleep with him again. I'd promised myself that I'd lay that groundwork immediately. But then, I'd promised myself never to be pregnant and unmarried again, too. Somehow when I was around Dennis Walker I forgot every agreement I'd ever made with myself.

It didn't bode well for the future.

DENNY LOOKED BETTER than any forty-eight-year-old man had a right to look. The few gray hairs on his head just served as interesting highlights to the dark brown hair I'd always loved. His skin was tanned, his muscles firm, and there was no sign of a middle-aged gut in evidence. The motorcycle he pulled up on must have cost him as much as my Lexus. He swung one long leg over the saddle, strapping the helmet he'd already pulled off onto the back of his bike, and I started to salivate. In faded jeans and T-shirt, he could easily have fulfilled any woman's biker fantasy.

I felt every wrinkle in my skin, every hint of cellulite as I stood there in a short-sleeved flowered cotton dress. I should've worn the black jeans with crystal studs that Kylie had talked me into buying on sale last summer after every eye in the store turned when I wore them out of the dressing room for her to see.

And with them, my favorite tight white top.

I should be braless.

And for having those thoughts, I should be hanged.

CHAPTER SEVEN

IT WAS ONLY A LITTLE past five, and we had our pick of stools at the bar of the Mexican café I'd chosen.

Denny, raising a brow when I ordered lemonade instead of a margarita, asked for a bottle of beer. Seeing him drink was odd—as though I was watching someone I didn't know. I'd felt the same way six weeks ago.

"We were too young to drink back then," I murmured aloud. Too young to do a lot of things.

"We're still too young to drink," Denny said, as he molded his mouth around the bottle of beer. "This stuff'll kill you."

I wanted to ask the obvious—why was he drinking it? But I didn't.

"Have you told her about me?" With one hip leaning against the bar stool he glanced at me out of the corner of his eye.

I could hardly swallow I was so hungry for him. "Yes."

What was the matter with me? I was forty-eight years old, not a teenager. I'd matured, learned control, grown emotionally. And I was pregnant.

He nodded.

"Just last night, though," I added as I watched melancholy steal across his expression. He cared about Kylie. Didn't want her hurt. Just looking at him, I knew.

"I told her you needed time to think."

He peeled at the label on his beer. "And she said?"

"That she understood." I forced myself to concentrate despite my rapidly beating heart. "She likes to think about things before taking action."

Did he see that she was like him in that way? Did he care?

"So that's why you called. To tell me she knew."

Sure.

I opened my mouth to say so. Met those deep, dark eyes and gulped instead. I could hardly breathe. Felt dizzy. How was it possible to still react so intensely to someone I'd only known for a couple of years when I was very young?

I ended up just shaking my head.

"Why, then?" He continued to watch me and even while my head told me what was happening, that I was falling under his spell all over again, that I'd determined not to, that doing so would only lead to disaster—I fell anyway. I sat there on that bar stool, clutching my lemonade, relegating all the surrounding conversation and myriad sounds of life to the background, shutting myself inside a private little room with Denny.

"You have a way of looking at a person, focusing on her, that makes her feel as if she's the only person alive."

"When I'm with you, you *are* the only person alive for me. It's always been that way."

With shaky fingers, I jerked my glass to my lips, hoping to relieve some of the dryness that was nearly choking me. I took a tentative sip, and then another. Slowly. Sticky liquid jostled over the side of the glass and dripped down to my fingers. My stomach was quavering.

And I blurted, "You're not going to believe this, Denny, but I'm pregnant."

My words were brutal, unfair, unpolished. They made my face burn and my hands tremble. But I couldn't think rationally while under Denny's spell.

I couldn't want him. Not this time. Not again.

Denny dropped his beer.

OUTSIDE, I HURRIED BEHIND Denny, not even trying to pull my hand from his grasp. I knew him—understood that trapped feeling he got. I felt a little guilty about the broken glass and beer we'd left all over the floor, but the twenty Denny had thrown on the bar would probably deal with that.

We raced past familiar shops—designer clothes, custom jewelry, colorful glass art pieces in the windows. I didn't ask where we were going. As long as Denny was taking me with him, I didn't care. I hadn't grown up at all.

We rounded a corner. And then another. Now we were passing homes instead of shops. And still the father of my child pulled me along behind him—and I kept up with him. It crossed my mind to be thankful for my years on a treadmill. And to worry about what would happen when we finally stopped.

Denny was perturbed. I knew that much, and I couldn't blame him. I just wasn't sure how equipped I was to deal with his reaction. I wasn't doing too well with my own.

Dusk had fallen and as much as I welcomed the fading light, the cool breeze on my skin, I knew our time was limited.

It's okay, Denny, I'm not holding you responsible.

I'm not going to ask you for anything.

It's okay, Denny, it's not yours.

Denny, really, I was kidding, can't you take a joke?

Scenarios played themselves out in my mind. Just as thirty-one years ago, I'd felt compelled to spare him from the effects of our passion. Just as thirty-one years ago, I felt responsible on my own.

What's with you? I imagined him saying, in my version of hell. *Thirty-one years ago you ruin my life with a child we can't even provide a tent for, then you show up suddenly wanting me to be a father to this same kid—and now you're telling me there's going to be* another *one?*

Amazing, really, that he was still clutching my hand.

Oommph. I ran into his back.

"Sit."

We'd arrived at the grounds of one of Palm Desert's many posh resorts. We were surrounded by cultivated grass, huge trees and a garden of flowers lit by twinkling lights. I sat on a pristine white bench.

"I don't know how to do this gently, Mel." Denny began, pacing in front of me. "We can't recapture the past, can't make up for what happened. The hurt's always going to be there."

Because I didn't disagree with a word he was saying and because I couldn't think of a single thing to contribute, I remained silent. I hadn't figured out what this had to do with our current predicament.

He knelt down, took one of my hands. Oh, God. He wasn't going to propose, was he?

What would I say? My heart raced. My breath quickened.

"I can understand you being overwrought," he said softly, his brown eyes tender as he looked at me. But I could only remember one other time I'd seen his mouth so pinched. It had been the night I told him I'd signed the papers giving up our baby for adoption. "Us seeing each other again, making love, wasn't the best choice but, Mel, you have to see that this so-called pregnancy is a figment of your imagination. It has to be."

He'd called what we'd done *making love*. Not having sex. My heart fluttered stupidly. And then crashed. He'd said it hadn't been a good choice.

A figment of what?

I stared at him.

"Think about it," he said, standing again, his hands on his hips. He wasn't breathing too well, either. "We were together one night—not even the whole night. You've been through menopause. You're too old to have a baby."

And I'd thought he was the smartest person I'd ever met.

"Denny, I'm *pregnant*."

Sitting down, he took one of my hands in his again. This time I caught on right away that it wasn't a proposal. "Mel, you can't…"

"I've been to the doctor. I'm due in November."

"You're almost fifty years old!"

"Thank you. I was aware of that."

"You weren't always sarcastic."

Wasn't I? Seemed to me I'd always been mouthy. At least inside. Maybe that was what I had to show for thirty years of growing up. I'd learned how to speak up.

"I don't want anything from you, Denny." I resorted to the trite lines I'd rehearsed. "I'm not trying to trap you, and I'm not asking for help. I just thought you should know."

He nodded. "I appreciate that."

Well good, then. I stood.

"Where are you going?"

"Home."

"Mel." He pulled me back down. "Give me a minute, okay? I'm feeling a little shocked here."

Taking pity on him, I stayed where I was and didn't run—as I longed to do.

"And I thought facing a thirty-one-year-old stranger was my biggest challenge of the year," he muttered a few seconds later, as if in the middle of a conversation with himself. "But now…a baby?"

CHAPTER EIGHT

HEADLIGHTS APPROACHED, passed, leaving taillights in their wake. And again.

I listened for sounds of birds, but apparently they'd decided our party was a bust.

"Can you do this?" Denny asked, after one of the longest silences of my life. "What did the doctor say? I'm assuming, since you've told me about it, that you're planning to have it. Is that safe? A baby's not worth the risk of losing your life, Mel."

Comforted by his concern, I focused on the realities. "I'm at higher risk for some things, but overall, I'm pretty safe," I assured him—hoping I was listening in, too. "More and more women are having babies in their forties these days. It's not as uncommon as it used to be." If I repeated Lynn's words often enough, I might eventually convince myself. "Right now, physically, everything looks great."

"What about birth defects?"

"The biggest concern is Down syndrome—a one in thirty chance, less than five percent. There are early tests that indicate the condition, but I can tell you right now that whatever that test shows I'm going to have the baby."

"You're going to be sixty before this child reaches high school."

I swallowed. Tried to calm the swarm of butterflies in my stomach.

"There's not much I can do about that at this point."

Except pray for energy.

He didn't say anything for so long I thought the conversation was over. And then, out of the blue…

"Thirty years ago I would have given my right arm to marry you."

Thirty years ago I'd have accepted. Thirty *minutes* ago I'd have accepted.

"I know."

"I have a different life now."

I tried not to feel crushed. Of course, he had a life. Hadn't I told Shane so just the night before? What had I expected, that he'd spent thirty years mourning for me and the love we'd lost?

As I had. The small voice inside me that was more enemy than friend took a potshot. But I had to sit there and be strong, to hear about the people who shared his life, to be happy for him.

I had to be able to walk away.

He leaned forward, elbows on his knees. "I have my place up north, but as I told you, I spend the majority of my days on the road," he said, looking away. "I come and go as I please. No ties, no expectations."

Tears filled my eyes at the thought of Denny so alone.

"I like it that way."

I could feel the truth of his words—his life was as he needed it to be. Knowing Denny, I understood those words. And because I loved him so completely, I accepted them.

"I can't imagine not being on a bike."

The teenager I'd known had never even ridden a motorcycle.

I rubbed my arms. The night air was cool, but I was chilled from the inside out.

"I can't think of one single good memory of family life."

I'd tried to give him some, to include him in the safe cocoon my parents had kept me in during my youth, but they hadn't been willing to accept Denny. Quite the opposite. They'd forbidden me to see him.

I'd seen him, anyway—for two years before they found out.

"Look at you and your parents. You said six weeks ago that they retired to Phoenix, which is just four hours away. Yet you see them—what, once or twice a year?"

"They never quite forgave me for…well…some of the choices I made."

"Me," he said, glancing at me.

I held that gaze, in spite of the darkness, connecting to Denny as completely as I always had. "I've never once regretted seeing you, in spite of their disapproval."

"I thought when I left, when you gave up the baby, they'd come around. It was obvious they loved you and just wanted the best for you."

"Their version of best."

He shrugged.

"They did come around," I said after a long moment. "For a while."

"What happened?"

"I got married."

Denny sat back. Stared out at the street. His silence was painful—mostly because I sensed that he was hurting.

"Let me guess. He wasn't good enough for them, either."

"No, he was," I said, bumbling a bit in my rush to explain. "He was the son of my dad's boss at Vector. My folks were thrilled. His folks were thrilled."

"And you." He turned to look at me. "Were you thrilled?"

"I felt dead inside, Denny." There was no room for pride when Denny was around. There never had been. "The minute you left my heart stopped feeling anything real at all." I paused, tried to detach my thoughts from the emotions that were building in my chest. Consuming me.

"Shane was a good friend—the best. And I didn't want to live alone."

"Six weeks ago you said you weren't married."

"I'm not."

"What happened?"

"Shane found his true love."

Sitting up straight, Denny turned to face me. "He left you for another woman?"

"No." I shook my head, allowing myself a small smile. "He left me for another man."

"Damn!"

"I knew he was gay when I married him."

I could only imagine what he thought of that.

"My father never forgave me."

"For marrying him?"

"For not being woman enough to 'cure' him."

"Your father has one hell of a lot to answer for."

"He does his best," I told him, straining to grasp the peace I'd worked long and hard to find with my parents—a peace that lasted, as long as I didn't see them very often. "He's old school, Denny. He can't help that any more than I could help loving you."

"You said you work at Vector, that you head the corporate sales team."

"That's right."

"Does Shane's father still work there?"

"No, he retired."

He nodded.

"Shane does, though. He's vice president now."

"You work for your ex-husband."

"Yes."

"Did you sleep with him?"

"Excuse me?"

"You said you knew he was gay when you married him. Was the marriage ever consummated?"

Call me stupid, but I hadn't expected the question. Some things just weren't meant to be said.

"Yes."

The burst of air he released was far more brutal than a sigh.

"Come on, Denny," I said, trying to work up enough anger to carry me through this. "You can't tell me you haven't had other women in the thirty-some years we've been apart."

"Thirty-two years," he said with exaggerated precision. "Thirty-two years, and yes, there have been women. Just no commitments."

I wanted to ask how many women, but knew I wouldn't handle the answer well. I had enough open wounds already without inflicting more.

"Shane and I experimented, trying to ignite real desire between us, but after the first year or so we gave up. We were afraid if we kept forcing things, we were going to lose the one thing of value that we had."

"What was that?"

"Our friendship."

"And in the end, did you lose that, too?"

I shook my head. "I still see him and Derek—his partner—on a regular basis," I told him. "As a matter of fact, I had dinner with them last night. Derek's the one who said I should call you and tell you about the baby."

"They know about you and me?"

I nodded. Would that make him angry?

"What did Shane say?"

"That I should wait for you to call."

"I'm glad you didn't listen to him."

Strange as it might seem, considering the fact that Denny wasn't going to have anything to do with the baby, so was I.

CHAPTER NINE

ON TUESDAY a letter arrived from Denny.

He'd walked me back to my car at the end of our conversation about Shane. He'd kissed me goodbye and made no promises. I didn't know if I'd ever hear from him again, until I found his letter waiting in my mailbox three days later.

I made myself go into the house. Change clothes. Fix the light dinner of chicken and fruit that Lynn had recommended. Eat at least half of it. And then, without doing the dishes, I tore open the envelope.

Dear Mel,
I hope you're well.

He followed that with apologies for choosing this form of communication, adding that he'd always been better at getting his feelings down on paper than expressing them in person—as if I hadn't already known that. He mentioned that I'd given him my home address, but not my e-mail address.

I hadn't even thought of it. When I was with Denny I slid back thirty years. E-mail didn't exist then.

But I still had every love letter he'd written to me during our time together. I'd read them all again on Sunday.

I stopped by your office a couple weeks ago. And it was as if the past thirty years of making a good life for myself had never happened. You were speaking with a couple of people, and their respect for you was obvious from the way they were hanging on your words—and joking with you at the same time.

I had no idea what he was talking about. Denny had been at Vector and I hadn't known? How could that be?

I was shocked by how small I felt again, standing there. How inadequate. You were the prom queen and I was a thorn in everyone's ass.

I could hardly read through the tears in my eyes. Thirty years before, his words might have been closer to the truth.

I did the only thing I know how to do, Mel. I left. I know this about myself—I am a leaver. I am content only when I'm going.

I know something else, too. I loved you completely. And I had to get over that love in order to survive. I will not tell you that I feel nothing for you now. That wouldn't be true. But I can't tell you what I feel. I don't know. I can't tell you that I'll be around when you have this baby. Or that I'll ever be a part of his life. I don't know.

I can tell you that I'm thinking about you. I wish things were different. If you get into trouble, if you have any problems, I want you to call me. I'm not asking you to, that wouldn't be fair, but I want you to know that I *want* you to.

This isn't over for me, Mel.
Denny.

This wasn't over for him? What was I supposed to do with that?

Kylie's reaction to the news wasn't much better than her father's. I'd decided to have her over for dinner the next day and come clean before I drove myself crazy worrying.

"You're pregnant," my daughter echoed me, with a deadpan expression and voice to match. We'd finished eating the Chinese chicken salad I'd prepared, but we were still sitting at the drop-leaf table in my kitchen.

Perpetua, in the empty seat across from Kylie, stared sadly at the food that remained. I didn't seem to be able to please any of my loved ones.

"I know it seems pretty incredible. Believe me, no one's more shocked or appalled than I am."

Kylie nodded, gazing at me until tears flooded her eyes.

I reached across for her hand. "What?"

Shaking her head, Kylie said, "I'm thirty-one years old and I can't have a baby to save my soul and you— you've gone through the change of life, you have sex once and end up with a baby. Doesn't seem fair, you know?"

"Oh, sweetie." I didn't know what to say, except that my heart was breaking. More for her than for me, and it was pretty broken up over my own circumstances. "I'd change places with you in a split second if I could."

"I know." The words were softly uttered, but I had no doubt she meant them.

"Come on," I said, agonizing over the pain in her eyes. "You said you always hated being an only child, that you wished you had brothers and sisters growing up. Now you'll have one."

"I wanted a playmate, Melanie. I have Sam for that now. Besides…" Her voice trailed off and she stood up, scraping the food from my plate onto hers, stacking the dishes for a trip to the sink. Perpetua perked up hopefully.

I grabbed Kylie's hand, stopping her from leaving the table. "What?"

She sat back down, and after a moment, met my eyes. "I'm sure this is incredibly selfish of me, but I've only just found you," she said. "I've had you for what, a year? And now I'm going to have to share you. And with a kid who's going to get everything from you that I never had."

"I never said I was keeping it." I was. But I hadn't said so yet.

Her jaw dropped. "You aren't?" And then, "Of course you are. It killed you to give me away. You never would've done so if you'd had a choice. You have one now. Not many people get a second chance, and you're too smart to let this one pass."

Tears filled my eyes. It had to be the hormones, I told myself. I'd never been the weepy sort.

"Thank you."

"For what?"

"For making it okay."

"It is okay." She paused, frowned. "Isn't it? Have you seen your doctor?"

I told her about the appointment with Lynn, the greater risk of diabetes, high blood pressure, thyroid problems, miscarriage, premature birth, Down syndrome. "She doesn't foresee any trouble, but she'll be watching closely. I'm going to have to have some extra tests."

Another thing I could barely stand to think about.

What was I going to do if there was something wrong with my baby? Could I give her every chance she needed? Would I have the energy?

"HOW AM I GOING TO TELL Mom and Dad? What are they going to think?" Kylie asked half an hour later, the dog lying in her lap. We'd washed the dishes together and I'd asked her to come to my office. She was sitting in my desk chair, holding the folder I'd collected from my financial planner that day.

"My guess is I'm going to lose some of their respect."

Kylie frowned. "You have to understand, Melanie, they're older than you by almost ten years. They grew up with different values…."

The comment hurt. But I didn't want Kylie to know that. "As I said, they may not understand."

"You have to admit, it is a little unusual."

I nodded. She was right. I'd admitted that about a thousand times. And the admission didn't change a thing. I was still ancient. And still pregnant.

I had another tough subject to approach that evening. But first it took me another half hour to convince myself I had a chance of seeming logical.

In the meantime, I'd asked my daughter to look over a contract drawn up by my financial planner. After thoroughly studying it, asking some questions I hadn't even thought of, she'd given it a tentative okay—depending on the answers I received.

"Boy, it's been a long day," she said, pulling her wire-rimmed reading glasses from her face, folding them up and reaching for their case. "I haven't talked to Sam since noon." Perpetua roused herself.

"Don't put those glasses away just yet," I told her nervously brandishing the manila envelope I'd been holding since we'd first come in. "I have one more thing I'd like you to look at."

"Sure." Kylie unfolded her glasses again. I took a deep breath.

"I met with Paul Ascott today." He'd been my personal attorney for years but Kylie had given her approval of him, as well. "I had him redo my will."

Without a word, Kylie took the document from me. I couldn't tell what she was thinking.

"I'm splitting everything between you and the new baby."

Before, Kylie'd had it all.

Kylie nodded, seemingly unconcerned. Glanced at the first page and then at me.

"I'm perfectly comfortable on my own, Melanie," she said. "I already told you that. And I'm also the beneficiary of Mom's and Dad's wills."

"I know." We'd been through this before. "You can give the money to the society of mice if you like, but this is something I have to do. You are my biological daughter and as such, my heir."

"One of them," she murmured.

"Yes, one of them." The reminder threw me for a second there. Maybe I still wasn't accepting the pregnancy quite as well as I wanted to think I was.

"Anyway, the other change is somewhat more significant."

"What?" she peered over at me.

"I want you to be the baby's guardian if anything should happen to me. Paul drew up papers for both of us to sign to circumvent or ease the red tape process in the event that I should die while the child is still a minor."

She pulled off her glasses and absentmindedly put one earpiece in her mouth, saying nothing.

Would she refuse? Was all our talk about being a family just that—talk? Was my daughter going to reject my baby?

Perpetua lay down again, plopping her head on her paws with an audible sigh.

"I'll need to speak with Sam about this," she said.

"Can you call him?"

She hesitated for a moment, then picked up the phone. Fifteen minutes later, our signatures were there on the stark white paper.

The sight brought me a comfort I'd never known before, a comfort I didn't recognize. My daughter and I were finally official—our names side by side on this legal document, biology and blood and love all mixed together.

"MELANIE?" KYLIE STOPPED on her way out the door, keys in hand, purse over the shoulder of her short black jacket.

"Yeah?" I'd already turned to go back to my office, intending to review a proposal one of my staff was going to present in the morning.

"Can we please not tell Mom and Dad about this? My signing for the baby? At least not yet?"

A little of the comfort I'd gained slid away, as I nodded. "Of course."

CHAPTER TEN

THE NEXT WEEK PASSED in a confusing mixture of panic and peace, fear and stoicism. I worked. I came home. I ate properly. I got plenty of rest. Or rather, I lay in the bed for the required amount of time. If I was not completely myself, no one at work seemed to notice. Not even Rick.

Or at least they weren't saying anything.

Of course, Shane might've had something to do with that. I hoped not. I didn't want special treatment. Or pity. I'd lived my whole life standing up for who I was and what I did, living with the choices I'd made clearly in the open. I wasn't about to change now.

Though sometimes when I pictured myself, obviously pregnant, in a sales meeting, seeing the raised brows and imagining the bitten-back remarks, the idea of change was tempting. If I'd been able to figure out a way to disguise the fact I was having a baby, I'd probably have given in to temptation and hidden this mistake.

Or poor choice.

Okay, no, my night with Denny wasn't either of those things. Nor was the child we'd conceived. It was a challenge. That was it. A challenge. I'd handled many challenges in my forty-eight years. I'd handle this one, too.

I went on the Internet and found a support group for pregnant women over forty-five. There was a session in a chat room that Saturday. I logged on. Early. And was the oldest one there.

It figured.

The following Thursday my cell phone rang while I was sitting at my desk, nibbling grapes for lunch. It was Denny.

He wanted me to go away with him for the weekend. On his motorcycle. Our destination would be a surprise.

Could I ride a motorcycle? Would the tiny child inside me be safe?

"I don't want to mislead you," he continued, when I didn't immediately respond. "I haven't found any resolution. I just want to see you."

I wanted to see him, too. But did I dare to agree, as vulnerable as I was?

"I can't stop thinking about you," he said.

"You've been on my mind a lot, too." Would he show me his home? "Okay, I'd like to spend the weekend with you." I was shaking, unsure, anticipating…what? What could possibly come of this?

"You're sure?"

"You talked me into it, and now you're trying to talk me out?"

"No." He chuckled. "I don't know."

"Look," I said, suddenly afraid I was going to lose this chance before I even knew what it was. "We're grown-up now, Denny. Each of us has proven we can make difficult decisions, that we'll do what we think best. Right now, we're facing something that involves both of us. Maybe spending some time together will give us a chance to talk, to get some clarity."

"That's what I thought. I feel horrible that once again you're bearing the brunt of the consequence of our actions."

"Hey," I said, frowning. "You aren't feeling sorry for me or anything, are you?"

"No, Mel." His voice was filled with the affectionate humor that had always melted my heart. "It's never crossed my mind to think of you as a woman in need of pity."

Okay, then. Just as long as we both understood that. "Thank you."

"You're welcome."

"Um, when were you thinking about going?"

"I have an order to deliver in the desert Friday afternoon. I can swing by for you after that. Say around four."

That was tomorrow. My knees felt a little weak. "I'll need to check with my doctor first, to make sure there's no danger in me riding a motorcycle."

"Of course. And Mel, when you call your doctor, could you ask her if it's safe for you to have sex?"

LYNN GAVE ME the go-ahead on both counts. For the next hour, I vacillated between cursing her and feeling eternally grateful. Sitting at my desk, trying to focus on reports I had to sign off on by Monday, I wondered if I should take my swimsuit. I probably wasn't going to be looking good in it for much longer and then...

Oh, no. What would my forty-nine-year-old body look like when all of this was over? Seventeen-year-old skin was elastic. Mine was not.

Losing weight at seventeen wasn't much of an issue. At fifty, it was an impossibility.

She'd also had me schedule an amniocentesis and chorionic villus, each of which involved a needle in my abdomen. The tests themselves carried a slight risk of miscarriage. And the results...

The first test wasn't for another four weeks. The amniocentesis was booked for three weeks after that. And

I had e-mails to answer. A proposal to approve. A client to placate.

Should I buy a negligee? I'd tried once with Shane. He'd gotten tangled in the silk and I'd just gotten sweaty. The damn thing hadn't breathed. But then, neither had I, in those days. I'd just existed.

At four-thirty, I gave up. I couldn't concentrate. It had to be hormones. Chemical. Something I ate. I called Kylie and begged off our dinner. Suddenly overprotective, she refused to let me off the phone until I told her why I was canceling and then she insisted on coming over to help me pack. She was bringing food, too.

What, now that I was eight weeks pregnant I was helpless?

Sometimes I felt that way—emotionally at least. I didn't remember buying a ticket for this roller coaster and it seemed highly unfair that I'd been put on the wrong ride.

I started to cry on the way home—tears of happiness now. My daughter loved me. Supported me. I wasn't alone.

"THE BLACK SWIMSUIT, no question." Kylie sat on the bed looking back and forth between the bright floral set I held in one hand and the low-cut black one-piece in the other.

I held up the black, raised my brows, and in response to her firm nod, slid it into the duffel. She'd already gone through my underwear—passable, but not great. My nightgown she threw back in the drawer, saying I wouldn't need it anyway. A pair of black studded jeans she accepted, but my slacks went the way of the nightgown.

My daughter knew how to take charge.

"I feel a little strange with you sitting here planning for me to have sex with your father."

She snorted. "That's a little after the fact, wouldn't you say?"

Maybe. What did I know? I'd lived most of my life not having the chance to behave like a mother.

"We aren't planning a future together. Sex should involve the future."

"Usually. But this situation isn't usual, is it?" Kylie said, folding and packing. "Sex is good, Melanie. It's healthy."

"It seems to get me into trouble."

Laughing, she hooked a finger through the strap of my serviceable white bra, then rummaged in my lingerie drawer for a barely there lacy pink one. Secretly I was glad. I wouldn't have dared take that, but if it was Kylie's idea…

"Did you know that statistics show that women who have three orgasms a week reduce their risk of certain medical malfunctions?"

"Sounds like some bunk a man came up with."

"No, really, it was in a report by a female doctor from some Eastern university. I came across it when I was in college."

"So what happens if she has four?" Nerves were making me ridiculous.

"Apparently there's a reverse effect and it's not so good—depletes the chemicals that it stimulated or something." Kylie started to laugh.

This was craziness. The fact that I was planning to go off for a weekend with a man who was promising nothing was crazy in itself.

"Let's face it, Melanie," Kylie said, following me into the bathroom as I packed my makeup and toiletries. "Your history with Dennis Walker makes this weekend a pretty open-and-shut case. It doesn't take an attorney to figure it out."

"I'm weak. I'm a fool."

She leaned against the marble counter. "You're a beautiful woman who's loved once in your life—passionately. Which makes you one of the envied few."

I stopped, toothpaste in hand, and looked at her. "Do you really think that?"

She nodded her head. Then glanced away with an odd, troubled look on her face.

"He loved you that way, too."

I froze. My hands. My breathing. How would she know that unless she'd spoken with him? Denny had called Kylie and hadn't told me? But then, why would he? His relationship, or lack of one, with Kylie had nothing to do with me. I sure didn't call to tell him our daughter was coming over to help me pack for our weekend away.

"He called you?"

She shook her head, suddenly quite interested in the toe of the forest-green pump that matched the suit she'd worn in court that day.

"I went to see him."

CHAPTER ELEVEN

I HAD NO REASON to feel betrayed. Hurt. Jealous. So why did I?

"Sam wanted a weekend in wine country, so on Saturday we headed upstate. It wasn't hard to find him, since I now know his full name. He's listed."

"He said he was on the road a lot."

She nodded. "But when he's not, he lives in a remodeled barn."

A barn. Kylie had seen it—had seen him—in his home. I had never once, in my entire life, seen Denny at home.

"It's the most amazing structure." Kylie's voice grew in strength, showing an eagerness to talk now that she knew I wasn't going to do anything stupid like fall apart on her.

I hoped she hadn't placed too much faith in me.

"It's all redwood and he built it himself."

I wasn't there to see my lover meet our daughter for the first time. Nor had I been there to watch him, sweaty and strong, building his home. Regret was a painful thing.

"Inside, it's more like a workshop than a house." Kylie's eyes glowed and just that quickly, meeting my daughter's eyes, I was lost in her tale, absorbed in her delight as I realized how much this meant to her. Kylie's happiness was far more important than mine. Her happiness made me happy. Truly happy—the bone-deep, sleep-with-a-peaceful-smile-on-your-face kind. "The place is one huge room and it's filled with these three-dimensional miniatures of rooms, places, skylines, all made of wood, metal, glass and fabric. They were wonderful."

Decorations. He'd said he made decorations in his spare time. That they were no big deal. Kylie wouldn't have been impressed by "no big deal."

"What did you think of him?" I wanted to see it all, know everything she knew and felt. I'd dreamed, countless times, of the moment when Denny would see the baby I'd had more than thirty years ago.

"He's gorgeous," Kylie grinned. "Even for an old guy."

I shoved her gently. "Kylie!"

Her face straightened. "I liked him," she said softly. "He seems kind. Gentle without being girlie."

Denny had been a hit with his daughter. Which didn't surprise me at all.

He was Denny. How could he not be?

"When we were growing up, everyone thought he was a hellion."

"Was he?"

"No." I thought back to those years, to the young man I'd known, still confused about a community that could so misjudge an innocent kid. "He looked like one," I said. "He had long hair, ragged jeans, a black leather jacket that he was almost never without, even in the summer. He wore a knife at his hip."

"A knife? No wonder people were afraid of him. Was he part of a gang?"

"No." I sat on the closed toilet seat, cosmetic bag still on my lap. "The knife was for show." Mostly. "Denny's mom took off when he was about two, leaving him with a drunk and abusive father."

"What a woman."

"Yeah." In all the growing up I'd done, I'd yet to learn forgiveness for a mother who'd put herself before her own child. "He was abusive to her, too, mind you. She was running for her life."

Kylie's eyes narrowed, her chin stiff. "But her son's life didn't matter?"

I shrugged; the question was rhetorical. Kylie knew far more about that kind of thing than I ever would. She saw it every day.

"The last time his father hit him, he was twelve. He went out the next day, bought that knife, and swore to his father that if he ever came near him again, he'd use it."

"Did he?"

"Not as far as I know."

I stood up, got back to packing before I talked myself out of going. Remembering was much harder than forgetting. Easier not to feel than to deal with all the hurt.

"He thought I was a buyer." The click of Kylie's heels on the hardwood floor followed me back to the bedroom.

"A buyer? He has buyers come to him?"

"Apparently, quite a few—not that I'm surprised. His stuff is magnificent." There was no doubting the pride in her voice and I took real pleasure in that, almost as if the credit were mine.

"What did he say when he found out you weren't?"

Kylie grabbed the duffel after I'd dropped in my makeup bag. She zipped it and lifted it off the bed. "Before I could tell him who I was, he gave me this spiel about how he's not interested in commercial production. His pieces are original, and yeah, he knows he won't get rich that way, but that was just fine with him. Then he told me he didn't have anyone to leave his wealth to, anyway."

She licked her lips. Hunched her shoulders.

"What did you say?" I could almost see the whole thing, my heart pounding as though I'd been there.

"I told him he was wrong about that."

DRESSED IN BLUE JEANS, white turtleneck, denim jacket and low boots, I was waiting in my driveway Friday after work when Denny's motorcycle roared around the corner.

Too little, too late, I know, but I didn't want him in my house, my space. It almost felt as though, if he went in, I'd never be able to get him out again—never be free of him.

After thirty-one years of failure in that area, there wasn't even a remote chance I'd ever be free of him.

"Hi," I said, handing him my bag to stow in the built-in compartment on the back of the bike. I loved looking at him. Those jeans wouldn't dare do anything other than fit his thighs to perfection. The soft black leather of his jacket hugged his waist and shoulders as if it'd been sewn onto him.

"Hi." He answered belatedly, with a smile that turned me to mush right there on my driveway.

It should be against the law for a grown woman to feel that way.

As if the law could save me from myself.

He held the bike for me as I climbed on. And sat obediently while he strapped a shiny navy helmet under my chin. It matched the one he was wearing. Then with nothing else said, we were off.

The cool air against my skin felt wonderful. The motor rumbling between my thighs, exciting and powerful. But it was Denny's sides and back and stomach that held most of my attention. The moment was perfect—filled completely with Denny—and my only job was to hold him.

We'd been on the highway for half an hour before I even wondered where we were going.

Sometimes I impressed myself.

Ninety minutes later, after a couple brief questions from Denny making sure I was okay, he signaled an exit. I'd been amusing myself imagining possible destinations, trying to figure out what he had in mind for our weekend. The mystery was fun. Exciting. Denny knew I liked surprises—and he'd always been great about providing them.

It was just after six; we were in Ontario, California. I looked around at all the billboards. He was taking me to Disneyland for the weekend? Not quite what I'd envisioned.

But I could adapt. I was flexible. I liked "It's a Small World" and, really, he was right. I had to get into the whole parent-kid mode. Yes, this was just the weekend getaway for me.

"You doing okay?" Denny asked, the second he cut the engine next to a gas pump on an impressive expanse of blacktop dotted with at least forty other identical pumps.

I nodded. "Fine." Surprisingly, I was—even with Disneyland in my near future. "It just feels good being with you, you know?" I asked.

He stopped, gas nozzle in his hands, looked at me and smiled. "Yeah, I know."

The knot that had taken up permanent residence in my stomach some thirty years ago released its fierce hold, allowing room for long-denied peace and contentment—temporary, maybe, but still very real.

"Ready?"

Tank filled, Denny was putting his helmet back on. I did the same, nodding. I'd used the restroom, though I would've preferred to wait until we got to our room, but already, in my pregnancy, I was finding it more difficult to postpone certain bodily urges.

"You up for another haul?"

Away from Disneyland and energetic kids? "Sure. You have someplace in mind?"

He nodded. "I have a time-share in Carmel that's free this weekend. It's another three and a half hours from here. You think you can make it?"

"I'm pregnant, Denny, not dead."

"And you're forty-eight—"

"I know, I know," I interrupted, raising my hand. If one more person reminded me that this was not a normal run-of-the-mill pregnancy I was going to scream. If I had to be pregnant, I wanted it to be normal. Surely it wasn't too much to ask to have *something* about my life happen in a perfectly ordinary, mundane way.

And if it was too much to ask, too bad. I was asking anyway.

OUR ROOM IN CARMEL was exquisite. Right on the beach. With plush red armchairs on either side of a pullout couch, and across the room…an ornate king-size bed with a wood canopy trimmed with a sheer white valance and drapes.

"This is your time-share?" I asked, dropping into one of the two chairs and gazing out across the blackness to lights bobbing on the ocean. A cruise ship? A freighter?

"Sort of," Denny said, placing our bags side by side on the luggage rack. "Mine is actually down the street. I traded with some people I know."

And then it hit me. Carmel was an artist's dream— the streets lined with shops that sold one-of-a-kind pieces that people all over the world paid exorbitant amounts to own.

"You sell your work here."

He sat down on the couch, stretching an arm along the back. "Some."

"Kylie told me about your home."

He nodded, watching me.

"What did you think of her?"

Glancing out the window, he was silent for a long time. Thinking—as Denny would before replying to such an important question. I knew he was feeling deep emotion, but I couldn't tell whether he was in the process of accepting, or rejecting, the possibility of a relationship with Kylie.

"She's everything we could ever have hoped for and more," he finally said, turning back toward me. I could barely make out his expression in the room's dim light.

"I look at her and I can't believe how beautiful she is." I was talking to my daughter's father about her. Like a real parent. The moment felt so good.

"Like her mother."

My chin trembled. If I started to cry I was going to be in serious trouble.

"We got lucky." He shifted his leg and I marveled again that it was Denny sitting across from me. After all these years, all the fantasies and dreams, it was finally true.

"How so?"

"She was raised by parents who loved her as much as we would have."

"I've spent a bit of time with them," I said, telling him how, after some initial hesitation, they'd welcomed me into their family circle. "They're almost ten years older than we are, and they're completely wonderful. And completely secure in Kylie's love. You're right, we got lucky."

I wanted to ask if he was going to see her again. Knowing Denny, it would be almost impossible for him to meet her face-to-face and be able to walk away. But did I still know him that well? Thirty years of life had intervened and wrought inevitable changes in the man I'd loved. Still loved…

I wasn't ready to test just how much change had happened.

CHAPTER TWELVE

IT WAS CHILLY OUTSIDE, but a fire was burning in the gas fireplace in our room. By the time we settled in it was after ten o'clock, and I was wide-awake. Wired.

Ready to…

"You hungry?"

We'd stopped for a quick bite a couple of hours ago.

"Not really."

I guessed we were finished talking about our daughter. Wondered when we'd speak of her again. But I wasn't going to push. Frankly, I couldn't push. I wouldn't do anything that might spoil this time with Denny.

So, I was weak. At least I recognized that about myself.

"We've never spent a whole night in bed together."

Aha, so his thoughts weren't far away from mine. My blood quickened at the idea of lying there with him.

And then I remembered that our daughter had taken my nightgown out of my bag. She'd said I'd be sleeping naked and I hadn't doubted her. What she'd failed to fill me in on, what I'd failed to ask, was just how I was supposed to get from fully clothed, with a man I suddenly realized I hardly knew anymore, to naked in bed beside him.

Six weeks before, thirty-two years before, it had simply happened. No planning or premeditation.

"You're awfully far away over there, Mel."

Funny how a few short words can change an entire world. "And lonely, too."

"I've got a solution." His eyes were half-closed, his body relaxed. Did he have any idea how sexy he was?

"What would that be?" I was enjoying our little game.

"Would you like me to show you or tell you?"

"As I recall, I always preferred the *show* part. Far less boring…"

I didn't even finish before I was in his arms—standing body to body, heat to heat, overwhelmed with hunger as he finally kissed me. I was home and there was absolutely nowhere else I wanted to be.

"TELL ME ABOUT HAVING HER." I'd been dozing, my head on Denny's chest, wallowing in the sensations of security and excitement nicely integrated in another perfect moment, knowing that for the first time in my life I would be spending the entire night with him. Falling asleep with him and waking up with him, too.

His hand was lying still on my lower stomach.

"What do you want to know?" I asked, sleepily. I was discovering something about myself. Making love took a lot out of me. Probably a good thing I hadn't been doing it all my life. I would never have been able to do this regularly and have a career, too.

Of course, having three orgasms in a row after having had three in a lifetime was a pretty big change in my routine.

Denny lay still, his naked legs intertwined with mine. "Were you alone?"

"No, my mom was there."

He was silent for a bit and then even though I wanted to doze again, I was suddenly wide awake. Remembering.

"As much as I still can't like her, I'm glad she was there." His voice was low, fading into the dark room. He'd turned off the fire, but I could still see ships bobbing on the ocean beyond our balcony door. "I hated to think of you going through that alone."

Yeah, well, for all intents and purposes I had. From the moment he'd driven out of town in his broken-down old Ford, the night I'd signed the papers giving away our unborn child, I'd been alone in every way that really mattered to me.

Until Kylie.

And now my new baby.

I wasn't alone anymore.

THREE O'CLOCK in the morning. The red LED readout on the nightstand radio glowed as I opened my eyes. I'd fallen asleep after all. And turned over. Lying half on my stomach, I was cuddled up to Denny, my leg thrown over his lower abdomen. His hand on my thigh held me there. Peace settled over me. My heart was safe; the world was firmly on its axis.

WE WENT WHALE-WATCHING in Monterey, half an hour's drive from Carmel. Denny had seen his first whale off the coast of Alaska. He'd worked on a cruise ship for a few years after high school. That morning we saw eight. They were beauties.

Just a few steps from the ship, he tossed a couple of bills to a little man of indeterminate age standing on the shore, dressed in bedraggled tweed overalls. With a nod from the guy, I sat on a nearby bench and his monkey jumped in my lap. I laughed when the audacious critter held out his hand for more money.

We stopped at a hot dog stand for lunch and split a foot-long loaded with onions and relish and mustard. I don't think I'd had one since I was a kid. Denny said the best hot dog he'd ever had was in Germany. He'd been there twenty years ago on a four-month-long hitch-hiking trek through Europe.

We went back to our room after that, took off our shoes and headed out to the beach. And we talked. About life and the world. Gay marriage. September 11th. Divorce rates. My parents' retirement. I confessed that I loved my job and he told me a little bit about how he got into the art of making miniatures. After his cruise ship stint, he'd taken a job on a fishing boat in Alaska and the captain of the ship had carved wooden furniture for his daughter's dollhouse during the long nights.

He'd offered Denny a knife and a piece of wood.

"Every time I'd sit down to carve, I'd start to see things in the wood," he said. "I'd listen to the rhythm of the knife against the shavings. Every other sight and sound in my mind would disappear." He grinned. "The silence was addictive."

"You saw things in the wood?"

"Yeah, you know, scenes. Rooms with people in them, celebrating, entertaining friends, paying bills."

"Sounds like it was your attempt to have home and family in your life." I told him exactly what I thought— just as I always had. I never had to weigh my words with Denny. He just seemed to understand.

"Maybe." He shrugged, walking beside me on the beach.

"You said you imagined people there. That they come alive in your hands…"

"Yeah, the same as with any other carver, I'd guess."

"Maybe." I slid my bare toes through the cold sand almost as if I were skiing. "Or maybe you were creating the one kind of home life you could control."

The afternoon sun was warm on my neck, mixed with the cool breeze that came in over the ocean. I was glad I'd packed my white sweater to go with the black jeans Kylie had insisted on. I wondered if our daughter was thinking about the two us—away. Alone. And if she was, what did she think?

Denny took my hand, stopping me. I turned to face him and went willingly, okay, eagerly, when he pulled me up against him. We had the beach to ourselves, but I wouldn't have cared if we hadn't. He had that effect on me.

"I've missed you, Mel," he said, his gaze troubled as he looked into my eyes.

Life wasn't going to be easy. It might not even be happy. I knew that was what he was telling me. "I've missed you, too."

He watched me for a while longer, then after one slow, deep kiss, he let me go.

And I knew I had to be prepared for that to happen again. And again. The kisses, maybe, but the letting go, too.

Just as the circumstances of my life had shaped me, Denny's had shaped him, too. He'd never had a lasting relationship in his life. He'd had no opportunity to figure out a working definition of what a lasting relationship might be. And at almost fifty, his boundaries were firmly established.

AFTER MUCH NAGGING, Denny relented and took me to a couple of the shops where his work was sold. The first one was empty except for three people huddled in conversation over a clock in the back corner. A lighted glass case in front had *Dennis Walker* engraved on a gold plaque at the top. I couldn't tear my eyes away. The intricacy of Denny's miniature three-dimensional rooms and landscapes astonished me.

"This detail is extraordinary," I said, staring into the glass case at the living room he'd created. There were tiny carved feet on the legs of the sofa, a quarter-inch leather-bound book on the glass-topped table.

"I wonder what the book is," I said, completely mesmerized.

"Frost, of course." Denny's answer shouldn't have surprised me.

I turned to look at him, my eyes filling with tears that I blinked away. "*'I took the one less traveled'...*" I quoted my favorite verse.

He nodded. "If you look closely, you can see the title of the book on the spine."

Maybe. If I still had the eyes of a seventeen-year-old. "If I had a magnifying glass," I said with a chuckle.

"I do all of this under magnifiers," he said, walking with me as I moved from piece to piece.

"Dennis!" An older woman broke away from the other two people in the back and approached us. "Why didn't you tell us you were going to be in town? We could've arranged something!"

"Barbara," Denny said, stepping aside and pulling me forward. "I'd like you to meet a friend of mine, Melanie Copperstone. Melanie and I went to high school together."

And had a baby together, too, I wanted to add. I didn't like the way the other woman was gazing at Denny—as if she had some kind of ownership.

"Melanie, this is Barbara Johnston. She and her

husband own this shop. Sorry I didn't call, Barb. Mel and I are just here for a couple of days, but she insisted on seeing these." He pointed to the piece in front of us—a skyline with tiny flowers on the balconies of one of the high-rises.

"You've never seen Dennis's work?" Barbara asked, eyes wide. I wanted to smack her when she took his arm. "You have to show her the garden," she said, pulling Denny toward a showcase built into the wall. "At twenty thousand dollars it's going to take a special buyer, but I know I'll sell it before the end of the season."

The piece took my breath away. Brightly colored flowers rioted across the entire square foot of space, interspersed with a gazebo and little white wooden benches along a meandering path with rocks and the occasional tree. In the back, toward the end of the path, was an angel fountain. My heart lurched when I saw the sad yet compassionate expression on the face of that angel.

It was Denny—a self-portrait. My angel. Sad. Compassionate. Alone in the garden of his life.

I bought that garden on the spot.

CHAPTER THIRTEEN

"So where are you off to next?" I asked Denny over dinner at Clint Eastwood's restaurant in Carmel that night.

He popped a bite of steak into his mouth. Seemed to really be aware of the taste of the meat, to savor and enjoy it. Something new I'd noticed in Denny. He'd always been attentive, focused, but now he'd developed a keen awareness of everything around him—a habit of being fully present in every moment.

"A month in the outback of Australia," he said when he'd finished the steak, eyes glowing as they did every time he mentioned his travels. "I want to do a series of nature miniatures from around the world."

If my new garden piece was anything to go by, they'd be an unqualified success. I told him so.

"You didn't have to buy that, piece, Mel. I'd have taken it back from her and given it to you."

"I wanted to buy it," I told him. "I can't even tell you why, because I don't know, but it seemed important at the time."

"You wanted to shut Barbara up."

Maybe. But there was more to it than that.

"I wanted it to be legitimately mine."

He blinked. Sat back. Stared at me. And I realized what I'd just said—and what it meant. Nothing about my relationship with Denny had been legitimate. Not our time together in high school, which had been spent hiding from my parents. Not the time we were spending now—this weekend, a time out of time. And certainly not either one of the children we'd conceived.

But I owned his garden.

It would have to be enough.

"WE'VE BEEN GIVEN a second chance."

I was dozing again, naked and replete after another bout of amazing lovemaking. The moon was shining through the patio doors of our room. Only a few more hours and our time would be over. It would be back to the real world—real life.

Life without Denny.

I didn't want to think about that now.

"Did you hear me?" he said, brushing the hair away from my forehead as he leaned over and gave me a kiss. The kind we'd often shared—as if our lips couldn't bear to part.

"Yeah."

"You don't agree?"

I didn't know what to say. Couldn't find the usual flippant response I protected myself with when anyone got too close to my heart. Problem was, Denny was my heart. Always had been.

"If you mean a second chance to say goodbye, I guess so."

"Hey." He sat up and pulled me against him, so that my head was lying against his shoulder. "What's this about? We're grown-up now, Mel. The choices are ours to make. We're in control."

"I love you."

"I love you, too."

But that wasn't the end of it. I used to think it was,

back when I was still a kid and believed that love conquered all—when I was still waiting for my knight in shining armor to come along. Before that knight appeared and my parents hated him and we were too young and had no way to support ourselves. Before he put his love for me before his own happiness and rode off into the sunset. Alone.

And because I loved him so much I had to put his happiness before my own, I was not going to start dreaming impossible dreams now.

"You're a traveling man, Denny. You live wherever life takes you, for however long. You could choose to settle down, completely alter your way of life—but odds are you wouldn't be happy. I can't take that chance."

"Maybe I'll change."

"If you ever do, I'll be available."

His hand brushed up and down my arm. I lay against him, my body moving in rhythm with his breathing. I was making "big girl" choices.

Funny how none of the self help books tell you that "being a big girl" sucks.

"I love you, Mel. I don't want to lose you again."

"You won't," I told him and I knew the words were completely true. "I knew when I was sixteen that I'd fallen in love with you forever. A lifetime without you hasn't changed that. Whenever you're passing through, I'll be here."

To my surprise, my eyes were dry. Some hurts were just too deep. Some choices, even excruciating ones, were just too right.

Because I loved Denny so unconditionally, I had to accept him as he was—and be satisfied.

A MONTH AFTER MY WEEKEND in Carmel, Lynn called me. I'd had the first needle-in-my-stomach test—to extract a small sample of the placenta. It hadn't hurt as much as I'd anticipated, but it hadn't been my bright-est day, either. And I'd been worried sick pretty much ever since.

Lynn was concerned about the test results.

Just what I needed. I was barely three months into the pregnancy—had already gained five pounds—and the problems were starting. How on earth was I going to make it through six and a half more months of this?

What if the baby wouldn't make full-term? What if it had Down syndrome? What if…

I thought about calling Kylie. But she'd had her in-semination procedure the day before and was staying flat in bed for forty-eight hours in spite of the doctor's assurances that bed rest wasn't necessary.

And, of course, I thought about calling Denny. When didn't I think about him? I'd seen him several times since Carmel. He'd been to my home—even spent the night a couple of times. And we met in Ontario a time or two, as well. He was due in town the next day—Friday—the day Lynn wanted to see me. He was just in for the afternoon before heading for L.A. to fly off to Australia.

I thought about calling Shane. He and Derek would hold my hands.

I didn't want hand-holding. I wanted promises for a healthy baby. I wanted Denny.

THE BOUNCE IN DENNY'S STEP almost made me weep that Friday at noon. I'd just come from my appointment with Lynn, but I couldn't think about that now. There was nothing immediately urgent and Denny was about to be off on an adventure. I wanted him to remember me smiling and sexy during his long nights under the stars.

"Hey, Mel!" He pulled me into his arms for a kiss

right there on the sidewalk outside the Mexican place we'd been to the night I told him about the baby. May was approaching and the corners and boulevards in Palm Desert were awash with glorious, colorful blooms.

I put my greeting into the kiss.

"Whew." He grinned down at me as we stepped into the restaurant. "If you're trying to tempt me into staying, that's the way to go about it."

I'd give my right arm to have him stay. But he'd be giving up his whole way of life if he did so. I couldn't ask him to pay that price.

Besides, I reminded myself, he'd be back. And I was a grown-up, now. I might love him to distraction, but I didn't need him. I didn't need anyone.

That miserable inner voice that hadn't been fond of me in years wondered why, if I was so grown-up, I felt so damn small and helpless.

I don't know how I made it through lunch, except that I knew I had to be strong. Of course, that hour with Denny was made easier by the fact that he was talking almost nonstop about his plans. He was happy and that just plain felt good. He'd be on the plane for twenty-four hours—he was going to spend a week in Sydney, and then travel to the outback. He and his guide would spend at least two weeks under the stars.

"You okay?" he asked halfway through the meal, glancing down at my barely touched plate.

"Fine," I lied. "Just a little morning sickness."

His eyes grew shadowed and I knew he was remembering. Horrible bouts of nausea were what tipped us off to the fact I was pregnant all those years ago. We'd been together the first couple of times it had happened. He'd held back my hair while I retched my guts out. And then he'd gone down to the stream near where we'd been parked to wet a napkin and tenderly wipe my face.

He'd had chewing gum, too, though I didn't know why I'd remember such an asinine thing after all these years.

"Maybe I shouldn't go."

"Yes!" I took a deep breath. "Yes, you should go. Worst case scenario, I'm going to get sick to my stomach. Most likely, I'm going to be ravenous an hour from now and will look like an elephant by the time I see you again."

God, I hoped so. *Please, please, let it be so.* True to the contrariness of human nature, now that my baby might be in trouble, I wanted him or her more than I wanted anything.

I'd only had a couple of hours to digest the facts, the results of the C.V. sampling, but there they were. My placenta was thin. I might be fine; I might have periodic bleeding and need bed rest; I might not be able to carry my baby full-term.

Wait, I'd said I wasn't going to think about that. There wasn't a damn thing Denny could do to protect our baby if he stayed.

I had to get him on his way to Australia so I could fall apart in peace—without worrying about him feeling guilty for having any part in putting me through this potentially heartbreaking pregnancy.

CHAPTER FOURTEEN

TWO DAYS AFTER DENNY LEFT, I woke up to a bed spotted with blood. I was so terrified, I don't remember much about what happened immediately after that. Apparently I called Shane, though I don't remember dialing his number. He and Derek called an ambulance and they met me at the hospital.

The next however many hours were a blur of panic, worry and pain. I swear the cramping was worse than labor pains. I slept as much as I could—more for escape than anything else. And it seemed as if every time I woke up there was at least one face peering in my hospital-room window from the hallway. They didn't come in, they just smiled. Kylie. Shane. Derek. Even Denny.

That's when I knew I was hallucinating. Denny was in Australia. I wondered if they'd put some kind of nerve-deadening drug in my IV, thinking that was causing me to imagine things.

None of the medical personnel talked to me about much of anything. Cheerful chatter. Innocuous, meaningless.

I was sure that meant I'd lost the baby. And, at some point, I made the decision to just keep hallucinating. If it was drugs, I hoped they'd just keep giving them to me. I was too old to recover from a miscarriage. I couldn't assuage my grief with the thought of another pregnancy. Another baby. This one had been a fluke.

But it had been my fluke and I'd wanted it. I hated myself for not realizing that soon enough. Maybe if I'd loved the idea of my unexpected gift from the beginning, been a little more grateful, I'd have been allowed to keep it.

It seemed as if days went by, though on some level I realized that not that much time had passed. Maybe one more night. Nurses came and went. Lynn seemed to be present a lot. And eventually, when I cared enough to notice, it occurred to me that I had wires coming out from under the bedcovers. They were attached to my stomach among other places.

I couldn't tell you what was in the room. I didn't bother looking. The fluorescent green lights on the monitors beside my bed drew what focus I had. When I was all slept out, I lay there staring at the monitors— following the waves and dots. A heart was beating. I recognized that much. Who wouldn't? The words *as seen on TV* kept floating in and out of my mind.

I didn't care beyond that. Couldn't think or make any kind of decisions. Just stared at those waves and dots. Watching the heart beat to know that I was still alive— letting it do the work for me. Eventually my gaze wandered to the second screen. More waves and dots. They were watching my heart twice. It was beating at two different speeds—one much more rapid than the other. Two different ventricles? Was one slowly stopping? Could they watch two different parts of the same heart? Did one heart beat at two different speeds?

Without warning I got hot from the inside out. A flash. I'd thought I was done with them. Had the pregnancy and miscarriage triggered another menopause?

The first monitor, the slower one, sped up as I tried not to think. To hope. Two monitors. Two heartbeats.

Wires on my stomach. Could it be? Was it possible that I'd been given a second chance to appreciate the great gift I'd been given late in life?

Was I still pregnant?

And if I moved, would I lose it?

Turning my head slowly, looking for another human being, someone to answer my questions—to either give me hope or dash it once and for all—I saw the window in the door to my room. The one that had figured so much in my dreams these past hours. The window with the faces.

DENNY WAS THERE. So my mind was still playing cruel tricks on me. *And you'd actually thought you were rational,* my mind taunted me. Apparently even tragedy didn't kill that small voice in my head.

I tried to focus, but my vision was blurred—by tears, probably. I blinked. And blinked again. Denny was still there, watching me, his gaze intent, as if he was saving the world.

Saving me?

I smiled. What the hell. I needed to be saved and if a mirage in a window could do it, then who was I to deny myself that salvation?

The image in the window blinked, looked around, said something behind him and turned back—all in the space of a second. And then, as I watched, Kylie's image appeared. And then Lynn's. And suddenly—now this was bizarre—my parents were there. And then Denny was back. Taller than the other two, he was slightly behind them, but between my mother and father.

My grin grew. What a great dream. What a great life.

And then the door pushed open. Lynn was there first, with two nurses I recognized. Everyone was smiling, but completely efficient and businesslike as they pulled the curtains on the window. The nurses stayed in the background, checking equipment and wires and lines, waiting for direction from Lynn.

"You sure don't do anything in half measures, girl," Lynn said, her fingers feeling the pulse on my wrist, gaze jumping from monitor to monitor, to my face and back. "And I thought you were my friend."

"I am." My throat was dry, my voice unrecognizable—crusty. "What's going on?"

"You ready to listen?"

I nodded, vaguely remembering telling Lynn to do what she must but to leave me out of it.

"You lost some blood," she said. "And you were in shock."

I met her gaze. "I almost died." Give it to me straight, damn it. "Didn't I?"

"No, but you might have if the bleeding hadn't stopped."

She moved the sheet aside, pushed gently on my stomach, looked lower, as well.

"Did I lose the baby?"

Glancing up, Lynn smiled at me. "Who, you?" she said. "Come on, Melanie. When have you ever given up on anything? You're the woman who loves a guy at sixteen and hangs on to that forever. You get divorced and keep your ex as a best friend. You give up a baby for adoption and become her mother thirty years later."

I couldn't look away from her. "Am I still pregnant?" I asked, angry, afraid, ready to cry.

"Ah, sweetie," Lynn said, tender in a way I'd never seen as she replaced the sheet and ran a hand lightly down my face. "You didn't lose your baby. And as of now it doesn't look as though you're going to, as long as you do as you're told. The bleeding was due to complications from the exam. Your placenta held up just fine. Everything looks good with the baby."

I kept the pregnancy?

"I'll do every single thing I'm told," I said, wide-eyed, crying and laughing. I grabbed the hand against my face. Kissed it. "Thank you," I told my friend. "Thank you."

"Hold on before you anoint me," Lynn said. Her voice was more abrupt now, but she was grinning. "You're going to be confined to bed rest for the next few weeks," she said. "Possibly for the duration of the pregnancy."

Bed rest? That was it?

"Thank you," I said again. I'd lie in hot wax for nine months if that's what it took to keep my baby inside me long enough to grow.

"I didn't do anything, Melanie," Lynn said, nodding to the nurses that they were ready to leave. "You're a fighter. Always have been. You did this."

It was her job to make me feel better, but how I wanted to believe her. I wanted to know that after almost fifty years of living, I'd finally gotten something completely right.

CHAPTER FIFTEEN

"I'M GLAD YOU'RE HERE." It was a couple of hours later, my bed was cranked up and I clutched Denny's hand for all I was worth. I knew I had to let go soon. Just not yet. Too many emotions fought inside me. I needed his calm, the strength he brought to my heart, while I sorted out all the confusion that was assaulting me.

"I wouldn't be anywhere else," he said. When he arrived he'd pulled up a chair beside the bed, but half an hour ago he'd carefully crawled onto the bed beside me. Kylie, who was pregnant and up for only small periods of time, had taken the biological grandparents she'd just met to her place—to meet their son-in-law and, tomorrow, to meet her adoptive parents.

Shane and Derek had been in, too. They were the ones who'd called my parents. Poor Shane, he'd first had to tell them about the pregnancy and then tell them I might be losing the baby—and my life, as well. They'd taken Perpetua home with them.

I wasn't there when Shane and Denny met. I'd have to wait for Kylie to tell me how that went. Shane's parents had come by to see me. They'd even been cordial to Derek. Apparently, my folks were going out to dinner with them the next night.

"Yes, you would, too, be somewhere else," I said now to Denny. I was too tired to be forceful, but tomorrow was another day. "You should be in the outback of Australia, seeing sights that inspire you to greatness."

He stared at me. "There is no sight that will ever surpass this."

I wanted to believe him. But I was not a pretender, never had been.

"Denny, nothing's changed…."

Reaching up he kissed me lightly. Gently. Stopping my words in the sweetest of ways.

"Everything's changed, Mel," he said, resting his head beside mine on the pillow.

"I was angry when I left all those years ago. Angry at life, at the bum rap I'd been handed. Angry at my father for beating me up instead of loving me, for being a weak drunk instead of a good father. Angry at myself for having gotten you pregnant, screwing up the one good thing that had happened to me. Angry with your parents for not making it better for us when they had the means to do so."

"I know." I swallowed back more tears.

"To some degree, I've been angry ever since."

That didn't surprise me, though I'd hoped he'd found some measure of peace.

"I was angry all the way to Australia."

"You were?" I turned my head so I could see him better. "Why?"

"That's the damnable part," he said. "I didn't know why. Couldn't figure it out. I'd put the past to rest, had you back in my life again, had my life just as I wanted it—what in the hell did I have to be angry about?"

I didn't know, but I hoped he was going to tell me.

"I was angry with you, Mel."

With me? How could he possibly be angry with me? How dare he? I loved him completely, had sacrificed so much. "I went through labor and delivery, buddy," I said. "At seventeen. While you were off gallivanting around the country and if you…"

"Shh." He put a finger against my lips. I wanted to bite it.

"I was angry at you for not needing me enough then, for being able to let me go. And angry, because you didn't need me enough now to make me stay."

"But, Denny…"

"I know," he said, carefully pulling me close to him. "As soon as I arrived in Sydney I turned around and caught the next plane home—intending to give you a piece of my mind."

"I missed hearing it, I guess."

"I didn't give it," he said. "I got Kylie's message as soon as I landed in L.A. I made it to Palm Desert in less than two hours and I've been here ever since."

That explained the duffel I'd noticed in the corner of my room.

"You don't look wrinkled or anything."

"They have a shower for family members' use."

Family member. That sounded good. He was forgiven for coming to yell at me.

"These past hours, while I watched you, waiting for you to come back to me, I did a lot of thinking, Mel. A lot of changing. I'm not seventeen anymore."

"I could've told you that," I murmured against his chest.

"And with the hindsight gained from fifty years of living, I saw that what I assumed was a lack of need in you was, instead, a love so great that you sacrificed yourself, your own needs, for mine."

"I'm no saint, Denny," I had to assert. If he put me on some kind of pedestal I was only going to come crashing down. "I just love you."

"And I love you, Mel."

"That still doesn't mean you're cut out to be tied to a family."

"It wasn't the ties that got in my way."

The monitor beside me sped up again. I'd be glad when they took me off the damn thing. It left a woman no privacy at all.

"What was it?"

"In my mind, when you became part of a family, you gave other people the right to run your life, control you, treat you as they saw fit, and you couldn't do anything about it. You just had to take it."

The waves and dots slowed again.

"In a sense, that's true, I guess."

"Of course it is. If there'd been no truth in what I thought, I'd have seen through it long before now."

"So?"

Did I say I was tired? Too tired to keep up with him.

"So, what kind of fool wouldn't give that right to someone who wanted his happiness even more than he did? Who would help him, and let him help her, to be the best they could be?"

I couldn't breathe. Was there a monitor that told them that, too? Out at the nurses' station maybe? He'd just used marriage words. Did they mean what I hoped they meant? Or was I being a fool again?

"You've shown me unconditional love, Mel. As much as any imperfect human being is capable of showing it. And now that I've finally got the picture, I don't ever want to be without it again. Not for a minute. A day. A week. And certainly not for a lifetime."

I was crying again. Sobbing. Uncontrollably. All over him.

"Will you marry me?"

He was kissing my wet face, licking my tears, holding me so close I felt completely encapsulated by his magic—his love—the promise of peace and joy and happiness that I was only going to find with him.

"Yes, Denny," I sobbed. "Oh, yes."

And three weeks later, I did.

It's a Boy!
Name: Samuel Nicholas Walker
Date of Birth: November 3, 2006
Weight: 6 lbs. 9 oz.
Parents: Dennis and Melanie Walker.
Mother and baby (and Daddy, too) are just perfect!
Big sister is six months pregnant—and ecstatic.

Dear Reader,

I'm a mom, so participating in the *From Here to Maternity* anthology was an honor. While I was writing *Promoted to Mom*, it was easy for me to remember the joy and happiness associated with being pregnant, as well as the stress over many decisions parents have to make. My hero and heroine, Braden and April, realize the enormity of the decisions they make that will affect their baby. While they are figuring out their lives, they fall in love all over again and understand they need to compromise to find their happily-ever-after.

When I celebrate Mother's Day this year, I will give thanks for my mother, whom I miss very much, as well as for my son, who is the greatest gift I will ever receive.

All my best,

Karen Rose Smith

PROMOTED TO MOM
Karen Rose Smith

To the women who taught me how to mother: my mom, Romaine Cacciola, my mother-in-law, Rita Smith, and my son's (as well as my husband's) godmother, DeSales Sterner. Thank you.

CHAPTER ONE

"I'M GOING TO HAVE a baby."

"April…" Braden Galloway's shock was evident in the low sound of my name.

We had stepped into a corner of the kitchen, away from the central hustle of Braden's restaurant. But now the room was silent as if everyone was eavesdropping.

When I couldn't reach Braden at home, I had phoned the Tin Roof and his staff told me he'd gone skiing for a few days. Today, even though he was supposed to be back, he still hadn't answered his home phone or cell and I hadn't wanted to leave a message. This was news I had to give him in person. And yet, a mixture of joy and fear about being pregnant had led me to blurt out my reason for being here rather than choosing my moment with more care.

I realized I'd just made a monumental fool of myself.

Turning on my heels, I rushed down the short hall to the ladies' room and slipped inside, bolting the door. Before Braden, I'd focused on my career. I'd been hesitant to fall in love because my father had controlled my mother's life. In addition to that, my sister Jenny's husband had deserted her when she'd needed him most. But when I'd met Braden, fear and hesitancy had evaporated into a haze of new love…until the night we'd argued.... Until I'd realized he hadn't loved me enough to work out our differences.

Tears came to my eyes and I blinked furiously. At thirty-five, I, April Renquist, was self-confident enough and savvy enough to handle whatever reaction Braden might have to the news he was going to be a father.

There was a knock on the door, a try at the knob and then a muffled oath. The door rattled with Braden's insistence. "Let me in, April."

Let him in when he hadn't contacted me once, since our argument four months ago? *Let him in* when, although I already loved this baby with all my heart, I still had so many fears about being pregnant that they kept me sleepless most nights? *Let him in* when he'd been too inflexible even to consider my dreams along with his own?

Knowing there was no point postponing the inevitable—I'd already put off telling Braden for too long—I flipped back the bolt.

He opened the door slowly, then stepped inside. I was only a foot away from him again and my pulse raced like a runaway train. To my amazement, even with so much tension between us, I found I just wanted to stand there staring at the smile lines around his eyes, his strong jaw, the wave that didn't always behave in his raven hair. The electricity between us had been as powerful as a bolt of lightning since the moment I'd met him at a Chamber of Commerce dinner the previous summer, and it still hummed between us now.

"At least we'll have some privacy in here." He looked at me with his probing green eyes, as if he were trying to see into my heart, but I was still too hurt to let him anywhere near.

"I'm sorry I told you like that," I apologized.

"You just announced it to the entire state of Oklahoma. Gossip carries from the kitchen," he added, more gently than I'd expected.

The silence that fell over us vibrated with the memories of words we'd shared in the dark as well as words said to each other in anger. The last night we'd been together, we'd lost ourselves in desire and made body-weakening love without protection. During those time-suspended minutes, I'd forgotten what had happened to my sister, Jenny. For those minutes I'd been crazily in love with my fiancé, showing him exactly how much I loved him.

"Is the baby mine?"

The fact that he had to ask made me turn away from him to face the sink. "Of course, it's yours."

His gaze met mine in the mirror. My light brown, chin-length hair was disheveled against the hood of my coat, and I had circles under my eyes. Braden's serious expression gave no clue as to what I might expect from him. I wondered if I should have consulted a lawyer. If Braden tried to block my move to L.A....

He put his hand on my shoulder. When he did, I could remember pleasure-filled moments we'd shared, our first date, his proposal in the museum garden.

"You know I want kids. I love the idea of being a dad."

I turned to face him and saw the pleasure he took at the mere thought of being a father. Four months ago, after we'd made love, I'd told him I'd been offered the promotion I'd been planning for all my adult life. But the promotion meant a move to L.A. Braden immediately reminded me that his restaurant was here in Oklahoma City...his family was in nearby Galloway...his roots were in this area. He'd suggested I turn down the promotion, marry him and start a family right away. For the first time in our relationship his attitude had been rigid, and I'd panicked, thinking I couldn't marry a man who'd turned out to be like my father. I couldn't marry a man who expected me to give up my dreams for his.

"I know you like the idea of being a dad. But, Braden, I was awarded the promotion and I'm moving to California by mid-February."

"You *can't* move. That's not fair to me, April. I don't want to be a father in name only."

His tone was determined and I knew Braden was used to getting what he wanted. But my life counted, too. My dad had destroyed my mom's ability to make her own choices. He'd dismissed her dreams, convinced her to settle for a life without an identity of her own and persuaded her to devote her life to him. I would *not* let that happen to me.

"I'm having a baby. And I'll be the best mother I can be. But I trained for this promotion. I've wanted it for years."

Braden knew I'd started out managing a cosmetics department in a store in Dallas, then transferred to Phoenix to become a field rep. When Natural Beauty Cosmetics opened a branch in Galloway, I'd moved here knowing I could grow with the company.

Someone pounded on the bathroom door. "Boss? We need you."

I recognized the voice of one of Braden's waitresses. I'd gotten to know his staff fairly well during our whirl-wind courtship.

With a frown, he turned toward the door. "In a minute."

The waitress called again, "We've got a table

unhappy with the corn dressing."

To me, he said in a low voice, "We can't talk here and we're not going to solve anything now. I have a meeting in Tulsa tomorrow. I'll call you when I get back."

"You still have my number?" After all, he hadn't called after our argument. I'd returned his engagement ring when we'd argued, yet I'd expected he might reconsider his stand on my promotion…might care enough about me to call and talk it through again. But he hadn't. I'd heard from a friend about a week ago that she'd seen him at Galloway's community theater with a short curly-haired redhead who had attended *The Nutcracker* with him. Had she also gone skiing with him?

"I have your number," he said evenly.

Studying his expression, unable to read his emotions, I had to admit I'd missed him so very much. Still I had my pride and that was going to get me through this.

Crossing to the door, I put my hand on the knob.

"How pregnant are you?" he asked, unable to tell because of my coat.

"Four months."

The line of his mouth tightened and his angular jaw set. I knew exactly what he was thinking—I hadn't told him right away. Unable to handle any more confrontation tonight, I went into the hall and hurried through the kitchen to the back door.

Outside, I took a few deep cold breaths and heard a car door slam. In another direction someone hummed "Jingle Bells." Hurrying to my car, I hit the remote to unlock the door and slipped inside. A few minutes later I was on the highway toward Galloway and the town house where I'd lived for the past ten years while I was working on my career.

During the drive home, I reexamined why I'd never revealed to Braden the real reasons marriage and starting a family had spooked me.

ONCE I'D GOTTEN HOME, I couldn't seem to stop the tears. At midnight, I stood in my bathroom, my nose red from blowing it. I told myself my upset was simply a matter of hormones, yet my heart knew better. While I applied one of Natural Beauty's soothing lotions to my face, I began to think about how my childhood and Jenny's stillborn baby had affected my relationship with Braden. But, maybe we'd never looked below the surface with each other. Maybe we'd seized on the passion between us, right there on the surface, so we didn't have to delve any deeper.

The phone rang.

I froze for a moment, then set down the jar of lotion. No one would call this time of night except—

When Braden and I were dating, he'd often phone after I was in bed, just to say good-night. He'd done so many wonderful things. He'd made me feel so special. Had he just stopped loving me when I'd given him back his ring? My heart hurt as I answered the phone by my bed.

"It's me," he said as if he needed an introduction.

"I know," I murmured back. Tonight I wouldn't be describing the peach silk nightgown I was wearing or teasing him with flirty banter.

"What are you going to do about the baby?" There was an edge to his tone. I wished I could do something to alleviate the tension between us, but I couldn't.

"What do you mean—what am I going to do? I'm already at sixteen weeks."

"Some women—"

"I'm not *some* women, Braden. Don't you know me at all?" Suddenly I realized my acceptance of Braden's proposal after six weeks of a swept-off-my-feet courtship might have been the most foolish decision I'd ever made. We'd fallen in lust and we hadn't had time to share our souls.

"I thought maybe you'd consider giving up the baby for adoption," he explained calmly.

My breath caught in my chest. Was he thinking about suing for custody?

"No. I won't consider adoption. I can make a good life for our baby…especially with the promotion."

Time ticked by and I could feel Braden's restrained frustration. "You know I want kids. When you have this baby, I intend to be a hands-on dad."

"With me in Los Angeles?"

"I'll fly to California whenever I can. But, April you know it would be better for you and our child if you don't move to L.A. You might have financial security if you take this position," he added, "but aren't your hours going to get even longer? Won't you have to travel? Have you thought about giving me custody when the baby's born. I have a large loving family. My mother or sister could babysit…"

"No!"

When Braden somberly asked, "You really want this baby?" I realized my forceful reply had surprised him.

With all sincerity, I answered, "Yes, I do."

At the moment when I'd checked the stick in the pregnancy test, happiness had rushed through me. I was pregnant…. Braden and I had created another life. Fear had soon crowded the happiness, though—and my sadness that Braden and I weren't together had overshadowed my discovery. I'd gone on with the idea of my new promotion as if it were even more important now because I had a baby to think of and plan for. Maybe I'd postponed telling Braden because he could change everything…including the way I felt about moving.

"Did you consider *not* telling me about the baby?"

I hesitated, then answered honestly, "Yes, I did."

"You asked if I know you. I *thought* I knew you… until you decided to throw everything away for a job."

I remembered my anguish, how torn I'd felt and how unsure I'd been as I handed back his ring.

"I'll get back from Tulsa around four tomorrow," he finally continued. "Can you free up your schedule for a couple of hours?"

My schedule was tight because I was in the midst of tying up loose ends before moving west. Right now, though, my baby was more important than my schedule.

"I'll free up some time." In spite of everything, I wanted to see him again. I had to find out if he'd dismissed me from his life simply because I didn't fit or because he'd never really loved me at all.

After Braden said goodbye and we'd hung up, tears came to my eyes again.

Hormones, I reiterated, determined to get my emotions under control by the time I saw Braden tomorrow.

"APRIL, DO YOU AGREE?" Frank Temple asked impatiently.

I'd been deep in worried thoughts of my own as my immediate supervisor, Charlie Rugland, droned on about projections for Christmas sales. I was reliving my teen years, the period during which I'd realized how unhappy my mother had been with my father. Yet she'd never had the courage to divorce him and make a life of her own. Had she stayed because of Jenny and me? Had she thought her unhappiness, her disconnect from dad, wouldn't affect her daughters?

When I'd started college, I'd decided my career would be more important than any man. When Jenny had married, she'd seemed blissfully happy, and after she'd gotten pregnant, she practically glowed! And then everything had gone terribly wrong. Jenny's contractions had started early and the baby had been stillborn. My sister had sunk into a depression and her husband had become impatient with her. Not considering Jenny's grief, Bill had wanted her to get pregnant again quickly to replace what they'd lost. But Jenny couldn't even consider it. Wanting a family, tired of dealing with a wife who couldn't get over her loss, her husband had divorced her.

Mom's disillusionment and Jenny's husband's desertion had taught me to find my course and stick to it, to search out happiness and fulfillment without a husband and maybe even without children. I'd been afraid that what had happened to Jenny could happen to me.

And I still was.

Ever since discovering I was pregnant, I'd been terrified something would happen to my baby. I thought of this little life inside me every waking moment. I was torn by what would be best for my child and what would be best for me. Our lives would always be intertwined.

How did this promotion fit in and what should I do about it? How was I going to tell Charlie Rugland and Frank Temple, who'd just offered me the job of a lifetime, that I was pregnant?

As the CEO of Natural Beauty vied for my attention

now, I answered him. "Yes, I agree. Christmas sales this year will equal or surpass last year's."

Gray-haired, robust, in his early sixties, Frank Temple took a no-nonsense approach to everything, including the quality of the cosmetics his company produced, the success of his sales force, and the enthusiasm and commitment of every one of his employees.

"Is there something wrong, April? You look a bit pale today, and you seem distracted," Charlie Rugland commented, regarding me with a kind look.

"I'm fine, Charlie. Mr. Temple, if I seem a bit distracted, it's just that I have a very long to-do list to tackle."

Charlie nodded in agreement. "You certainly do. You have your replacement to train in the next six weeks, as well as tying up all loose ends. As we've told you, we'd like you in L.A. by February fifteenth. Then, of course, there's business as usual…" He trailed off. "I did notice you came in late this morning. An appointment with that mover we discussed?"

I still hadn't made a decision about my furniture—what to keep and what to sell. But this morning a mover hadn't detained me. I'd had a check-up with my obstetrician. "No, sir, that wasn't today. I have an appointment with Overland Moving the first week in January." I wasn't going to explain further unless I was pushed. Charlie's raised brow said he'd like a detailed reason for my tardiness, but Frank Temple didn't seem to care.

Apparently sensing something, though, Mr. Temple asked, "Are you unsure about this promotion, April? You seemed thrilled four months ago when we proposed it. When I announced I'd be moving you into our corporate headquarters, I don't think I've ever experienced a more enthusiastic or spontaneous thank-you. But now—"

"I want this job, Mr. Temple. I studied for it, I trained for it, and now I have the experience that you're going to need for me to be a successful Vice President of Sales. You won't be sorry you promoted me." My enthusiasm and confidence were good cover for my doubts, which had begun as small worries but were taking over more and more of my thoughts.

"That's what I like to hear," Temple responded, standing now, signaling the meeting was over. The papers I'd given him a half hour earlier were lying on the conference room table. "I appreciate all the work you've put into these reports. As usual you've gone beyond the call of duty. I seriously consider every note you write, every comment, every suggestion."

"It's my job." I thought about Christmas next week, and my hand went to my stomach, envisioning the holidays a year from now and how everything was going to change. Where would I be living? Would Braden be in my life—as well as his child's life?

A few minutes later, Charlie walked me out into the hall. Frank Temple strode off toward the elevator as Charlie and I veered toward my office. The firm was housed in a smoked-glass and steel building on the outskirts of Galloway. An up-and-coming company, it was already making its mark in the world market. I wanted to make this move desperately for a multitude of reasons.

"What *is* wrong, April?" Charlie asked.

"I have a stack of work to finish before my move."

"All right. But if you need a shoulder, I'm here."

At fifty-seven, Charlie was twenty-two years older than I was. He was a handsome, well-built man, and he'd been my mentor ever since I'd taken a position with Natural Beauty.

"Thanks, Charlie. I know that. I'll let you know if I need to talk. I know I was late coming in this morning, but I've worked a lot of evenings this month. I'm also going to need a couple of hours this afternoon for personal affairs, but I'll be here earlier than usual in the morning."

After studying me for a moment, he responded, "I know you're dedicated to Natural Beauty. You take the time you need before you leave for L.A." Then with a smile, he turned to head in the other direction.

When I looked down the hall, I stood perfectly still. Braden was standing at my office door. He was an hour early. As I took a few steps forward, everything I'd ever felt for him flooded through me all over again.

I was five foot six without shoes, and even when I wore high heels Braden towered over me. Today he was wearing a charcoal gray suit, pale blue shirt, and gray-and-blue tie. The suit coat fit his shoulders as if it were custom-made for them, and maybe it had been. He was unsmiling, and I realized I'd give anything to see the playful twinkle back in his eyes, to have him tease me about the conservative cut of my suits. Whenever he'd turned his crooked grin on me, I melted.

The night we'd broken our engagement, we'd been poles apart in terms of what we wanted in life. Were we still?

As I reached Braden, he said simply, "I finished up in Tulsa early. How about taking a drive with me to the cowboy museum? It's quiet this time of day. It's always been a special place for us. Maybe walking and talking there will help us sort things out. I have a commitment later tonight, but we'll have a good chunk of time now."

Until our argument, Braden had always been chival-rous, reasonable and unbearably sexy. The National

Cowboy and Western Heritage Museum had been one of our favorite places to visit together. In the garden there, he'd proposed. Was this his way of telling me he wanted to reconnect? Yet if Braden had a "commitment" later, did that mean he had a date…maybe with the redhead?

"Let me gather some work together to take home, and then we can go."

It only took a few minutes for me to stuff personnel reviews into a folder and close that in my briefcase. Then I called the receptionist to say I'd be out of the office the rest of the afternoon.

All the while I was on the phone, Braden stood casually in the doorway watching me, assessing my red suit, his gaze sending me messages I couldn't begin to understand.

When I hung up, he went to the coatrack and took my coat from the hook, holding it for me. "It's still windy. You'll want to bundle up."

"It's always windy," I returned with a small laugh, hoping to lighten the atmosphere a bit.

I slipped my arm into one sleeve. As Braden held my coat, I was so aware of his presence behind me. His cologne was a woodsy musk, the same scent he'd worn when we dated. As I glanced over my shoulder at him, I could see afternoon stubble already shadowing his jaw. He had had a thick beard and the erotic sensation of its bristles on my skin had always been a sensual pleasure I loved.

I remembered whisperings in the night as he'd told me about growing up in Galloway and I'd shared with him the information that we'd moved around a lot when I was a child before my father settled into a career as a venture capitalist. But I'd only met his family once, for our engagement dinner, and he'd never met mine. Why hadn't either of us probed deeper? Had I been afraid of becoming too vulnerable? Had he?

His eyes were mesmerizing, and I felt turned inside out. Then he moved and helped me with the other sleeve of my coat.

As I buttoned and belted it, he asked, "How have you been feeling?"

"Mostly fine. A little nausea now and then."

"You're seeing a doctor?"

There was a caring in Braden's tone that wrapped itself around me, urging me to believe that at the least we could be friendly coparents.

I kept my voice low, so that anyone passing by in the hall couldn't hear. "I know there can be complications for women thirty-five and older, but I'm not taking any chances. At first I thought I had the flu, and I didn't take a pregnancy test until I was about two months pregnant. But then I saw an obstetrician right away."

After studying me for a long moment, he motioned toward the hall and I preceded him out the door.

As we walked through the parking lot toward Braden's SUV, the December wind buffeted us and I wished we could fall into the camaraderie we'd experienced from the moment we'd met. We'd laughed together. We'd teased each other. Braden had shown me affection like I'd never known, taking my hand, draping his arm over my shoulders, kissing me on the spur of the moment. I'd loved the feeling of belonging that his attention had given me.

"Have you been to any of the art shows at the museum lately?" I asked to make conversation. I knew Braden enjoyed going there because of his Oklahoma

roots. He had a keen sense of history and a strong connection with the pioneers who had been his forefathers.

"I haven't had the time. Officially, I'm opening the
restaurant in Galloway on New Year's Eve and I've been
caught up with the details of that. I managed to fit in a
few days skiing just to take a break before the new year
gets too hectic."

I wondered if his commitment tonight had to do with
the new restaurant, but I didn't feel I could ask. Maybe
later I could find out if he'd been skiing alone.

Braden used his remote to unlock the vehicle.

When he opened the passenger door, I looked up at
him and teased, "Maybe we should take *my* car."
Braden's SUV was one of those that was built high off
the ground, and I never could maneuver well in high
heels and a straight skirt.

"I'll help you," he offered as he had many times before.

However, today, so much was different. Instead of me
using his arm as a support, instead of him offering me
a hand, he lifted me off my feet. I was in his arms and
staring up at him, totally breathless and surprised. He'd
swept me off my feet…again. Had he wanted to touch
me as much as I'd wanted to touch him? Did he miss
the closeness we'd once had?

For the briefest of moments our lips were so very
close, our breath almost mingling. Then he deposited
me on the leather seat, closed my door and climbed in
the driver's side.

Maybe we were both rattled by the close contact
because we didn't talk during the twenty-minute drive.
The museum was located on Persimmon Hill in north-
east Oklahoma City. At the end of summer we'd walked
the colorful gardens hand in hand. Braden had proposed

by one of the more secluded waterfalls, and I felt a lump in my throat now just thinking about it.

After we parked and walked inside the building, Braden insisted on paying for both of us. As I checked my coat, I felt him study me all over again. I'd had to pin the waistband on my skirt because already my middle was thickening a little. It was so odd to think about the life inside me changing my body. Yet each day brought more of an awareness of that precious life and I cherished each change, even as I continued to worry. Jenny had gained weight month by month and had regular checkups. There'd been no indication of a problem before her premature contractions began. When I thought about that night in the hospital when my sister had lost her baby, I got chills.

"Do you want to sit or walk?" Braden asked, moving through the entrance area.

The cowboy museum was light and airy and shiny, peach and white and tan. There were comfortable leather couches that were deserted now. But sitting beside Braden just didn't seem wise. "Let's walk."

We strolled by an immense plaster statue—*End of the Trail*—then took the hall toward the galleries. Passing a security guard, we entered the room that housed masterpieces by Remington, Russell and Reynolds.

"Are you certain you're all right?" Braden asked quietly, gazing at me.

"Nope. I'm pregnant," I returned lightly. "I'm still coming to grips with that and… It feels strange to be back here again. With you."

"I thought coming here would be easier than going to your place or mine."

He was right. There was so much tension and awkwardness between us right now. Along with mutual attraction. Our shoulders were almost brushing, and I realized how much I wanted Braden to hold me, to assure me everything would be all right. Yet I pushed away that fantasy.

After a few moments, Braden asked, "Did you tell me about the baby because you wanted to involve me in your pregnancy or because you thought it was the right thing to do?"

I felt as if I were about to step onto a minefield. "I don't think I can separate the two."

He turned to me, ignoring the paintings around us. "You knew if you told me, I could disrupt your plans."

I shook my head vigorously. "No. I knew if I told you, my choices would be more difficult, but they are still *my* choices to make."

"You can be *so* stubborn," he muttered.

Before I could respond that he could be just as rigid, my cell phone beeped in my purse. As I reached inside to retrieve it, Braden stayed my hand. His skin was warm on mine, getting hotter.

The cell phone continued beeping.

"We need this time together. Let your voice mail take it."

Braden was waiting to see how I would respond, and I realized that whatever I did now could affect the rest of my life.

Closing my purse, I looked up at him. "Okay." Even if we didn't come up with any solutions today, we needed to get in touch again.

In touch. I wanted to run my fingers through his hair as I had before. I wanted to lay my head on his shoulder.

I wanted him to reassure me that we could work out our lives together.

The quiet of the art gallery provided a respite from my hectic work life and from the Christmas bustle. This place seemed to be a world set apart. Apparently Braden had known that it would be.

As we moved around the room, I barely noticed the scenes of horses running free and cowboys at work.

When we stopped before a bronze of a cowboy rounding up steers, Braden's voice was low. "Why are you scared of settling down?"

"I'm not." After all, I had accepted his marriage proposal.

"I don't believe that. At the first mention of family, you were ready to run."

How could I tell him everything all at once? The time and place just didn't seem right—or else I still wasn't ready. "I'm going to settle down in Los Angeles in a position I've always wanted to have. Since I learned I was pregnant, I've never had any doubts about keeping this child."

"But you wouldn't have chosen to become pregnant now or any time soon."

Honestly, I had to admit, "No, I wouldn't have."

He thought our broken engagement was all about work and my promotion. That was a huge part of it. Still, I wasn't sure Braden could understand the other reasons why I hadn't wanted to get pregnant—simply because he was a man, a man who had rejected me because I wanted something other than what he wanted. Most likely that was the real reason I couldn't pour out my heart to him yet. But there was another reason, too—I needed to know if he'd really gone on with his life as if our relationship hadn't mattered.

"You said you have another commitment tonight. Is it a date?"

Did I see a glint of satisfaction in his eyes?

"Not in the sense you mean. Would you like to come with me?"

"Where?"

"Say yes, and you'll see."

This was the playful side of Braden I'd fallen in love with. I thought about the work in my briefcase and my to-do list. Somehow none of that seemed to matter tonight. "All right. I'll come with you."

"Good. I think we'll bypass the Western Performers Gallery today in favor of getting something to eat."

That gallery was a favorite of Braden's. I remembered the Roy Rogers CD he'd given me as a surprise one evening and had to smile. It was nostalgic and pure and romantic—as romantic as the pink roses he'd often brought me. So much about us being together had been good.

Why had it been so easy for us to throw it away?

Because neither of us knew how to compromise? Or because Braden had decided I couldn't fit into his world and I wasn't the type of wife he needed in his life?

Maybe I'd find out tonight.

CHAPTER TWO

AFTER A QUICK BISTRO DINNER and a short drive Braden parked in front of an older two-story home in a residential district of Oklahoma City. I glanced at him, puzzled. "A relative's?" I asked.

"Nope. No one in my family lives here."

Although I'd met Braden's parents, sister, brother and their families when we'd eaten dinner together at the Tin Roof, I'd never seen their homes. Now I wondered why. Had the two of us been so wrapped up in each other we'd cut out everyone else? That was the obvious explanation. Yet now I was determined to find the *real* explanation. I'd fallen in love with Braden the first night we'd met. Attraction had been part of it, of course, but beyond that Braden had made me *feel* so many things. Definitely excitement. There had been something in those green eyes of his that had told me he was a kind man, a man who knew how to treat a woman with tenderness, a man who could make me feel safe for the first time in a very long while.

Throughout my dating years I had protected myself with an armor that had kept most men at a distance. With Braden, my armor had begun to crumble, and today I was having a lot of trouble lifting it back into place. Our dinner tonight had included some fairly awkward silences, and

I hadn't felt free enough to ask my questions. Still my heart pounded hard whenever I was near him.

As Braden unfastened his seat belt, he said, "Come on. I have to get something out of the back. I'm playing Santa Claus."

"Santa Claus?" The notion was so far from what I'd been thinking, it took me a moment to grasp it.

I soon learned exactly what Braden meant. The house was set up for families of children who were ill and in the hospital. They could stay here and not have to worry about hotel bills.

As Braden carried the Santa suit over his shoulder, he explained, "These parents and kids are away from their homes at a time of year when they want to be home the most. People donate toys and books for the children, then I play the part of Santa and give them out."

"Have you been doing this long?"

"The past few years."

"How did you become involved with it?"

"Remember Melissa?"

I nodded. "Your niece."

"When she was in fifth grade, her English class collected books to donate here for Christmas. Melissa is always bursting with ideas. She suggested they find a Santa Claus to give them out. Then she recommended me. Without asking me first," he added with a grin. "After I played Santa that year, I was hooked."

The tone of his voice told me he might occasionally be exasperated with his niece but his affection for her was lasting and deep. I looked forward to seeing him in action with these children. I'd get a hint as to the kind of father he'd be.

A minute later inside the house, Braden introduced

me to the housemother and then went to change for the Christmas party. My heart was full of admiration for a man who could be so busy with his restaurant yet find the time to involve himself with a project like this. It shouldn't have surprised me. I'd had several discussions with Braden about our philosophies of life. His natural generosity led him to give not only to his family and those he loved, but also to the community in general.

Everyone welcomed me, and I soon struck up a conversation with a young couple whose baby was in the neonatal intensive care unit. They also had a healthy four-year-old who was playing with another child across the room. I scanned the parents who were gathered there. Many of them looked tired and worried. Yet tonight, they were trying to concentrate on their other children—the ones who weren't ill.

My sister came to mind, the hours I'd spent in the hospital with her throughout a long labor that had ended so sadly. Eventually after her divorce, she'd pulled out of her depression. She'd begun a career she loved as a veterinarian and she now showered her love and attention on her furry patients. Yet I still saw the sadness in her eyes when we were together, and I knew she'd never forget the child she'd lost or forgive Bill for deserting her when she was at her lowest.

I thought again of the day Braden had proposed. Although the idea of getting pregnant had still scared me, I'd considered it for the future…because I loved him. Yet when he'd talked about having a family as soon as we could and about wanting lots of kids, I'd panicked. He'd wanted me to give up my chance to succeed, my chance to make my mark, and so I'd had no choice but to return his ring. I'd so desperately wanted him to see my side, not to eliminate my aspirations as if they didn't matter.

How much had *I* mattered to him, if he could let go of all we'd shared so easily?

When Braden appeared in the living room dressed as Santa, the children were wide-eyed and open-mouthed and their parents were smiling. He'd added some padding under the suit, but not a lot. The fake white beard had slipped sideways a little, and his mouth wasn't quite centered under the moustache. The hat, with its attached white wig, had to be uncomfortable, but he didn't look as if he minded any of it at all as he "ho, ho, ho'ed" his way into the room, carrying two huge laundry bags. Speaking in a voice deeper than his usual one, he greeted the children and told them he'd come to bring some Christmas cheer. And then he began to call their names, handing out presents the volunteers had chosen and wrapped with care.

I felt a lump in my throat as I thought about being part of something like this, not just this time of year, but *all* year long. Maybe I didn't give back enough. Maybe my life had been too focused on my career. Maybe my life had been about running all these years from a relationship with a man and true intimacy because it had been too scary to consider. I'd considered it with Braden. Had I run again, or had I simply chosen the wrong man to trust?

My pregnancy was making me look at life differently.

After Braden had given out the toys and disappeared back to the North Pole, refreshments were set out on a large pine table in the dining room. There were Christmas cookies and fruit breads along with pretzels, chips and soda. I picked up a can of cola and took it down the short hall to the room into which I'd seen Braden disappear. That suit was probably hot and he'd appreciate something to drink. Without thinking twice, I opened the door and went in.

Braden had apparently just stepped into his trousers. The button was unfastened, the belt unbuckled. Shirtless and bare chested, he was hanging the Santa suit on a hanger.

I stopped and stared. It had been four long months since I'd seen him without clothes…four long months that I'd longed for his body close to mine, four long months during which I'd analyzed and regretted and hurt, even though I'd convinced myself I could live my life perfectly well without him.

Overwhelmed with emotions that were turning me inside out, I moved to leave, but Braden said wryly, "Come on in. There's nothing here you haven't seen before."

A hint of amusement accompanied his words and I felt foolish. Although we'd once touched each other intimately, made love until we hadn't cared if the sky was falling, I now felt awkward with him—as if we were almost strangers.

Yet I wanted to get much closer. I wanted to touch him again and have him touch me. I needed to understand everything he wanted from the future and what that future had in store for us as parents.

Thinking about the two of us together again made my palms damp, and I had a difficult time ungluing my gaze from his chest.

Concentrating on his tousled hair, the sparks of humor in his eyes, I offered him the can of soda. "I thought you might be hot."

There was a pause, rife with the electricity that

zipped between us. When he reached out to take the can, our fingertips brushed.

"I am hot," he agreed in a husky voice, his gaze still connected to mine. He popped the top on the soda can and took several long swallows. When he was done, he set the can aside on a desk and I saw that we were surrounded by bookshelves. This was a den or an office.

"You could have been my helper tonight." He was appraising my red suit in a way that told me he was looking at more than the suit. Was he trying to identify the changes in my body? "You look good in red," he added. "You don't wear enough bright colors."

"I work with men, and there isn't a red or purple suit among them," I joked. "I don't usually like to stand out, but with Christmas coming I wanted to look festive."

"You can't hide who you are the rest of the year." His voice had dropped deeper and gotten serious.

"I don't do that."

"Yes, you do. You did it with me. Sometimes when I asked questions, you'd give me short answers without telling me the real truth underneath."

Braden's comments weren't accusatory but probing, as if he was looking for answers, too. I knew he was talking about my parents and my sister and my childhood—all subjects I had avoided with him.

"We knew each other such a short time."

When he took a step closer, my breath caught. "We fell hard and deep, but some things you kept on the surface and I'm not sure that would have changed with time."

Was he right about that? I'd always been a private person because I didn't want anyone to see my hurts or disappointments. If Braden and I had continued our courtship, had gotten married, would I ever have let my armor fall away completely?

"You're wrong about that." I thought again about the way we'd made love the last night we were together and how in our desire for each other, we hadn't used protection. I'd started the pill a few weeks before and had gotten so caught up in loving Braden I'd forgotten the medication wouldn't be effective for a month.

The room was small and we were standing so close. Braden shook his head slightly, as if regretting what he was about to do.

After he raised his hand, with one long finger he pushed my hair from my temple. "I can't believe you're carrying my baby."

"I can't believe it, either." My voice was shaky. His touch had always affected me that way.

Now in this quiet room with more privacy than we'd had all day, his hand slid to my neck and under my hair. "I want to be part of every decision you make in this pregnancy. I want to be a *real* father."

"I want that, too." Yet if I was in Los Angeles and he was in Oklahoma, how could he be an integral part of his child's life? He was wondering the same thing...I could see it in his eyes.

Then he was bending his head, drawing me to him, and I felt the heat of his lips on mine. Braden's kiss always took me out of myself and into him. As his tongue slid into my mouth, I wrapped my arms around his neck.

As his hot mouth built a fire inside me, I couldn't help but run my hands over the taut skin of his shoulders. Lacing my fingers in his hair, I inhaled his scent. Four months melted away and I was being loved by Braden again.

We always fit together perfectly. When he pulled me close, my jacket lapels had slid apart. My silk blouse wasn't much of a barrier and my nipples hardened against his chest. I knew he could feel them because he moved a little, rubbing against me. I moaned, and he angled the kiss more, deepened the intensity of the response he wanted from me. I could feel his arousal and when he rocked his hips against mine, I yearned for the touching and holding and fulfillment he'd always given me. When Braden kissed, there was never anything half-hearted about it. Now, my physical need rivaled his. I knew his desires were strong, but I'd never known how strong mine were until I'd met Braden.

When Braden's hands pressed the small of my back, I melted into him. Apparently he didn't like the feel of my jacket hiding me from him. His hands slid under it onto the silk of my blouse. I could feel the imprint of each of his fingers. As they slipped lower, he pulled me closer and erotically caressed my backside. Our contact was tantalizing, tempting and so sensual I was dizzy.

Braden groaned and I remembered what that meant. It meant everything would escalate and—

Suddenly, unbidden thoughts washed over me, bringing my hands to his shoulders. Upset, I pushed him back and broke our kiss.

His eyes were intensely green with desire.

"Why did you do that?" My voice came out shaky.

"You have to ask?"

"I have to ask. I have to wonder if you're using our…chemistry…to convince me to stay."

"Would that be so bad?" He sounded matter-of-fact, not nearly so shaken by our kiss as I was.

"I can't stay just because we'd have great sex."

His black brows furrowed. "Just what *would* make you stay?" he asked.

"I don't know. I've worked for this position for so long. I'd have to rethink my life, figure out a way to keep my independence…" Giving up the promotion still seemed unfathomable to me.

"Damn your independence," Braden muttered. "You need to think about what's best for this baby."

I pictured my mother, her lack of joy, her resignation. "What's best for this baby is me being happy and fulfilled as a woman."

He grimaced. "Are you repeating something you heard on *Dr. Phil*?"

"I don't have time to watch *Dr. Phil*. You know that." Braden did know a lot about me…more than I'd let any other man know.

"I know that you're driven. I know if you want to be a good mother, you might have to let go of a few of your other dreams."

"What about you? Why can't *you* change your life?"

"Because that doesn't make sense. My family's here. I'm going to have two restaurants here."

"And my promotion and dreams are in California." Except the truth was—not *all* of my dreams were in L.A. Ever since I'd met Braden, he'd been part of them.

"Then I guess we're at an impasse." He reached for his shirt, which hung over a cane-backed chair. Shoving one arm into it and then the other, he pulled the front together. "You frustrate the hell out of me."

"Because I won't give in?" I asked sadly, thinking about how my mother had given in over and over until she hadn't known who *she* was.

"That's the problem. You see it as giving in. If you stay, I see that as the best decision for our baby."

His fingers went to the buttons on his shirt and he started fastening them. I wanted to button it for him. I would've loved to be that close to him again, but I couldn't be.

After I glanced at the door, I moved toward it. "I'd better go back out there. Everyone might think—"

"What could happen almost did?"

When my cheeks grew hot, I blew out a breath and changed the course of the conversation. "You did a good thing here tonight."

He shrugged. "I like kids. What could be more fun than playing Santa Claus?"

I knew the answer to that. More fun for Braden would be playing baseball with his son, lifting his daughter onto his shoulders, buying his child an ice-cream cone or wiping his or her sticky fingers.

"April?"

My eyes met his.

"What are you doing for Christmas?"

"I don't have plans. I was going to call a friend."

"My family opens presents on Christmas Eve at my sister's house. Then on Christmas Day we have dinner at my parents'. Why don't you join us for dinner?"

Was pulling me into his family another way to tie me to Galloway? I didn't see ulterior motives in his eyes. I only saw the longing to be a father to this child.

"All right. That sounds nice."

He smiled at me, and looked relieved that I'd accepted. Before our attraction drew us back together again, I slipped out the door into the hall. I was looking forward to Christmas Day, looking forward to spending more time with Braden.

FROM THE MOMENT I joined Braden's family on Christmas Day, I could feel the tension in the living room. On the drive over, he told me that he'd informed his parents I was pregnant. That added an extra layer to the eggshells I already expected I'd have to walk on.

Braden's sister and brother had children, and the place was bedlam. From the moment I walked into the Galloway home, his mother Shannon's eyes were cool and disapproving. His sister, Carol, was aloof, although his brother, Collin, and Collin's wife, Joan, were friendly. Joan spent some time talking with me while Braden mingled.

Carol and her husband Joel's daughter, Melissa, was thirteen, a strikingly pretty girl with long black hair and green eyes like Braden's. During the hour before dinner, she smiled tentatively at me a few times and I felt almost friendly vibrations from her. After I excused myself to use the restroom, she was waiting for me in the hall as I came out.

"I just want to tell you, I love your outfit."

I was wearing royal-blue, faux-suede slacks that matched a long tunic top with a mandarin collar. I'd bought it because I knew the top would hide the early stages of my pregnancy.

"Thank you. You look pretty sharp yourself." With her green stretch leggings, Melissa wore a red turtleneck and a green-and-red vest decorated with puffy and sparkling white snowmen.

The teen wrinkled her nose. "Mom bought me the outfit

for Christmas and I figured I'd better wear it. It's so...so childish. She won't let me buy the clothes I really like."

Her tone made me smile. Obviously she wanted to grow up faster than she was being allowed to. "What kind of clothes do you want to wear?"

"You know, trendy stuff—crop tops, low-cut jeans. My friends wear them, but Mom says I can't." Brightening again, she tilted her head to one side. "I heard Gran and Mom talking about you. You work for a cosmetics company, don't you?"

All of a sudden I felt self-conscious about being the subject of family conversation. "Yes, I do."

"I think that's awesome. Do they give you lots of free stuff? You don't wear much makeup." She was scrutinizing me as if trying to analyze every cosmetic I'd used on my face.

I laughed. "I do get samples of all the product lines and I have a few kits from the sales counters. But you have to remember, I work for *Natural* Beauty Cosmetics. They enhance the way a woman looks...they don't proclaim it too loudly. Our lines are about taking care of a woman's skin as much as about eye shadows, lipsticks and foundation. Not that you need to worry about any of that right now."

With a giggle, she said, "I'm glad you came today." She'd almost slipped by me into the bathroom when she stopped. "You know, don't you, that everyone's kind of mad at you because you hurt Uncle Braden. He didn't come around to visit for a couple of weeks after you two broke up."

"I didn't mean to hurt him." I couldn't defend myself to this teenager and tell her that her uncle had hurt me just as badly.

Just then, Braden appeared in the hallway. "Dinner's ready."

With an "I'll be right out," Melissa slipped into the powder room and closed the door.

"Afraid I got lost?" I teased.

"I was concerned you might be upset. My family's not being their usual friendly selves."

"It's okay, Braden."

"No, it's not." He looked as if he might want to scold anyone who hadn't welcomed me with open arms.

"Collin and I had a great conversation earlier," I assured him.

"Collin understands what happened with us—two adults, two careers."

"And the others don't?"

"You have to realize my mother believed taking care of children was the most important aspect of her life. She never thought of working outside the home. My sister and sister-in-law have done the same."

Carol's husband was an electrical engineer. Joan's was the chief financial officer for a medical foundation in Oklahoma City. Both women were comfortable letting their husbands provide. I wasn't that type of woman. I needed to contribute. Even if Braden and I had gotten married and had children, I would have wanted to work.

Joan and Collin's four-year-old daughter, Darcy, came running into the hallway straight for Braden and wrapped her little arms around his knees.

"Uncle Bwaden! Uncle Bwaden! Come eat turkey."

Scooping her up, Braden set her atop his shoulders. As she smiled shyly at me, he looked up at her. "Are you going to eat turkey?"

Her head bobbed up and down. "And mashed potatoes and gwavy."

His niece was looking down at him with such an adoring gaze, my throat ached. Braden would be like this with his own children—warm and accepting.

"Come on then. Let's go get some turkey while it's still hot." Glancing over at me, he captured my hand. "You're okay?"

"I'm okay," I assured him. I couldn't be upset that his family resented me because I had hurt one of their own. That meant they cared. If I stayed in Galloway, our child would have an extended family to care about him or her.

My hand in Braden's as we walked into the dining room felt right and I held on to that thought for now.

At dinner, Braden included me in conversations and asked my opinion. He wouldn't let anyone at the table ignore me. Melissa had managed to sit on my other side and she smiled at me often, telling me about her activities at school.

Braden's nephew, Danny, who was about two, sat in a high chair and took most of Joan's attention. I noticed she'd hardly touched anything on her plate and realized that this was what it meant to be a mother—not only hugs and kisses and prayers at bedtime, but putting someone else first twenty-four hours a day.

Putting a child first.

What decisions would be best for this child?

Braden must have seen my attention riveted on his nephew, and on his sweet little chubby cheeks as he stuffed mashed potatoes into his mouth with one of his thumbs. I wanted to hold him and play patty-cake with him. Maybe I'd get the chance later.

Leaning close to me, Braden murmured, "Do you want a boy or a girl?"

His lips almost teased my earlobe and a deliciously warm sensation skipped up my spine.

"That's a tough choice," I responded. "How about you?"

"It doesn't matter."

As I turned, his lips did brush my cheek, and I saw in his eyes that he just wanted a family. He didn't really care if I had a boy or a girl.

When Braden leaned away, I missed his warmth. I missed the possibility that his lips might cover mine. His knee grazed mine under the table, and I didn't think that was an accident.

However, when I looked up and saw his mother watching us, I wondered what she was thinking…and then I wondered if I even wanted to know.

CHAPTER THREE

As MANY TOPICS rolled around the dinner table, I caught Braden's mother glancing my way often. Although I knew speaking to her might be awkward, I had to do it. I just wasn't exactly sure what I was going to say.

Throughout the meal Braden was protective of me. He joined in on some of my conversation with Melissa, smiling when we seemed to speak the same language. I could see he liked the idea that his niece and I were getting along so well. His arm brushed mine often and so did his knee when he leaned toward me so I could hear better what he had to say. His cologne spun my head and his low, deep voice had butterflies fluttering in my stomach.

Had I ever fallen out of love with him? Was I falling deeper now? What was *he* feeling? Could we ever forgive each other for breaking up?

Braden's father, an older version of his son, broke into my reflections. "I was talking to Wayne Rumson yesterday. We ran into each other while I stopped at the grocery store to pick up a few things for your mother."

Shannon explained to me, "Wayne Rumson's the mayor of Galloway," as if I lived on another planet.

Diplomatically, I just nodded. Although I didn't often have time to read the newspaper, I did see the mayor's name mentioned now and then.

"Was he razzing you about my decision to give up my council seat?" Collin asked.

"No. He said he understood time constraints for a family man." After Braden's father put down his fork, he turned his gaze on Braden. "I think you're going to be getting a phone call."

"He wants me to run for the council seat?" Braden asked, brows raised.

"He sure does. Since our forefathers founded this town, he feels it's only right that someone in this family has a say in what goes on here."

"Maybe a female Galloway should run," Braden's sister, Carol, interjected with a sly smile.

"You'd want to help run the town?" Melissa asked her mother.

"That could be interesting, don't you think?" Carol returned.

With a frown, Shannon Galloway shook her head. "I'm not sure you're cut out for the shenanigans that go on behind closed doors."

A stubborn expression settled on Braden's sister's face. "It can't be any worse that what goes on at the board of the community theater. Women can be as cutthroat as men."

"April, do you find that's true?" Braden's mother asked me, looking as if she really wanted to know.

"I work with both men and women—mostly men, though," I admitted. "As long as we concentrate on business, we don't have problems. We might have disagreements, but nothing we can't work out. I guess working with men during my professional life, I've adjusted my management style so that it fits with theirs."

"Men and women work differently?" Melissa asked, intrigued.

"Sometimes. In my experience, men tend to do business in a more cut-and-dried way. Women can bring a softer, sometimes more creative touch to the table. In a business like mine, men and women balance each other. The company is always concerned with the bottom line, yet we have to weigh that against a woman's needs and what campaigns will catch her eye most effectively."

There was a sudden silence around the table as if everyone was thinking about my promotion, but no one wanted to mention it.

Finally to break the awkwardness, I asked Collin, "Can you pass me the salad?" That seemed to do the trick, and everyone started chattering again. I breathed a sigh of relief.

After we finished dessert, Braden stood by my chair ready to escort me to the living room.

"I need to speak to your mother," I told him.

He looked concerned. "About?"

"About everything. I feel as if there's a wall of ice between us and I need to put a crack in it."

"Mom has set ideas," he warned me.

"Don't we all?" I asked lightly.

"Maybe you're right. Just don't forget her world's very different from yours."

"Because I have a career and she never has?"

"Not only that." He glanced toward the kitchen where his mother had gone. "Our world—yours and mine—is much bigger than hers. We've traveled. We've spent time outside of Galloway. She was raised on a farm ten miles from here and she's only been out of the state of Oklahoma twice—once for a vacation Dad insisted they

take to the Wisconsin Dells, and the other for a conference that was church-related in Atlanta. She likes her
life here and doesn't see the need to expand it."

"Is that why you didn't bring me home to meet your
parents while we were dating? I mean, I met them the
night we announced our engagement, but that was all."

"Let's face it, April, you and I didn't want to see
anybody else. We wanted to be alone with each other."

I thought about our nights in bed, making leisurely
love. I knew he was right. Still…

"*We* were what mattered." His tone was very serious.

I wanted to ask him if *we* mattered now, if there even
was a "we," but laughter broke out in the living room.
Little Darcy came running through the dining room.

She ran smack into me and caught a handful of my
tunic to steady herself.

Smiling, I crouched down to her. "Whoa! Are you
okay?"

With wide eyes, she stared at me. "Mommy says I
shouldn't run in Gran's house."

"That's probably a good idea." I couldn't help
ruffling her curly brown hair. "Did Santa bring you
what you wanted?"

"Santa and Uncle Bwaden," she assured me. "Santa
left a baby doll. She cries. Uncle Bwaden got me
blocks." Moving over to him, she tugged on his hand.
"Come build wif me."

As I straightened, my gaze locked on Braden's. He'd
obviously been watching me with Darcy. There was so
much tenderness in his eyes that my heart lurched.

Breaking eye contact, he gave his attention to Darcy.
"What do you want to build?"

"A bathtub," she exclaimed and he laughed.

"A bathtub it is."

After a last smile at Darcy, I assured Braden, "I'll keep in mind what you told me about your mother." As I opened the swinging door into the kitchen, I stepped into Shannon Galloway's domain.

She was loading the dishwasher, trying to decide what she could fit in and what she couldn't.

"I thought you might need help with some of those pots and pans."

"It's nice of you to offer," she replied formally, "but I can handle them. Joan will be in in a few minutes after she changes Danny. I'm not sure what happened to Carol, but she'll be in, too."

Braden's mother looked at me speculatively. "But now that you're here— I think you should know how Braden feels about being a father."

"He's told me."

"I'm not sure he's gotten across to you how important it is to him or you wouldn't even be thinking about moving to California."

Whoa! Apparently she didn't pull any punches. I had to be honest with her. "This job offer in Los Angeles isn't something that just happened."

"I understand that. They offered it to you about four months ago and that's why you broke up with Braden."

I decided to slide over my breakup with her son. "The promotion was offered to me four months ago, but I've been working for it for the past ten years. When I moved to Galloway to take a job with this company, I knew what I wanted. My aim was to work to the best of my ability, earn respect and be asked to take a position in the highest echelon at corporate headquarters."

Shannon Galloway's eyes were sad. "So this is a dream you've had for years and you've finally achieved it. Tell me, what new dream will you have when you reach Los Angeles? When you achieve success with this dream, what comes next? CEO? And when you become CEO, will you find that job and the salary solace when you're all alone?"

Her words hit me hard. "I won't be alone. I'll have a child."

"Don't think Braden's going to let you cut him out of this baby's life."

"I don't want to cut Braden out of this baby's life. If I live in Los Angeles, we'll figure out a way Braden can see his child."

Mrs. Galloway lifted her hands in frustration. "See his child? When? Every other weekend? A few weeks in the summer? Oh, April, that's no way to be a parent. That's no way for a child to grow up."

"Families are different now than they used to be," I protested, trying not to be defensive.

"They might be different, but that doesn't mean they work. They might be different, but that doesn't mean it's good for the children. I'm not sure this whole situation is about a baby at all. Isn't it about you wanting to keep your independence?"

Wasn't that exactly what I had told Braden—that I wanted to keep my independence. I couldn't tell his mother that wasn't a big part of it. "Maybe so."

"Parents sacrifice for their children. That's the way it's supposed to be." Braden's mother didn't sound angry, just terribly concerned.

"You've given me a lot to think about," I said sincerely.

"I expected you not to like anything I had to say."

"I didn't say I liked it," I admitted wryly. "I said I'd think about it."

With a chuckle that seemed to break that ice between us, Mrs. Galloway shook her head. "At least you're honest. Come on, you can help me with the pots and pans."

Joan swung into the kitchen then, carrying glasses that had been sitting around the living room.

"April's going to help," Braden's mother announced, and Joan gave me a tentative smile to assure me that was all right with her.

SPENDING THE DAY with Braden's family had given me much to consider, especially his mom's question about what dream came next for me. Once I was in Los Angeles…in the perfect job…with the baby, then how would I feel? What would I want? What would I strive for? Was giving my child the best of everything my new goal? Would giving my child two parents in one place be the best of everything?

"You're awfully quiet," Braden remarked as he parked in front of my town house. "For a while there I thought you were asleep," he teased.

"Not asleep. Just thinking."

"About?" he prompted.

"Everything."

"Just like a woman," he complained. "I ask for simple and I get complicated."

"The thing is, you asked and I answered. I can't always tell you what you want to hear."

The night we'd argued, he'd asked me if my promotion was more important than a life with him. I'd hesitated, then I'd told him honestly that I didn't know. He hadn't been able to accept my doubt, my wanting to explore the idea of moving to L.A. He hadn't been able to explore it with me.

Unexpectedly, he turned to me now, took my face in his hands and kissed me. It was quick and fast and over in an instant, like a clap of thunder or a flash of lightning.

"What was that for?"

"Your honesty. It always impressed me about you from the very beginning."

"Even though it frustrates you sometimes?" I asked.

"Even though it frustrates me."

I couldn't let Christmas end yet. I wanted a little time just for the two of us. Also, I needed his opinion on tests that could affect my pregnancy. "Do you want to come in for coffee? There *is* something I need to discuss with you…about my pregnancy."

In the darkness I could feel him tense. "Is there something wrong?"

"No, at least I hope not. Let's go inside."

As I unlocked the door and we stepped into the living room, Braden looked worried. His gaze passed over the peach-and-cream sofa and chair, the oak-and-glass tables, the sculpture of cattails hanging on the wall.

"Nothing's changed," he remarked as he glanced into the eat-in kitchen, where a wrought-iron chandelier hung over the table.

I felt everything had changed as I went toward the kitchen, shrugging off my coat on the way. "Coffee?" I asked, "Or something stronger?" I would be drinking milk no matter what Braden had.

"That depends on what we're going to discuss. Do I need something stronger?"

I hung my coat over a kitchen chair. Braden hadn't worn one. His red-and-black ski sweater made his shoulders look impressively broad. His black jeans made his legs look so long. A thrill of excitement went through me, with the awareness that we were alone here in my town house.

"Forget the drinks for now," he decided, motioning to the sofa.

We sat side by side, hip to hip, and I almost forgot we weren't a couple anymore. "I have a decision to make because I'm thirty-five and pregnant."

"What does being thirty-five have to do with it?"

"There are tests available and advisable for women thirty-five and older. My obstetrician laid it all out at my appointment this week."

"Tell me about the tests."

Gazing into Braden's green eyes, I was glad he was here to talk to about this. "I can have amniocentesis to diagnose genetic or chromosomal abnormalities, but with amnio, there's a small risk of miscarriage."

He placed his hand over mine on my knee. "Do you have another option?"

"Yes. Instead, I can have a multiple marker screening test and an ultrasound."

"Does this screening test have a name?"

"It's called the alpha-fetoprotein blood test."

"Is your doctor recommending one over the other?"

"No, she isn't. She gave me literature to read on the amnio and the AFP in combination with an ultrasound. Would you like to look at the pamphlets? I can make coffee for you while you do."

"Are you bound and determined to give me a caffeine high?"

I laughed. "I've got decaf, too, if you'd like. I don't want to hover while you look over the information."

"I could just take the pamphlets along."

"Yes, you could."

His hand was still covering mine. The heat we generated together seemed to fill the whole living room. I'm not sure what happened next—if I leaned toward Braden or he bent toward me. But sitting there like that, the months seemed to fall away and we were a couple again. As his lips captured mine, as I let the whirlwind of emotion I felt toward him swirl about me, I knew I still loved him. I'd never stopped loving him.

As Braden's tongue moved erotically against mine, I longed for him to make love to me again. I forgot about fears and goals and a job waiting for me in L.A. All that mattered was having Braden's arms around me. All that mattered—

Abruptly Braden broke the kiss and leaned away. His expression was troubled, and I could see our kiss had caused more turmoil than pleasure. "I shouldn't have done that. We don't want to muddle this up any more than it is."

"That kiss was like old times," I murmured.

"We can't go back."

"We can go forward," I offered, not knowing what I wanted from him.

"We can make decisions about our child together. But when it comes to you and me—"

He looked straight ahead rather than at me and his hand was a balled fist on his knee. "I felt betrayed when you gave back the ring. The fact that you would choose a promotion over us spoke volumes about the relationship we *didn't* have. Afterward, I swore I'd find a woman who wanted a home and a family as much as I did."

Facing me once more, he asked, "You might be pregnant now, but nothing else has really changed, has it?"

There was hope in his question. Yet he wasn't willing to consider changing *his* life. The odd thing was, I felt as if my world *was* changing, and I might have to re-adjust my priorities to fit those changes. I didn't know yet what that meant to me and Braden.

"We're going to have a baby. That's a huge change." I stood and went to the rolltop desk by the stairs. Lifting the lid, I took out the pamphlets and brought them to him. We wouldn't be able to resolve anything else tonight.

As he rose to his feet and took them from me, I said, "We have to learn to trust each other again."

"Maybe we do. But once trust is broken, it's not so easy to get it back." He checked his watch. "I'd better be going."

When he walked to the door, I followed him. "Thanks for inviting me today."

The tension between us lessened as he joked, "You didn't feel outnumbered?"

"Maybe at first."

"Melissa took a real liking to you."

"I took a liking to her."

"Did you miss not being with your family on Christmas?" he asked.

"I spoke to Mom and Dad last night and Jenny this morning."

Lifting the pamphlets, he asked, "How soon do you have to make a decision on this?"

"Soon."

"I'm opening the new restaurant in Galloway on New Year's Eve. The night before we'll have a run-through for friends and family. Would you like to come?"

This was a milestone for him and I got the impression he'd like me to be there. He was trying to bridge the gap between us, and I wanted to bridge it, too.

"Sure, I'll come. What time?"

"Around six-thirty, seven o'clock. There might be people there you know. I told my friends they could bring friends."

"It will become the new hot spot in Galloway."

"I don't know about hot spot. I just want plenty of patrons night after night."

"Same kind of food as Tin Roof number one?"

He laughed. "Same kind of food."

I hadn't felt awkward with Braden all day, but now I did, maybe because he'd pulled away from our kiss, maybe because something was happening between us again and neither of us knew exactly what to do about it.

"I'll see you Friday night."

Moments later, after a goodbye, he was gone and I knew I'd be counting the days until I saw him again.

TIN ROOF TWO, as I dubbed the new restaurant, was located in a small shopping plaza in the northern end of town. At the restaurant's end of the lot, parking places were at a premium. Thinking about seeing Braden again made me feel practically giddy. I'd dressed tonight as if dressing for a date in a soft lilac sweater and wool slacks. As I left paperwork on my desk in order to go home and change, I didn't regret leaving my files instead of taking them with me. Were my priorities changing? Or had I just gotten caught up with seeing and being with Braden again?

When I entered the restaurant, it was almost filled to capacity. Round, plain hardwood tables were accented by wrought-iron chairs. Trestle tables and booths lined the walls of one large room. An archway led into a smaller room. Enlarged photos telling the story of Okla-

KAREN ROSE SMITH   147

homa's history—from cowboys riding the range to oil
rigs dotting the peaceful landscape—hung on the walls.
The aroma of barbecued ribs, grilled onions and sizzling
steak beckoned.

Hanging my coat on a rack in the foyer, I smiled at
the maître d' who was dressed in a white snap-buttoned
shirt, black bolo tie and black jeans. He took a menu
from a stack on the table beside his podium.

"Will you be meeting anyone here tonight?" he
asked, as if that's what had been going on all evening.

"No." Unless Braden joined me. I knew he'd be busy.
Running a restaurant required so much behind-the-
scenes activity. I'd seen that when we'd dated.

After studying his seating chart, the man made a
notation and smiled at me. "I'll see you to your table."

As I followed him, I looked over the array of people. I
wondered if Braden's family was here but I couldn't see
into the other room. After I was seated, I spotted Braden
chatting with a petite woman in a far corner. She had curly
red hair that bounced attractively on her shoulders. Was
this the redhead Braden had taken to *The Nutcracker*?

Suddenly the redhead laid her hand on Braden's
forearm. The gesture was familiar. Had they been dating
long? Apparently he'd invited her here tonight, too!

I felt like a fool, unreasonably hurt and much too
emotional to stay. Why should it matter if I did?

Gathering my purse, I slid out of the booth and
headed quickly toward the foyer. The maître d' wasn't
at his spot so I didn't have to make explanations. I just
grabbed my coat from the rack and left.

Sadness and regret wrapped around me like a
blanket. As I entered my town house, I knew why I felt
devastated. I loved Braden. I loved him in a way I'd

never loved anyone…except maybe the baby growing inside me. When we'd become engaged, time hadn't tested what I'd felt for him. Now, with over four months apart, it had.

Yet love wasn't a glue that could hold a relationship together if there wasn't trust and commitment and unconditional acceptance. What would it take for a man to follow a woman anywhere, not the other way around?

I was in the kitchen pouring myself a glass of milk when my doorbell rang sharply twice. I wondered if it might be my elderly neighbor, wanting to visit.

When I opened the door, however, I was stunned to see Braden. "What are you doing here? You have guests and a restaurant opening—"

"Yes, I do," he agreed, sober-faced. "But I saw you leave. I was worried. Are you feeling okay? Is the baby all right?"

Calling on as much composure as I could muster, I responded, "It wasn't the baby. And I'm fine. I just saw you with that…redhead. Have you been dating her?"

"How do you know that?"

"A friend saw you with a redhead at *The Nutcracker*. She described her. I can't believe you invited both of us to the Tin Roof tonight!"

"You're jumping to conclusions," he returned, looking angry now.

"Did you take her to the ballet?"

"Yes, I did."

Tears came to my eyes, and I tried to blink them away. I didn't want him to see how much I hurt.

Suddenly his hands were on my shoulders. "But I didn't ask her to the restaurant tonight. She came along with a friend. We dated one time. That was it."

"She's beautiful. One date? She didn't go skiing with you?"

"She did *not* go skiing with me. I went alone. We only had one date because we didn't have much to talk about. We didn't have anything in common. We—" He stopped as if he didn't want to share too much.

Tipping my chin up, he asked, "Don't you know I'd never put you in a position like that? April, you're the mother of my child. I'd never hurt you that way."

"Oh, Braden."

Bending his head, he kissed me possessively, in a way he'd never kissed me before. His desire was primally hungry and I responded to it instantly without hesitation. As his tongue thoroughly explored my mouth, I held on to him tight. Because if Braden left my life, I'd feel lost in a way I'd never felt lost before. For this moment, I felt found. His kiss wasn't about the past or about recriminations or consequences. It was about right now and needing each other.

I needed Braden and I held on to him, hoping he needed me, too.

CHAPTER FOUR

BRADEN WAS PROVING he desired me with each stroke of his tongue, each caress of his hand down my back, each erotic movement against me. Tall and muscled and lean, he was hard with desire now. When his hands settled on my backside and he lifted me to him, rockets exploded.

I moaned.

He must have heard that small sound because he let me slide again to the floor. His hands tunneled under my sweater, then caught my breasts and stroked them.

Finally he broke away and stared at me. "I want you."

"I want you, too." That was all I could say…all I needed to say.

After he lifted my sweater over my head, he made quick work of my bra and then cupped me in his hands. "You're bigger," he muttered, his voice thick.

"You like that?" I asked softly, reveling in the way he was looking at me.

"I've always liked the way you look," he answered tightly before he bent to my breast and kissed close to the nipple.

"Oh, Braden," I murmured again as a shiver skipped through me.

My nipple was instantly hard and as he sucked it, I didn't think I could stand the pleasure. I laced my fingers in his hair, caressed his neck and wanted his clothes off.

When he raised his head again, he kissed me once more. Somehow we made it the short distance to my living-room carpet, but no farther. Our clothes had left a trail. The sofa wasn't so far away, yet it seemed too great a distance as he kissed my breast again, my neck and then my navel. When we both collapsed to the floor, the plush carpet was enough of a bed. I don't think either of us would have cared if it had been a hardwood floor. Nothing else mattered but the desire between us. Nothing else mattered but touching and kissing and belonging again. At least that was the way I felt.

With our clothes strewn around us, Braden's hands slipped between my thighs to see if I was wet. I was more than wet. I didn't even have time to feel self-conscious about my thickening waistline as he raised himself on his forearms above me, kissed me once, twice, then smoothly and swiftly thrust inside me.

I felt tears come to my eyes at the completion…at the pleasure…at the wonder of having Braden inside me again. When I lifted my knees, I contracted around him and he shuddered.

"You've always made me crazy. You've always made me want too much," he rasped hoarsely as he thrust into me again and again and the meaning of his words eluded me.

I was wrapped up in excitement and passion, sliding my fingers down his slick back when my climax shook me so forcefully, my breath caught in my chest. It was a cascading explosion of need and dreams and pleasure. Never had it been so powerful, so bone-shaking, so deliciously unending.

The pulses of that were still reverberating as Braden's release came, too. He shuddered in my arms and kissed me as if the world was about to end.

As my body cooled and quieted, I had no idea what might come next. Where would we go from here?

A few seconds later, Braden rolled apart from me and onto his side. "I sure didn't plan for that to happen tonight."

I couldn't read his expression—if he was pleased or frustrated or sorry. "As eventful as opening a new restaurant?" I asked lightly.

Not answering me, he ran his hand down my breast, over my midriff and onto my stomach. His large hand rested there. "Your body's changing."

"I know. Sometimes I look in the mirror and imagine how big I'll be in a few months."

With a frown he asked, "Do you resent gaining weight? Are you—"

I cut in before he could go on. "No, I don't resent it. I love this baby, Braden. Whatever changes my body has to go through to make it the best place for him or her, I don't mind."

When he looked at me for a long moment, I could see he was weighing the truth of what I'd said.

Hiking himself up on his elbow, he blew out a frustrated breath. "We have to talk, but I don't want to rush it. I need to get back."

"I can't believe you left."

"I can't believe I did, either. It probably wasn't the smartest thing I've ever done." Rising to his feet, he reached for his clothes.

I picked up my sweater and pulled it over my head, suddenly not wanting to be naked anymore. "When do you want to talk?"

"It's going to be late, but I could come over after I close the restaurant. You don't work tomorrow, do you?"

Tomorrow was Saturday. "I have an early meeting with Charlie, because he's going out of town for a few days."

"Then we'll do it some other time," he responded gruffly.

He'd left his restaurant opening tonight to make sure I was okay. Now I needed to put the two of us—the three of us—first, too. "No. Come back tonight. I don't need a lot of sleep and I can always get a nap tomorrow after I get home."

"You're sure?"

"I'm sure." I wanted to find out exactly what Braden was thinking.

After he buckled his belt, he slipped into his shoes and pulled his sweater over his head. Coming over to me, he crouched down. "Are you all right?"

It was sweet of him to ask. "I'm fine."

Although I wished he would kiss me again, he didn't. Rather he straightened. "I'll see you in a few hours." Moments later he'd left.

Sitting on my living-room floor half-dressed, I wondered if what had just happened had really happened.

When Braden returned, would we make love again?

ALTHOUGH I WAS DISTRACTED, I sat on the sofa reviewing notes I'd taken at a recent meeting. Suddenly I heard a knock and my front door opened. When Braden came in, he said, "You shouldn't leave your door unlocked."

As he strode toward the sofa, tall and fit and handsome, I relived what had happened earlier. After Braden had left, I'd showered and pulled on a set of pink sweats. After all, I didn't want to presume anything when he returned. We *did* have to talk.

Quickly I made a pile of the papers in my lap and laid them on the coffee table.

"I left it unlocked for you." Perhaps that was a symbolic gesture. I'd opened my heart to him again, and I hoped he realized that.

"Was tonight successful?" I asked.

Lowering himself beside me, he nodded. "We experienced a few kinks, but hopefully they'll be worked out before tomorrow night."

"Ringing in the New Year with a new restaurant. I hope it goes well for you." I sincerely meant that. I wished Braden nothing but success.

"I hope so, too. I want to leave my son or daughter a legacy. Besides that…" He looked uncomfortable for a moment then went on. "We have to decide about child support. Would you prefer to hire a lawyer to draw up something formal?"

If he was thinking in terms of lawyers, maybe he wasn't even considering the two of us getting back together. Was *I* seriously considering it? Did I want a long-distance relationship? Did I want an ongoing affair?

Pushing those questions aside, I admitted, "The idea of a lawyer scares me." That's probably why I hadn't made an appointment with one yet. "Can't we work this out on our own?"

"I don't know. As I said before, it will be hard to be a dad long-distance. I'm going to want joint custody…at least."

A knot wound tight in my stomach. "Even when this baby's an infant? How can you possibly handle that?"

His shrug was casual, but I could feel his hard body

beside me and that it was taut with tension. Was he afraid I'd shut him out altogether and turn this over to a lawyer? Had what happened earlier been a persuasion tactic? I didn't want to believe that.

"I can take time off when I have to," he said. "I have a good manager at the restaurant in Oklahoma City. I am in the process of finding one for here. I also know Mom and Carol would be glad to help."

"And Joan," I added, thinking about Braden's family, how close they were, how they could depend on one another.

When he stretched his arm across the back of the sofa and shifted toward me, he reminded me of a man on a mission and I wondered what was coming next.

"Do you realize how much you hold back with me?"

When Braden and I had dated, I'd been lost in the euphoria of new love. Even in that euphoria, though, I'd protected myself. I hadn't shared my innermost thoughts. Because I'd been afraid he'd use them to hurt me somehow? As my dad had hurt my mother? He always seemed able to manipulate her into doing whatever he wanted. Because she loved him too much? Or because she'd never learned how to stand up for herself?

"I didn't hold back tonight," I said truthfully.

His fingers now rested on my shoulder, stirring the excitement and desire that had exploded between us earlier. "No, you didn't. And in bed you didn't hold back. But afterward, I always felt as if you put up a shield when I asked specific questions."

"What do you want to know?" Opening myself completely to Braden was a risk I had to take.

"I want to know about you, and why you drive yourself so hard. You've only told me bits and pieces about your family. Will they be involved with our baby? Will you visit them? Would you trust your mother or sister to take care of an infant?" He sliced his hand in the air in frustration. "I don't know much about them, except that your mom works with your dad and your sister's a veterinarian."

Nights when we'd both worked late, we had fallen into each other's arms and made love until morning. I'd thought we were communicating by touching. I'd thought making love was *showing* love. I now realized when we'd been engaged, I'd wanted to keep everything romantic and easy. Maybe I'd thought my fears would push Braden away and being vulnerable to him would take away any power I had.

Now Braden's hand settled on my shoulder as if to reassure me. "You've spent some time with my family and I want to know more about yours. Why didn't you go home for Christmas? Because you're pregnant? Have you even told your family you're pregnant?"

Where did I start? Could I trust Braden to understand? It was suddenly important that he did. "I didn't go home to Dallas because Mom and Dad went to a resort on San Padre for Christmas. I called them there. And Jenny—"

Braden just waited and I took the jump into sensitive territory. "Jenny worked on Christmas Day."

"Veterinarians are open on Christmas Day?"

"Emergency veterinary care is. Christmas Day has always been hard for her and she prefers to work."

"Why?"

So this was it—time to make a decision about how vulnerable I wanted to be. Yet if I didn't take this step, how could I expect Braden to?

After I picked up a throw pillow and held it to my chest, I tried to keep my explanation simple. "When Jenny got married, all she wanted was a family...all her husband wanted was a family. She's four years older than I am and I was in college then. A year into her marriage she got pregnant. She and Bill were so happy. The baby was due around December eighteenth and they planned to name a little girl Noel or a little boy Nicholas. But Jenny went into labor prematurely and...then the baby was stillborn." The pillow didn't seem to be nearly enough protection over my heart.

All of Braden's attention was riveted on me now. "I'm sorry. It must have been a devastating time for her."

I swallowed hard and shoved the pillow aside. "It was. She went into a serious depression afterward, but I think some of the reason for that was Bill's attitude. That baby had meant the world to him, and he wanted Jenny to try to get pregnant again right away. But she couldn't even contemplate it. Bill was determined to be a father, and if he couldn't do it with Jenny, then he was going to do it with someone else. He asked her for a divorce."

I felt Braden shift beside me, but he remained silent and listened.

Pushing my hair away from my face, I remembered that year all too well. "I spent that summer with her, and by the end of it, she'd decided to earn her veterinary degree. But she never got over losing the baby, and every year when Christmas rolls around, she makes sure she's busy."

"And you witnessed all this firsthand?"

"A lot of it. I was home on break and at the hospital with her through her labor. Bill was her coach but she wanted me there, too. After the baby died, I could feel Jen's pain. It scared me."

As if Braden had just fit the pieces together, he said in a husky voice, "That's why you balked when I said I wanted to get married and have a family right away."

"That was part of the reason," I admitted.

"Why didn't you tell me that?"

"What would you have said if I had? That I'm not my sister and I shouldn't worry because statistics are on my side? That the joy of having a family is worth the risk?"

Looking troubled, his brows drew together. "I might have said some of those things."

"And maybe you'd have gotten angry when I wouldn't listen to you? When I wouldn't agree?"

Frowning, he shook his head. "I'm not your sister's husband. What makes you think men are so inflexible?" He suddenly stopped, maybe realizing how inflexible *he'd* been. Then going in a different direction, he returned the focus to me. "Why have you worked so hard to succeed?" he asked again as if the answers I'd given before hadn't satisfied him. "Why do you want this promotion so badly?"

I felt as if I was exposing too much. But making love with Braden had left me completely vulnerable and thinking about second chances. If he could understand why I wasn't willing to push my goals aside in favor of his, would we be a step closer to a compromise?

All at once, our whole conversation seemed too big…too important…too overwhelming. "Would you like something to drink?" I asked.

"I'd like the answers to my questions. Are you trying to avoid them?"

His gaze was piercing and this time I knew he wouldn't leave until he got the answers he wanted. "I'm not avoiding them. I'm just postponing answering for a few minutes."

"Fair enough." He relaxed against the sofa and was looking at me differently. As if we had a bond again? Had sex done that? Or had the revelation of my fears?

The coffee brewed quickly and as I stood in the kitchen pouring it into a mug for him, I felt the inexorable pull toward Braden and everything he represented—dreams, a home, stability. Wasn't that what I'd always wanted?

Yet, I wanted more, too.

"How about ice cream?" I called in. "I've been craving raspberry ripple and I bought a half gallon." Knowing Braden, he might have tasted food at the Tin Roof in the beginning of the evening, but then he'd gotten caught up in the people there.

"Sure. Have you had any other cravings?"

"Not pickles." I wrinkled my nose. "Peanut butter, cream-filled doughnuts, cheesecake and waffles with maple syrup."

When he laughed, I loved the sound of it. It was deep and rich and hearty, and I remembered again all the good times we'd had.

"Sounds to me as if this baby's going to like sweets."

"Or maybe I'm just craving fat," I admitted as he came into the kitchen to fetch his ice cream and coffee.

"You don't have any to spare on you. That could be why."

The way Braden's eyes were caressing me, I almost dropped my bowl of ice cream. Often after we'd made love, he'd run his hands over my breasts and—

Cutting off that train of thought, I explained, "Except for the cravings now and then, I'm eating healthy and take long walks a few times a week. I want to make sure I do everything right for this baby."

When he came a few steps closer to me, he pushed my hair away from my cheek, then ran his thumb from my temple to my chin. I could have purred from the gentleness of his touch.

"You aren't your sister," he assured me, understanding my fears.

I wanted to dive into his chest and let him tell me everything was going to be all right. Yet I didn't really want a protector. What I needed from Braden was so much more than that.

"I know," I replied softly. "But I'm still afraid. There's a reason I haven't told my parents or Jenny I'm pregnant. What if something goes wrong?"

His arms encircled me and drew me close. Yes, we were attracted to each other. Yes, my body was tingling to repeat what had happened earlier. Now, though, for these few moments, only tenderness emanated from Braden, a tenderness that had urged me to fall in love with him.

Before that tenderness turned into passion, he leaned away and dropped his arms. Then he picked up his ice cream and his mug of coffee and headed to the sofa. As I followed him, I hurt again for what we'd had and what we'd lost.

He took a few swallows of coffee. "So why do you want to become vice president of sales?"

"This isn't simply about becoming vice president of sales."

He was listening and waiting.

After a spoonful of ice cream, I began, "My mom met my dad the summer after she graduated from college. She had a scholarship to go to med school but she had to work that summer to earn more money."

OFFICIAL OPINION POLL

Dear Reader,

Since you are a book enthusiast, we would like to know what you think.

Inside you will find a short Opinion Poll. Please participate in our poll by sharing your opinion on 3 subjects that are very important to all of us.

To thank you for your participation, we would like to send you your choice of **2 FREE BOOKS** and a **FREE GIFT!**

Please enjoy them with our compliments.

Sincerely,

Pam Powers

Editor

P.S. Don't forget to indicate which books you prefer so we can send your FREE gifts today!

What's your pleasure...

Romance?

Enjoy **2 FREE BOOKS** that will fuel your imagination with intensely moving stories about life, love and relationships.

OR

Suspense?

Enjoy **2 FREE BOOKS** that will thrill you with a spine-tingling blend of suspense and mystery.

Whichever category you select, your **2 FREE BOOKS** have a combined cover price of $11.98 or more in the U.S. and $13.98 or more in Canada.

Simply place the sticker next to your preferred choice of books, complete the poll on the right page and you'll automatically receive **2 FREE BOOKS** and a **FREE GIFT** with no obligation to purchase anything!

*We'll send you a wonderful surprise gift, **ABSOLUTELY FREE**, just for trying our books! Don't miss out —* **MAIL THE REPLY CARD TODAY!**

Order online at
www.FreeBooksandGift.com

YOUR OPINION POLL
THANK-YOU FREE GIFTS INCLUDE

▶ **2 ROMANCE OR 2 SUSPENSE BOOKS**

▶ **A LOVELY SURPRISE GIFT**

OFFICIAL OPINION POLL

YOUR OPINION COUNTS!

Please check TRUE or FALSE below to express your opinion about the following statements:

Q1 Do you believe in "true love"?

"TRUE LOVE HAPPENS ONLY ONCE IN A LIFETIME."
○ TRUE
○ FALSE

Q2 Do you think marriage has any value in today's world?

"YOU CAN BE TOTALLY COMMITTED TO SOMEONE WITHOUT BEING MARRIED."
○ TRUE
○ FALSE

Q3 What kind of books do you enjoy?

"A GREAT NOVEL MUST HAVE A HAPPY ENDING."
○ TRUE
○ FALSE

Place the sticker next to one of the selections below to receive your 2 FREE BOOKS and FREE GIFT. I understand that I am under no obligation to purchase anything as explained on the back of this card.

Romance

193 MDL EE4P

393 MDL EE5D

Suspense

192 MDL EE4Z

392 MDL EE5P

0074823 ‖█‖█‖‖ ‖█‖‖ ‖█‖‖   FREE GIFT CLAIM # **3622**

FIRST NAME	LAST NAME

ADDRESS

APT.#	CITY

STATE/PROV.	ZIP/POSTAL CODE

(TF-SS-06)

The Reader Service — Here's How It Works:

Accepting your 2 free books and gift places you under no obligation to buy anything. You may keep the books and gift and return the shipping statement marked "cancel." If you do not cancel, about a month later we'll send you 3 additional books and bill you just $5.24 each in the U.S., or $5.74 each in Canada, plus 25¢ shipping & handling per book and applicable taxes if any.* That's the complete price, and — compared to cover prices of $5.99 or more each in the U.S. and $6.99 or more each in Canada — it's quite a bargain! You may cancel at any time, but if you choose to continue, every month we'll send you 3 more books, which you may either purchase at the discount price...or return to us and cancel your subscription.

*Terms and prices subject to change without notice. Sales tax applicable in N.Y.
Canadian residents will be charged applicable provincial taxes and GST.

"How did they meet?" Braden asked, possibly guessing where this was going.

"At a barbecue given by a mutual friend. My dad is seven years older than my mom and he dazzled her…or his maturity and his vision of the future did. By the end of the summer they'd decided to get married. So, of course, she didn't accept the scholarship, because my dad would have been too far away. They were in love and she wanted to be with him. I think she always intended to earn her degree somehow, but then she got pregnant. My dad insisted that raising kids was more important than becoming a doctor."

"Did your mom believe that?"

"I think she did. Then. But after Jen and I were in school, she sent for college catalogs again. When he saw them, Dad insisted he could use her help in his business."

"And she didn't take another look at the catalogs," Braden guessed.

"Oh, I think she looked at them, and that was the sad part. When I was in my teens, she sent me to the cedar chest in her bedroom for a tablecloth. They had invited business guests of my dad's for supper. There I saw the catalogs and the pages turned back. The next day I asked her about them."

Braden's gaze on mine urged me to go on.

"I'd never seen her look quite as she looked when she answered me. Tears came to her eyes and she seemed so…resigned. She told me she'd put her dreams aside for my father's, because she couldn't have both med school and a marriage. I asked her if Dad had ever encouraged her to go back to school. Almost resentfully she told me, 'He didn't think I needed to expand my horizons. He expected me to do what *he* wanted.'"

I'd lost my appetite for the ice cream and I set the bowl on the coffee table.

"What would have happened if she'd enrolled in college again after you were grown?"

"I don't think she had the courage to find out. I think she was afraid that if she didn't do what my father wanted, that would be the end of their marriage."

"You don't know that."

"I know how forceful my dad is. I know my mom always gives in to him. I know as I was growing up I always felt a distance between them. I don't know if that was resentment on her part, or an unwillingness to bend on his. I just know that after my conversation with her, I vowed never to let a man run my life or kill my dreams."

While we were talking, Braden had set his ice cream aside and held on to his mug of coffee. Now he leaned toward the coffee table, set the mug down, too, and faced me on the sofa. "I understand that *you* have plans and aspirations. But a child changes them."

"I'm not sure a child *has* to change them."

Braden ran his hand through his hair, looking frustrated, as if there were a whole book of things he'd like to say. Yet apparently he knew all of them might push me away rather than change my mind. "When I came here earlier tonight, I didn't intend to have sex with you. I mean, it wasn't a calculated move."

If I didn't know that earlier, I knew it now. I trusted that he was telling me the truth because Braden had always told me the truth. I needed more of it. "The woman I saw tonight…"

"I can read the question in your mind, and the answer is—we weren't intimate." After he studied me, he asked, "Is there a possibility you'll stay in Galloway?"

Although it was silly, my heart was singing because he hadn't made love to the redhead. Tonight was changing my perspective on everything and I answered him honestly. "I don't know. This meeting with Charlie tomorrow morning... I'm going to tell him I'm pregnant. Natural Beauty could rescind the promotion offer."

"So you'd stay here by default?" Braden swung around to face the coffee table as if not expecting an answer.

We'd been as close as a man and woman could be a few hours before, but now I felt as if Braden and I were separated by a chasm. Still I wanted him to know I wasn't cutting him out of my decision making. "Did you look at those pamphlets you took along?"

"Yes, I did."

I slid closer to him and laid my hand on his arm. "What do you think?"

"I think you should have the AFP test since it's simply a blood test and then have the ultrasound. If anything questionable shows up, then consider amnio-centesis. You already have fears about losing this baby. Don't add to them."

"That's what I've decided."

Taking my face in his hand, he asked me somberly, "Did you really need my feedback?"

Whenever he touched my face, I felt so cared for. Somehow I spoke around the lump in my throat. "Yes, I did. If you had felt strongly about the amniocentesis, I would have reconsidered."

While he studied me, I wondered what he was thinking.

Dropping his hand, he stood. "I'd better go."

Quickly rising to my feet, too, I walked him to the door, wishing he'd stay. I longed for him to hold me through the night, yet I knew that wasn't the answer to anything.

"Good luck with the restaurant opening tonight," I told him.

"Do you have plans?" he asked.

I shook my head. "If I'm awake, I'll call Jenny and we'll watch the ball drop together."

When he tipped my chin up, I wasn't sure what to expect. His lips were fiery and taut and hungry on mine. Then he pulled back and walked away.

I still loved Braden, and yet loving him could break my heart.

CHAPTER FIVE

MY STOMACH TWITTERING with anxiety, I picked up the phone to call Braden. By the end of the first week in January, I'd learned what the CEO of Natural Beauty thought of my pregnancy.

"Galloway."

When Braden answered I immediately remembered every detail of making love with him again…his compassionate expression as I'd told him about my family…

"Hi. It's April." Not wanting to plunge right in with news Braden might not like, I asked, "Did the opening go well?"

"I think it went great. Lots of people who came for New Year's Eve also stopped in for dinner this week. I matched faces with names from the guest book. I'm drawing residents from Norman, too, and a food critic is scheduled to come in at the end of January. I think he wants to surprise us. By then, everything should be running smoothly. What's going on with you? Any new cravings?"

Our conversation was so surfacely casual, my stomach sank. I'd thought about Braden every day. Had he thought about me at all? Had he thought about second chances and risk and being more than coparents?

"I told Charlie about my pregnancy and he had a conference call with Frank Temple."

"And?" Braden prompted, his voice wary.

"And it seems they've never had anyone in exactly this position before. They still think I'm the right person for the job in L.A., but they want to make sure I'm committed to it. If I am, I can start on schedule and work with the present vice president of sales. He can stay on an extra eight months before he retires, which would give me three months at home with the baby."

"Then what?" Braden asked.

"I'd have to hire a nanny or find day care."

At Braden's silence, I knew he was restraining his response.

"Anyway, in the meantime before I start training a replacement, Frank wants me to fly to California for two to three weeks to see exactly what my job there would entail."

"What about flying during your pregnancy?" Braden asked.

"I checked with my doctor. As long as I'm in a pressurized cabin, it's fine."

"I don't think you should go."

"Why?"

"Because you're pregnant! You're trying to operate as if this is business as usual, and it's not. You need to take care of yourself."

"You think I'd do a better job of that if I'm here, or do you think *you* can do a better job of that if I'm here?"

"Is it so wrong for me to want to watch over you?"

There was a gentleness to his words that took the wind out of my sails as nothing else could. "You have to trust me to find a balance. I need to spend this time in California to really get a taste of the lifestyle and the offices and the people who work there. This will also give me the opportunity I need to see exactly what the job is going to encompass."

"You're gathering information for an informed decision?" he asked wryly.

"Something like that. I'll be leaving on Tuesday and I just wanted to let you know."

Silence fell over the line again, lasting until Braden asked, "Are you working tomorrow?"

This weekend I was sorting through closets. I'd postponed my appointment with the movers and planned to set up a new time with them when I returned from L.A.

"No, I'm not working this weekend."

"I want to show you something. Why don't I pick you up around nine."

"What do you want to show me?"

"I'm thinking about buying a house and I'd like you to see it."

His words shook me a little. While I was flying off to California, he would be putting down deeper roots here.

"Nine is fine." A few seconds later, after I'd hung up, I thought about the trip some more and about everything I had to do before I left.

Then I thought about Braden buying a house. The statement he was making was clear—*he* wasn't going anywhere.

TENSION PRACTICALLY buzzed between us the following morning as we drove about a mile out of Galloway. I glanced over at Braden. "When did you first look at this house?" I asked.

"I went through it twice last week."

If he'd gone through it twice already, then he was really interested. "Is it new?"

"It's about ten years old. It sits on three acres and has been well kept."

When we turned down a secondary road, I saw trees dotting the properties we drove past—amur maples, tall oaks, red cedar. Soon after we passed a ranch-style house, we came to a mailbox at the end of a lane. Braden slowed, then turned onto the gravel.

We pulled in beside a blue sedan that was parked in front of a two-car garage. A woman my age climbed out of the car and came over to greet us.

After introductions, she said to Braden, "I've opened it for you. Take as long as you want to look around. I have a meeting with another agent and I'll be back to lock up."

As the agent pulled out of the driveway, my gaze fell on the house once again. It was charming. A courtyard wrapped around the front of the house and a wide, wrought-iron gate beckoned to us. The exterior was sturdy two-tone brown brick and the roof was low-pitched like the roofs on so many Oklahoma homes. It looked huge from the outside and I wondered how big it actually was.

"Come on," Braden said with a smile. "Let's explore."

Explore a life we could have together? If I stayed in Galloway, maybe that would be possible.

As we walked along the flagstone path across the court-yard to the front door, I imagined us living here and caring for our baby. I could imagine it so easily. Yet was I ready to give up everything I'd worked so hard to accomplish?

Braden opened the door and let me precede him inside. He was wearing a suede jacket today and as I passed him, I caught the scent of his aftershave along with the smell of leather. I focused my attention on the ceramic-tiled foyer, which stretched ahead of me.

Motioning to the right, Braden informed me, "This is the living room. It leads into an open dining room."

The area was spacious and bright. Oak hardwood floors gleamed in the sunlight that streamed through a picture window. Without even trying, I could imagine a table under the brass chandelier.

Instead of entering the living room, Braden nodded to the left. "There are three large bedrooms, but let's go into the family room first." He pointed straight ahead.

The house *was* huge. The family room was wonderfully large, with a cathedral ceiling.

"There's space for a wide-screen TV," I joked.

"Sure is, and a sectional couch, too—you know—with recliners on the ends."

I laughed. Braden had always said he wanted one of those, but the living room in his apartment wasn't large enough. The walls in this room were attractively painted a soft yellow and the whole house was immaculately clean.

A doorway off the family room led to a home office or den, one wall of which was completely lined with bookshelves. A sunroom was adjacent.

Braden hadn't followed me and now I returned to stand beside him, looking into the spacious kitchen before us. The sage-green counter and tile floor, oak cupboards and the spotless white appliances beckoned to me.

"There's enough space there for a table, too," Braden said as if I couldn't see it. "A utility room off the back part of the kitchen leads into the garage."

"This house is immense."

"I want some space. I've lived in an apartment long enough."

"You said it has three bedrooms?"

"Yep. I like the way they're gathered on one side of

the house." When he headed toward them, I found myself reluctant to follow.

As Braden stepped into the large master suite with its comfortable, spacious bathroom and walk-in closet, I asked, "Are you seriously thinking about buying this?"

"Yes, I am."

"Why now?"

"Because when my son or daughter is born, I want him or her to have a place to call home and plenty of room to play. I want a child to know I'll always be here and that there is one place to depend on."

My heart beat faster as I anticipated Braden asking me to live here with him so we could raise our child together.

However, he didn't ask me that question. Instead he said, quietly, "I'd like you to seriously think about giving me custody."

"I can't do that. I *want* to be a mother." The idea was becoming a reality and I wouldn't let Braden take my baby from me.

When Braden clasped my arm, he did it gently. "Think about this. Really think about it. I don't believe you can have the career you want *and* raise a child."

"Lots of women do both."

"Maybe. But how *well* do they do it? Do you know any working single moms who aren't run ragged?"

In turmoil, I pulled from his hold. "I know single moms. And yes, raising children alone is tough. But it can be rewarding, too. *You* have a career. What's so different about you being a single dad?"

"I own my own business, and I can make sure my hours are flexible. I don't have to report to anyone else. Isn't that the bottom line?"

Upset, I left the master suite and found myself

walking straight out of the house. In the courtyard, the wind blew my hair and I watched narrow white clouds skitter across the blue sky.

The door opened and closed and Braden's footsteps sounded on the walk. Then he was standing behind me.

"We'll work this out."

"Will we?" I asked sadly. "Or will we end up in court in a custody battle. I don't want that, Braden."

When he reached out and dragged a thumb over my cheekbone, he assured me, "It won't come to that. I know that would be the worst thing for a child and so do you. We're smarter than that."

We were smart, but we both wanted what we wanted.

"You're afraid to lean on me. You're afraid that somehow I'm going to take over your life. That's *not* what I want to do."

Whenever Braden touched me, I felt as if I could melt into a puddle at his feet. But physical attraction wasn't going to fix this mess. I wasn't sure what would. "If I'm on the West Coast and you're here…"

"I like the amount of space in this house for lots of reasons," he said, "but especially for one very big reason. Whenever you fly in from L.A., there will be plenty of room for you and our child."

"That might work at first."

"Why only at first?" He looked genuinely curious.

"Because when you start dating somebody seriously, she's not going to put up with that."

For a moment, I thought he might say, "I don't want to date anyone else seriously. I want to date *you*." I was looking for some sign that we could be more than co-parents and more than fifteen-minute lovers. But

Braden was silent and my disappointment made me feel almost nauseous.

Fighting it, I took a deep breath. "I have an appointment with my obstetrician Monday morning," I offered softly. "I'm going to have blood drawn for the AFP test and the doctor will perform the ultrasound then. I don't know how much of the baby we might be able to see."

"Are you asking me to go along?"

"If you want to."

When he took me by the shoulders, he gazed into my eyes. "You don't have to go through this pregnancy alone, April. I want you to know that. Of course, I'll come along. If I can get a glimpse of my son or daughter, nothing will keep me away."

This baby was everything to Braden and I was just part of the package. Had he ever really loved me? Or had I simply been a road to the family he always wanted? That idea chilled me.

Swallowing my disappointment, I stopped looking for answers in Braden's green eyes. I had to find my own.

"So what do you really think about the house?" Braden asked, dropping his hands.

"I like it," I admitted.

"After I take you home, I'll put in an offer on it."

I pictured myself flying back and forth, playing house when I was here with him, being lonely for him when I was in L.A.

Joint custody didn't seem to be any solution at all.

ON MONDAY MORNING, I arrived at my obstetrician's office before Braden. We'd agreed to meet there since we'd be going our separate ways afterward. When the nurse called me back to an examining room, I told her that Braden would be joining me for the ultrasound. I had no doubt that he would arrive in time to catch the first glimpse of our baby.

After blood was drawn, I followed the nurse to the room where the ultrasound machine was housed. She handed me one of those flimsy, cotton gowns that was supposed to tie down the back. Afterward she left, saying she'd be back shortly. There were two hooks on the back of the door, and I hung my suit and blouse on one, panty hose and underwear on the other. I set my high heels under a chair. I was standing beside the examining table unfolding a sheet when there was a rap at the door.

"April? It's me," Braden called. "The nurse sent me back."

When I opened the door feeling much too scantily dressed, Braden practically filled the entire space. "Do you want me to come in or wait till the doctor comes?"

"Come on in." I was very aware of the flap at the back of my gown. Reaching behind me, I held the gown together and backed up to the table. I saw the amused glint in Braden's eyes. My efforts to keep my back covered made my breasts protrude more.

"I promise I won't look until you're up on the table."

Although Braden was obviously trying to hide his amusement, there was a tenderness in his tone that made me relax a bit.

"I gained another two pounds."

"You're *supposed* to gain weight."

Lifting the sheet from the end of the table, I hiked myself up and let my legs dangle. "I'll soon have to wear maternity clothes."

"Have you bought any?"

"No. I thought if I had time I'd do some shopping in L.A. while I was there."

The amusement faded from Braden's eyes. "Do you have a ride to the airport tomorrow?"

"Yes. My neighbor's taking me when she goes into the city for work. She said she'll pick me up when I fly back, too. Then I won't have to leave my car at the airport."

"I could have taken you."

I felt as if Braden and I were precariously perched on a ledge. One false move and we'd topple off. Asking him for help made my balance unsteady, so I preferred not to ask him for support unless it directly concerned the baby.

Dr. Felton rapped on the door, then pushed it open. As usual, she was wearing a kindly smile. In her fifties, with short black-and-gray hair, she never seemed to be rushed or hurried. I didn't know how that was possible with babies being born every hour of the day, every day of the week. Her serenity was one of the things I liked about her.

After I introduced her to Braden, a nurse joined us. With natural ease, Dr. Felton motioned to a chair on wheels.

"Roll it over here so you can see the monitor clearly," she directed Braden. "April, why don't you lie back now. You'll be able to see the monitor, too. At almost nineteen weeks, I might be able to tell if this is a boy or a girl. Do you want to know?"

"If April does," Braden said, his voice deep and husky.

"If we know the sex, I can prepare a little better," I mused out loud.

"Blue or pink instead of yellow and green?" the doctor joked, and I nodded with a smile.

"You had blood drawn for the AFP test?" Braden asked me.

"Yes." Then I addressed the doctor. "How soon will I know the results?"

"In about a week. I know you'll be in California, but I have your cell phone number."

During the next few minutes, the nurse prepared me for the ultrasound and Dr. Felton took the wand in hand. She pressed buttons on the computer keyboard. "Listen," she directed us and turned up the volume. I heard "thump, thump, thump," like the ticking of a fast metronome.

"That's the heartbeat," she said.

I listened to each wonderful beat as I watched the screen, totally entranced with the images of my baby...*our* baby. Tears blurred my eyes as the mystifying concept of carrying a baby became a reality.

"You're going to have a son," the doctor added with a wide smile.

A son! A baby boy. I pictured him with black hair and green eyes...Braden's smile.

Apparently affected by the picture of our son on the monitor, Braden covered my hand with his as we gazed at the screen together. We both needed the contact. This was an experience like no other we'd ever have, and I felt so close to this man who was going to be a wonderful father.

After we simply listened to that heartbeat for a while, Dr. Felton pointed out what we were seeing on the monitor, then took the measurements she needed to accompany the results of the blood test.

All the while, Braden and I stared at our baby. When my eyes locked with his, I knew I'd never witnessed such a tender look there before...such gentleness...such warmth. My heart overflowed with love for him and our child.

The physician read off her observations to the nurse and printed out data. Cold reality set in once more. I was glad I would be busy for the next week, so I wouldn't be sitting by the phone waiting for Dr. Felton's call. No matter what happened I would be keeping this child who came from my love for Braden, praying there would be no abnormality present to worry us. The truth was, I didn't know if Braden was the type of man who would walk away if a difficulty arose.

After all, he'd walked away from *me*.

Fifteen minutes later, I was dressed again. Braden had left the examination room after the ultrasound and I didn't know if he'd be waiting or not. But he was.

After I checked out at the receptionist's desk, he said, "Let me buy you breakfast."

"I really don't have time," I began, checking my watch.

"If you're going to take care of yourself, you have time."

"I *have* been taking care of myself. I've been eating regularly and all the right things." I patted my waistline under my suit. "That's why I'm getting bigger."

"You're getting bigger because our child is growing. I've never seen anything so awesome as the sight of our baby on that screen."

"I know what you mean. I can't wait to buy baby clothes in blue."

He laughed. "And there's furniture and room decorations." There was a long, empty pause before he added, "I guess we'll both be buying those."

I wanted the tension between us gone. I wanted to be in agreement with Braden about something, so I said, "I'll come to breakfast with you on one condition."

"What's that?" he asked warily.

"We don't talk about my promotion or Los Angeles. We can talk about the baby and our dreams for him, colleges we might want him to go to."

He thought over what I suggested. "All right. And we can talk about Melissa's admiration for you. She told me she wants to go shopping with you sometime. That's a high compliment. She doesn't want her mother anywhere around her when she shops."

"When I get back from L.A., I'll call her. Or do you think Carol would mind? I don't want to step on her toes."

"Phone me when you get back and I'll have Melissa call you. Then we won't have to worry about Carol."

"We will if I take Melissa shopping."

"I'll deal with that when the time comes."

With his hand protectively on the small of my back, he motioned toward the door. "Ready?"

"Ready." I was looking forward to this breakfast, and to bonding with Braden in a way we hadn't before.

TWO AND A HALF WEEKS had never gone by so slowly. My time in L.A. had been taken up with meetings, meetings, and more meetings, lunches, dinners and tours of the area. I even looked at a few condos, but all the while I was waiting for the results of my test and…I was thinking about Braden. Los Angeles seemed like another planet compared to Galloway. I thought that was what I wanted, but Shannon Galloway's questions kept ringing in my ears. *When you achieve success with this dream, what comes next? CEO? And when you become CEO, will you find that job and the salary solace when you're all alone?*

Exactly a week after the tests, Dr. Felton called me in L.A. The AFP test in conjunction with the ultrasound indicated my baby was developing as he should be. My baby. Braden's baby. I had called him immediately and the sound of relief in his voice had been obvious.

As I opened the door to my town house at 7:00 p.m. on Friday, I realized that the trip home from L.A. had tired me out more than I ever imagined it would. My neighbor had dropped me off, and all I wanted to do was take a nap before I put my notes in order for my meeting with Charlie the following week. But then, I noticed the blinking message light on my answering machine.

I pressed Play.

"It's me," Braden said. "I'd like to know that you returned safely. Give me a call."

His concern wrapped around my heart, bringing tears to my eyes. His caring had always touched me and this instance was no different.

Torn between calling his apartment and leaving a message or phoning his cell, I decided to phone his cell.

When he picked up, I said, "I'm back."

"Good. How do you feel?"

"Tired," I admitted. "Otherwise fine."

"Do you have any food in the house?"

Now that I thought about it, I had to admit I didn't. "No, not fresh anyway. I can open a can of soup."

"You deserve a welcome-home dinner. I'll bring something over from the restaurant."

"You don't have to. I mean, I know you're busy."

There were a few beats of silence. "I'm in Galloway and everything's running smoothly here. The specials tonight are stuffed chicken breast and prime rib. Which would you like?"

"Chicken breast," I answered automatically.

He chuckled. "I should have known."

As soon as I hung up, I looked down at the sweater I'd worn on the trip. It was part of a maternity outfit I'd bought in L.A. But now I just wanted to be comfortable. So taking a rainbow-colored caftan from my luggage, I changed in my downstairs bathroom, and felt fatigue wash over me again.

After I unlocked the door so Braden could come right in, I went to the sofa and decided to just close my eyes for a few minutes before he arrived. In the throes of a marvelous dream in which Braden and I were alone in the moonlight on a desert island, my heart longed for more than a dream. When Braden lifted his hand and ran his fingers through my hair, I—

Suddenly coming awake, I realized I wasn't *in* a dream. Braden *was* running his fingers through my hair.

"Hey there," he whispered close to my ear.

I had turned on my side and was facing the back of the sofa. Now I shifted around and gazed into his eyes. He was crouched beside me and I was so glad to see him.

"I must have fallen asleep."

"Must have." Standing, he motioned to the bags on the coffee table. "I brought supper."

I shook my head. "I'm not hungry. I think I'm just too tired to eat."

For a moment he looked as if he was going to argue. But he didn't. Instead, he took the bags and went into the kitchen. A moment later I heard the refrigerator door open, then shut.

At the sofa once more, he slipped one arm in back of me, the other under my knees. "Come on. I'm going to put you to bed."

"You don't have to—" I began.

Instead of listening, he bent his head to mine and kissed me. "I know I don't have to. I want to."

Then I was in his arms and he was carrying me up the stairs to my bedroom.

I'd been so tired, but now all my senses were awakening. Braden's black sweater brushed my arm as I looked up at him, inhaling his cologne, trying to make sense of what I was feeling. Sleepiness was fast fading and my body was tingling from being held so close to him. Two and a half weeks had caused more changes in my figure. What would he think of them?

At my bedroom, he didn't hesitate and didn't even switch on the light. Bright moonbeams cascaded through the window. Braden set me down next to the bed and then quickly drew back the covers, but I didn't get in. He was staring at me in the moonlight, and I realized the silky caftan hid nothing from him. While I was in his arms, he had felt my body against him. Now he was looking at my breasts as if he wanted to touch them.

I needed his touch so badly…as much as I needed the answers to all my questions. Somehow I believed they were hidden in the stirrings of my heart, which spoke to me whenever Braden made love to me.

I'd taken risks in my professional life but I had rarely taken them in my personal life. When Braden and I had fallen in love last summer, everything had been so easy. Now nothing was easy. I knew I'd have regrets for the rest of my life if I didn't act on what I was feeling.

"Stay with me tonight?" I asked softly.

From the set of his jaw, I could tell this wasn't a decision that was easy for him to make.

I had risked my pride and now I was embarrassed. Crawling into bed, I pulled the covers up to my chin.

"Never mind. Thanks for supper. I'm sure I'll wake up in a few hours ravenous."

I expected him to leave. Instead, he just stood there, and I braced myself because I knew I probably wasn't going to like what he had to say.

CHAPTER SIX

"DON'T YOU THINK we should talk about your trip to L.A.?" Braden asked.

On the flight back to Oklahoma, I'd been thinking about the trip and everything this job would entail—the hours, the workload, the commitment and the responsibility. I'd also been considering my new responsibilities to my baby.

"Let's not talk tonight," I suggested. Whether Braden left or he stayed, I wasn't ready to line up the pros and cons or make a decision.

His guarded stance seemed to ebb away and I saw the sparks of desire in his eyes as they'd been there the night we'd first made love…the sparks that had been there all those nights before our engagement had ended. After he lowered himself to the bed, he cupped my chin in his palm and kissed me—a hard, sensually arousing kiss.

Breaking away, he shook his head. "This won't solve anything."

I knew he was right, but I wanted tonight anyway.

When I was still silent, he swore and then kissed me again. That kiss tore down the dam on any restraint either of us might have had. Minutes later, my caftan was on the floor beside his clothes and he was running his hand over me, erotically discovering all the changes.

He was so tender with me, so unhurried and gentle. With each stroke of his hand, I fell deeper and deeper in love with him. After he reverently kissed my breasts and laved the nipples, I felt tears come to my eyes because I wanted Braden in bed beside me every night.

Our bodies glistened from foreplay, our breathing came faster from passion, our tongues mated and danced while our hands explored. Nothing else existed but the two of us right here…right now. Soon neither of us could wait a moment longer. As we lay face-to-face, Braden drew my leg over his hip. I knew he was choosing this position to make sure I was comfortable…to protect me.

Slowly I guided him inside me. When he groaned, I rubbed his nipple with my thumb, wanting to give him even more pleasure. As he ran his hand over my back, I contracted around him. Our climaxes built as we rocked together and our bodies knew ecstasy simultaneously. He shuddered. My orgasm seemed to go on and on until I finally kissed his neck and he held me tight.

Neither of us moved. We just breathed in each other's scent and marveled at the unity we felt. At least I hoped that was what Braden was feeling, too.

We stayed joined, and he brushed my hair from my forehead. "Do you want me to stay the night?"

"Yes."

As he caressed my cheek, he kissed me and then asked, "What now?"

"I don't know." I thought he might list all the reasons I should stay in Galloway, but he didn't.

"The coming week is going to be a bull," he muttered. "The food critic's going to be coming and I have to be at the restaurant every night to make sure I'm there when he makes an appearance."

"I understand." I took one of those risks again. "But you have to sleep somewhere…sometime."

"Yes, I do." Quiet for a few moments, he finally said, "Carol and Joel are going away overnight this weekend to an inn in Tulsa. I told them I'd stay with Melissa. How would you like to keep us company tomorrow and Sunday?"

Thinking about Carol and her attitude toward me, I asked, "Do you think that would be all right with Carol and Joel?"

"Knowing Carol, it will be fine as long as we sleep in separate bedrooms."

"She has to set a standard for Melissa." I didn't disagree with Carol's thinking.

"Yes, I guess she does. Do you want to come?"

"I'd like to keep you company."

As Braden ran his hand over my shoulder and down my arm, I felt him stir again inside me. I knew from experience that he had stamina. I also knew I could keep up with it.

"You need to sleep," he murmured, starting to pull away.

Feeling so much love I had to express it, I tightened my arms around his neck. "I need *you* more."

When Braden kissed me, I gave myself up to the chemistry between us. I gave myself up to my love for him. No matter what decision I came to, I knew Braden would always own my heart.

WHEN BRADEN AND I picked up Melissa after her piano lesson on Saturday afternoon as prearranged, she climbed into Braden's SUV with a wide grin. "I told Mom I didn't need a babysitter, but the weekend

might be great with you two. What are we going
to do?"

Braden laughed. "We have to 'do' something?"

"We could go shopping," she offered innocently.

Shifting in my seat, I gazed at Melissa in the back.
"We didn't clear that with your mom and I hate to bother
her on her getaway." At Melissa's frown I hurried on,
"But I brought along one of my cosmetics kits. We
could dabble with that tonight."

A worried expression crossed the teenager's face,
but just as quickly it was gone and I thought I had
imagined it. "That will be great." She flipped her hand
through her long hair. "And maybe we could find a new
style for this. What do you think?"

"I think I'm going to be in the way," Braden grumbled.

"No, you won't be in the way," I teased him. "You
can buy the pizza for supper."

"Or I could take a run to the restaurant and bring back
real food," he offered.

"Do you need to check in?" I asked.

"Not necessarily. I hired a manager who knows what
he's doing. I can't be two places at once, so I have to let
go of the hands-on management somewhat."

"I'd rather have pizza," Melissa informed us. "Mom's
watching her carbs and we never order it anymore."

"Pizza it is," Braden agreed.

At Carol's house a short time later, I admired its
precise, just-cleaned look. The cherry-wood furniture
was beautiful. The rooms were spacious, the fabric on
the love seat and sofa as well as the window treatment
were fine quality. As Melissa showed me to her room,
I saw it was a little girl's dream, all white organdy and
pink roses and a white canopy bed. But there was some-

thing incongruous about it and I soon figured out what it was. The dolls and stuffed toys on a set of bookshelves as well as the frilly and flowery decorations on the walls didn't give the impression that this was a teenager's room.

There was a CD player on the dresser. After I placed the large cosmetics case on the bed, I looked through the CDs.

"I don't have my good ones there," Melissa told me.

The CDs in the small rack were mostly classical.

Crossing to a closet, Melissa disappeared inside. A few moments later, she reappeared with a shoe box. As she sat on the bed cross-legged, she flipped off the lid. Inside was an assortment of music, mostly from male pop idols.

"When do you play them?" I asked.

"I have a portable player with earphones. I also dig them out when Mom's not around. Dad wouldn't have a clue as to who's singing what, so I don't have to worry about him telling me I should be listening to something more worthwhile."

"What else do you have stashed in there?" I asked teasingly.

Her face flushing, she asked, "How did you know?"

"Just a guess."

For the next half hour, she showed me teen magazines and posters of heartthrobs. I had to wonder if Carol really knew her daughter at all.

Melissa was telling me about a concert she'd like to go to when Braden poked his head into the room. "Ready for pizza?"

"Sure," she answered him. "Then April and I can spend the rest of the night on makeup and nail polish and everything else."

When Braden gazed at me shoulder to shoulder on the bed with Melissa, my legs crossed like hers, a warm look came into his eyes.

Out of nowhere, Melissa asked, "Are you two sleeping together tonight?"

There was no doubt in my mind what the answer should be to that inquiry, but before I could answer, Braden's expression grew serious. "That's not a question you should ask."

Unruffled, Melissa shrugged. "I just wondered. I don't care. Since April's pregnant and all, why wouldn't you?"

"We're sleeping in separate rooms tonight," I replied. "Your mom prefers that and this is her house."

"She's got so-o-o many rules," Melissa complained.

"Don't you know that's what parents are for?" Braden joked. "To make up rules that irritate kids."

Melissa smiled then. "Well, mine do a good job of it."

When Braden and I exchanged a look, I knew that he, like me, could see both sides. Being a parent would never be easy. And raising a child alone…

I'd rather have Braden by my side and not miles away it seemed, and I found I was seriously considering *not* taking the promotion in Los Angeles. This was the first I'd admitted that to myself. There were so many reasons to stay in Galloway, not only so our baby would have two parents close by, but because I loved Braden. If I stayed, maybe we could build on what we'd clearly had in the beginning.

When he left the room to order pizza, Melissa turned to me. "Are you going to marry Uncle Braden?"

"I don't know," I answered honestly, understanding now that Braden's proposal might be what I was waiting for in order to make my decision. The question was, would he ask me again and risk being turned down? Up until now, my career had been more important than our relationship.

During the evening, Melissa and I had fun. When she got her first look at everything in my kit—eyeshadow, lip glosses and lipsticks, nail polishes and lotions, she giggled. "I want to try it *all*."

"You can try it all," I assured her with a laugh. "But remember, I work for *Natural* Beauty. We believe in enhancing a woman's own look, not turning her into someone else. That's especially true for someone your age."

When Melissa frowned, I wondered what she was thinking, but then she smiled at me with thirteen-year-old enthusiasm. "Let's get started."

Her hair took no time at all. We found curlers in the linen closet and used them. Long ago I'd learned a trick of using a curling iron, then setting my hair in rollers. The heat helped hold the wave. Melissa took note of all of it. When we got to the makeup, she played with some different colors and then washed them all off. I showed her how to use foundation to cover imperfections. Smoothing a bit of plum shadow on her eyelids, I taught her how to make her eyes look larger. Afterward, I applied a touch of blush that looked natural, then she chose a pretty mauve lip gloss.

"Can we take some pictures with my camera?" she asked. "We can print them out on the computer, then I can show my friends. They won't believe it's me."

"Sure they will. It's just a dressed-up you."

"Are you sure I don't need mascara?"

"I'm positive. Your dark lashes are beautiful, just as they are. Remember, natural is what matters."

"Can you do my nails?"

I checked the clock. "It's getting late. Why don't we take some pictures and do your nails in the morning? We can always reset your hair and apply makeup again tomorrow if you want."

"No," she said quickly. "I mean…we can do my hair again and then my nails. We don't have to do makeup."

"All right. I think Braden would probably appreciate a home-cooked breakfast. How are you at scrambled eggs?"

"I'm great at scrambled eggs. How are you at pancakes?"

I laughed. "I'm great at pancakes."

After we'd taken pictures and gotten a snack with Braden, Melissa turned in for the night. I heard the CD player—a boy band playing in the background.

When I returned to the living room, Braden switched off the TV and patted the sofa next to him. My heart started jumping because I could see in his eyes that he wanted to kiss me. We hadn't been physically close all day and even though I'd spent my time mostly with Melissa, I felt as if Braden and I had been emotionally close.

As soon as I sank onto the sofa cushion, he put his arm around me. "You're going to make a terrific mom."

"Because I can relate to Melissa?"

"It's not just Melissa. On Christmas Day I watched you with little Danny and Darcy, too. You like kids, don't you?"

"Sure, doesn't everybody?"

"Absolutely not. Sometimes when families come into the restaurant, I see expressions on diners nearby. They don't want to be anywhere around kids."

I shrugged. "Melissa's wonderful. I can't help but

love being around her. But—" I wasn't sure I should go on or not.

"But?" Braden prompted.

"I get the feeling if Carol doesn't loosen her restrictions a little, Melissa could rebel."

"You're probably right about that." He bent his head close to me. "I don't want to talk about my sister."

Amused, I tilted my face up to his. "What do you want to talk about?"

He rubbed his nose against mine. "I'd rather not talk at all. In fact, I'm damn sorry I told Carol we'd sleep in separate bedrooms."

"It's the right thing to do for tonight."

"And what about tomorrow night?" he asked and my heart began singing.

"You want to have a sleepover at my house?" I kidded, afraid to hope he wanted a whole lot more.

"A sleepover. Now *there's* a thought. How about if we stop at that little gourmet shop and pick up chocolate-covered strawberries?"

"That sounds like a wonderful idea." Maybe if we took our time making love, maybe if we spent that intimate time together, Braden would admit he still had feelings for me...that he still loved me. If he was trying to convince me to stay in Galloway, he was doing a great job of it. I just had to make sure that having sex was more than convenient physical fulfillment for him...that having sex was more than a way for him to secure rights to his baby.

However, when Braden's lips covered mine, I forgot about questions and doubts and decisions I had to make. His kiss and his touch filled my world. I knew we wouldn't be going to our separate rooms until much later.

MAKING BRUNCH with Melissa and Braden gave me a sense of family I hadn't had for a very long time. Braden helped, frying the bacon, while Melissa scrambled eggs and I made pancakes on an electric griddle. The three of us laughed and teased and talked seriously about what Melissa might want to major in at college.

While Braden and I still sat at the table talking, Melissa printed out the pictures from her digital camera and brought them back to the kitchen. She looked absolutely adorable. We'd taken some photos with a hat, others without, some with sunglasses perched on top of her head, others with her just grinning into the camera.

"You look terrific," I said again.

"The kids won't believe it's me."

"They'll believe it's you," Braden assured her.

Just then the front door opened. Braden's sister called, "We're home."

Melissa froze and I didn't understand her stricken expression. "I didn't think they'd be home yet."

The pages of photographs were spread across the table, and she quickly began brushing them into a pile.

"Something smells good in here," Melissa's father said as he and his wife came into the kitchen.

"Brunch," I responded lightly.

"We have a few leftover pancakes if you're interested," Braden joked.

Although Melissa had picked up most of the sheets of glossy photographic paper, there was still one by my place and Braden was holding one in his hand.

"What have you got there?" Carol asked, taking off her jacket and hanging it on a hook by the door.

As she crossed the kitchen to peer over Melissa's

shoulder, her daughter dropped her hand with the photographs to her side. "Nothing."

I wondered why Melissa was reluctant to show them to Carol.

"We were just having some fun," I offered.

Now Carol picked up the loose photograph on the table and her expression changed from politely friendly to downright angry. "What is this?"

I didn't understand why Melissa looked so miserable and her mother so disturbed. "I brought a cosmetics kit along last night. Melissa and I just spent some girl-time having fun with it. She asked if we could take some pictures with her camera to show her friends, so that's what we did. She just printed them out."

"Melissa knows I've forbidden her to wear makeup until she's fourteen. Did she tell you that?"

Melissa's face flushed and her stance was defiant. She answered Carol before I could. "No, I didn't, Mom. Because it's another one of your *stupid* rules. Do you think I don't carry lip gloss to school in my pocket? Do you think I don't borrow eye shadow and blush from Kristi and then wash it all off before I come home? Kristi's mom understands that she wants to look pretty and she's not a baby anymore. April was great last night. We had so much fun. Why can't *you* be like that?"

"Melissa," Joel warned sharply.

I felt so bad for Carol. If my child ever thought she couldn't confide in me or even just talk to me, I'd be devastated.

Entering the fray, Braden put his hand on Melissa's shoulder. "Honey, maybe you'd better go to your room and let me talk to your mom."

Braden's niece looked up at him. "Talking won't do any good. She doesn't listen!"

Then with the photos clutched to her chest as if they were the most precious things in the world to her, she ran to her room.

Addressing his sister, Braden motioned to the chairs. "Why don't we sit down and talk about this."

"There's nothing to talk about," Carol replied tersely. "This isn't any of your business. She's *my* daughter." Glaring at me, she said pointedly, "This is all your fault. If you hadn't brought your cosmetics in here, this wouldn't have happened."

I thought about the treasures Melissa kept in her closet and I wanted to tell Carol about them, but I knew that was probably the worst thing to do right now. "She just wants you to listen to her," I suggested quietly.

"You're pregnant and suddenly you know everything there is to know about kids? Let me tell you, April, I've taken care of Melissa since she came home from the hospital. I've been here day after day, night after night, not off earning a reputation for myself, not trying to compete with men but nurturing my child."

Braden stepped closer to me. "Don't do this, Carol. Go to Melissa and talk to her."

"Do you think talking's going to help this…this rebellion of hers? By treating her like a grown-up, April has made the situation ten times worse."

"I didn't mean any harm," I began, hurting for Melissa as well as Carol.

"You never mean any harm, do you? I guess you didn't mean any harm when you chose a promotion over Braden's love for you. Do you know how devastated he was? Do you know—?"

"Carol!" Braden's voice was louder and rougher than I'd ever heard it.

His sister went quiet and from the expression on his face, so did I. In an instant of anger, Carol had raised the specter of our breakup again. I saw the pain in Braden's eyes and I realized that his dreams had been even bigger than mine. When he'd given me a ring he'd envisioned a wedding, two lives united on one course, building a family. My fear and ambition had shut all that down.

After Braden laid the photograph of Melissa on the table, he said to me, "I'll get our things. Let's go."

Without another word to us, Carol went to Melissa's room. I put on my coat and picked up the cosmetics kit.

Looking awkward, Joel met us at the door. He said to me, "I'm sorry about what happened in there. I know she'd never admit it, but Carol is jealous of you."

That shocked me. "Why?"

"She sees what you've accomplished, your confidence and independence, and I think part of her wishes she had that, too, especially now that Melissa's growing up and building boundaries between them. Carol knows she's going to have an empty nest soon, and I think she's afraid of that. It's not an excuse, but it might help you understand."

I *did* understand. I'd be raising a son only to have to let him go. There was an old expression for that—giving a child roots and wings.

On the drive to my town house, Braden was silent. In the parking lot, he switched off the ignition. When I looked at him, I knew I had to bring up our broken engagement.

"When I gave back your ring, I thought I was doing what was best for both of us. We wanted different things—"

"You didn't break off our engagement because it was best for both of us. You broke it off because it was best for *you*." The anger and hurt he'd never expressed were in his voice now. "You were too scared to take the plunge into marriage, to give up any of your independence. You were afraid to have a baby and you didn't even tell me!" He swore, then demanded, "Why did you say yes, when I asked you to marry me?"

Obviously he'd been holding in all the pain and anger, maybe hoping it would diminish or vanish on its own. It hadn't. "I said yes because I loved you," I returned quietly. "I said yes because I thought we'd be engaged for a while, married for a while, and *then* we'd have a family."

"Your fear wouldn't have disappeared just because we got married," he pointed out, aiming another angry glance in my direction.

"No. But I guess I hoped in time, with your love and your trust, it would fade away. I know you were hurt and maybe you'll never be able to forgive me, but maybe you need to think about something else, too. I didn't break off our engagement, *you* did—when I wouldn't agree to stay in Galloway. Yes, I gave your ring back, but only because I saw you wouldn't change your mind. You didn't even *try* to change my mind! You just let me go, as if our engagement hadn't mattered to you at all. You just dropped me and the idea of *us* because I didn't fall in with your plans. After we broke up, it seemed to me you regretted jumping in so fast."

"I *did* regret jumping in so fast."

His words hung in the car between us and I'd had enough heart-wrenching emotion for one day. I opened the door and got out.

Again he didn't come after me.

Once I was inside my town house, I realized I'd left my cosmetics case and overnight bag in his car. I didn't care. At that moment, I figured Braden had always liked the idea of having a family but had never truly loved me.

BY TUESDAY MORNING I'd cried all my tears. In my office, I called Charlie and set up a meeting for the following day. No matter what had happened, Braden and I would still be coparents. The best decision I could make for our son would be to stay in Galloway.

The guard in the lobby buzzed me to say that a messenger was coming to my office. When I went to the door, the uniformed man handed me an envelope. Inside was an invitation requesting my presence at the Tin Roof in Galloway at eight o'clock that evening.

My first thought was to make an excuse and be busy doing something else. But if Braden and I were going to be parents successfully, we'd also have to be friends—no matter how much my heart hurt right now.

THAT EVENING I was surprised to see very few cars in the parking lot of the Tin Roof. However, there were lights on inside. I went to the restaurant and opened the door. When I walked in, the lobby was dim and no maître d' stood at the podium. As I stepped into the main dining room, the scent of flowers surrounded me and I saw there were pink roses everywhere. The tables were devoid of tablecloths except for one in the center of the room. There was a globed candle in the middle of it and two place settings, as well as a beautiful crystal vase. It didn't hold any flowers. Then I spotted the instruments on a small dais in the corner of the room—a cello, a violin and a clarinet.

I heard the door from the kitchen open and turned toward it. Dressed in a suit and tie, Braden came into the dining room. He was so devastatingly handsome I wanted to cry.

His expression was serious as he came to me, took my purse from my hands and laid it on the table, then unbuttoned my coat. I felt as if I was in a daze when he lifted it from my shoulders and stowed it on a chair away from our table.

From a nearby table, he picked up a bouquet of pink roses and handed them to me.

I'd worn one of my new maternity outfits, teal-blue slacks and a matching embroidered blouse. But Braden didn't seem to care what I was wearing as his gaze locked on mine. "Tonight is for *you*."

"Braden?" I wasn't sure what this meant and my heart was beating so fast I could hardly breathe.

"Everything between us from the very beginning happened too fast and got muddled. When I asked you to marry me, I was absolutely in love with you. When we broke up I was hurt, but it was my pride that kept me from calling you…my pride that kept me from coming after you. I can't let pride stand in my way anymore."

Taking the roses from my hands, he settled them in the empty vase. Then he pulled out a chair at the table, and I saw that there were two boxes on it.

He picked up one of them. "I have two gifts for you. Open this one first."

My fingers fumbled as I set the white bow on the table and tore shiny blue paper off a small box. When I lifted the lid, I found a beautiful diamond necklace inside.

"That's the diamond that was in your engagement ring, the one you returned to me. I want you to wear it to remember how much I loved you then, as well as how much I love you now."

My eyes began swimming with tears as he took the box from my hand and set it down. Then he handed me a velvet ring box.

"Open it," he encouraged.

When I lifted the lid, I saw a beautiful engagement ring—a marquise cut with small diamonds surrounding it. I didn't know what to say.

"I love you, April, and I realize now that you need proof of that. I was arrogant to think my life couldn't change or that it might have to follow a different course than I planned in the beginning. I have good managers at both of my restaurants. I know how much this promotion means to you. So… I think we should move to California and I'll open another restaurant there. I can fly back to Oklahoma now and then, but my life will be with you and our baby."

Absolutely stunned, I asked, "You'd leave your family? I know how much they mean to you. And what about the contract on the house?"

A house that I really liked.

Taking the ring from the box, he carefully slipped it onto my finger. Then his arms were enfolding me, drawing me close. "I haven't settled on the house yet. And as far as family… Over the past few days I've realized just how much I want to make a life with *you*. We'll create our *own* family."

In technicolor I remembered Christmas Day with Braden's parents, sister and brother—the laughter, the joking, the conversation, the bonds. I remembered staying with Melissa and making brunch with her and the sense of connection I felt. With a blinding flash of insight I understood I'd hung on to my ambition because I thought I'd never find unconditional love. I never thought I would find a man who could fill my life as much as my work always had. But Braden *did* fill my life…and I loved him.

Stroking his jaw, I knew I was making the right decision. "You don't have to leave everything you hold dear. Last night I decided our son is more important than any job in California. He's going to be the center of my life for a while. I'm hoping Natural Beauty will keep me on part-time so I can keep my hand in. In a few years, when our son starts school, it will be about time for Charlie to retire. Maybe he'll recommend me for his position," I confided with a smile.

"Are you sure?" Braden asked, looking worried. "I don't want you to ever regret staying here."

"I won't have any regrets. I love you. And I want our son to have family around him. I want your mom to spoil him and Melissa to babysit him."

I could see nothing in the world would stop Braden from kissing me then. His lips were on mine—possessively, masterfully, lovingly.

When he broke away, he assured me, "I'll never swallow you up. I'll always remember that you need to be successful in your own right, too."

Wrapping my arms around his neck, I whispered, "I know you will."

Then he was kissing me again and we promised each other the rest of our lives.

EPILOGUE

"COME ON, APRIL. One more giant push and you can celebrate your first real Mother's Day," Dr. Felton encouraged, peering at me over her mask.

I felt as if I'd been pushing for many hours, though
in reality it had only been about two. Braden had been
by my side every minute since I'd gone into labor the
previous evening. We'd come into the hospital at seven
this morning, when the contractions had been a mere
three minutes apart. He was a wonderful coach…and a
wonderful husband. We'd been married on Valentine's
Day. Two weeks later we'd settled on the house Braden
had shown me and moved in.

My husband's eyes were filled with love as he
squeezed my hand, bent close, then whispered, "Come
on, sweetheart. Let's meet our son."

As my due date had drawn closer, I'd become in-
creasingly afraid that what had happened to Jenny would
happen to me. But in those anxious moments, Braden
had taken me into his arms, held me and reassured me.

With all my might, I summoned what energy I had
left and pushed with my heart and soul and body.

With his cheek next to mine, Braden held my shoulders, supporting the effort I was making.

"There he is," the doctor announced jubilantly.

Almost in a sitting position, I peered over the sheet, and then I heard the sound I'd yearned to hear for nine long months—my baby's first cry.

"We have a son!" Braden kissed me. His voice was thick and I caught the sheen of moisture in his eyes right before his lips covered mine. My cheeks were wet from happy tears, and I knew we'd never forget this moment for as long as we lived.

"Everything's fine," the doctor assured me as she suctioned our son's mouth and then let Braden cut the cord. After the nurses cleaned him up and wrapped him in a blue blanket, Nathan Michael Galloway was nestled in my arms. He'd stopped crying as soon as the nurse settled him there.

Running his thumb over our baby's black hair, Braden decided, "He looks like a Nathan."

"I think so, too." We'd spent weeks picking out the name and now it seemed to fit perfectly.

"I know you need to rest, but the nurse just told me my whole family's here. Are you too tired to see them?"

Over the past few months, I'd gotten closer to Braden's family, even closer to Carol. At our wedding reception, she'd admitted to me that she and Melissa had talked...really talked for the first time in a long time. She apologized for her comments that Sunday and confided she had always wanted a career of some kind. I suggested it wasn't too late.

Because of my blossoming feelings for Braden's family, I'd become closer to my own family, too. My mother was thrilled she was going to be a grandmother. Taking a stand, she said she would visit me this summer. If Dad couldn't take time off work, she'd come alone and nothing would keep her away. Jenny was flying in next week, using her vacation days so she could help me adapt to motherhood. When I asked if that wouldn't be too hard for her, she told me she needed the practice. She'd found an unwed mother who was giving up her baby for adoption, and she was going to become a mother after all.

Gazing up at my husband, knowing exactly how much he loved me, I said, "I'm not too tired. I want everybody to meet the newest member of the Galloway family."

The doctor and nurses had moved away to give us a few moments of privacy. Braden kissed my temple, kissed my lips, and then ran his index finger over our son's cheek, gazing at me all the while. "Do you know how much I love you?"

"Yes. As much as I love you."

We were equals, partners, lovers and friends.

No matter where life took us, we would face the challenges and the journey together.

"We have to give him wings so he can fly on his own some day," I mused.

Braden's large hand covered mine. "We will."

Braden's promise was as strong and true as his wedding vows had been. With my heart so full of happiness I could hardly absorb it, I knew our son would be our joy and would bring us even closer together—hour by hour...day by day...year by year.

Side by side with Braden, I looked forward to every moment of the rest of our lives.

Dear Reader,

I loved writing *On Angel's Wings*. I wrote the story after discovering Bridge of Hope, a real-life program where older Russian orphans come to the United States for a one-month stay with a host family. Many of these children end up being adopted by their "summer" family. The stories I read from both children and families who had participated made me wish for a way to bring this program to my own community.

After speaking with the wonderful people at Cradle of Hope in Silver Spring, Maryland, I learned that this was indeed possible. Along with a group of wonderful women from my church, we formed a committee, then set about raising the money to bring the children to our community and getting the word out to potential host families. It was an absolutely incredible experience. Our first group of children arrived in July 2005, and I know I will never forget the image of their sweet, hopeful faces as they met their host families for the first time.

To see children with no family of their own end up with a mother and father who love them beyond words is like witnessing a miracle. I feel so blessed to have been a part of this program. Although my story is a complete work of fiction, I do hope it gives honor to the intentions of such efforts.

In *On Angel's Wings*, Rachel and Clay have suffered the loss of a child, a tragedy that nearly destroys them. They have both come to accept that they will never again know real happiness. Until, that is, a little girl named Sasha walks into their lives, and they begin to realize they have so much left to give.

I hope you enjoy this story. For a look at my other titles, please visit my Web site, www.inglathcooper.com.

All the best,

Inglath Cooper

ON ANGEL'S WINGS
Inglath Cooper

For the Bridge of Hope families and their children.
In my eyes, heroes and heroines, each and every one.

CHAPTER ONE

"WILL IT HURT, Dr. Foster?"

I'd been a practicing pediatrician for fourteen years now, but still hadn't gotten used to being asked this question. I wished I could say no. I wished it didn't hurt.

"Just for a second," I said, putting a hand to the child's shoulder. "It will be over before you know it."

"Come on, Molly," the little girl's mother said, lifting her up onto the examining table. "Ice cream on the way home, remember?"

Our office had been swamped today. Rather than prolong Molly's misery by having her wait on a nurse, I decided to give the shots myself. At five years old, Molly was braver than most children her age who had long ago figured out what trips to the doctor usually meant. She lay very still on the table, one hand locked in a please-don't-let-go grip with her mother's hand. I swabbed the area on her thigh with alcohol, quickly injected the needle, withdrew it and popped the cap back on the syringe. Just as I stuck a Band-Aid on the spot, Molly began to cry, the sobs reluctant as if she didn't want to, but couldn't help it. The emotion echoed through me. I bit my lip and turned away, dropping the used syringe in the biohazard disposal hanging on the wall.

I got through the next two as swiftly as I could, and then said, too brightly, "All done. Thank you, Molly, for being such a big girl."

Molly nodded, fat tears rolling down her cheeks, the kind I had never been able to witness without a twist in my heart. Molly's mother pulled her into her arms, hugged her tight, consoling as only a mother can. "What a brave girl you are, sweetie," she said.

Watching them, I thought of Emma and the times when I had consoled her exactly that way. My arms ached with the memory, and it was all I could do to keep my face free of the pain.

I took a roll of stickers from my pocket. Winnie the Pooh. Tigger. Sand buckets and stars. Molly chose three, a small smile now replacing the tears.

The rest of the day disappeared beneath a full schedule of appointments. I finished seeing patients at five-thirty, but worked at my desk until eight, sipping a tepid Starbucks coffee one of the secretaries had gone down the block to get for me before she left. Such acts of kindness were a jolt to me, as if I had forgotten that good could actually exist in a world that had shown me too much of the bad.

When even the janitorial staff had left for the evening, I still couldn't bring myself to go home. I glanced around an office where I spent too much of my time. Framed diplomas from Georgetown and Johns Hopkins adorned the walls. As a girl who would have gone to neither had it not been for academic scholarships, a stint as a swimming instructor and a knack for waitressing, I had once taken such pride in seeing them there. The walnut desk in front of me held a convincing pretense of work, files stacked neatly in each corner, my laptop open and blinking in the near dark of the office. I liked it this way, no lights, dimming the focus of a life at which I tried not to look too closely.

The cell phone to the right of my computer rang. I glanced at the caller ID, hesitated at answering, then quickly punched the green button before I could change my mind.

"Let me guess. You're still at the office?"

Cathy's voice was chastising. I considered a half truth—on the way home—offered up with a cheerfulness she would be surprised to hear. But I decided she wouldn't believe me, anyway. She knew me too well. "Just getting ready to go," I said. "What's up?"

"I have a favor to ask," she said, to the point as always.

Cathy and I became friends as undergrads at Georgetown, had remained so in the years since. She worked for the Angels in Our Midst Adoption Agency in Washington D.C., and while I used to want to hear about the wonderful work she did there, it was now the elephant in the living room around which we both tiptoed.

Her voice held something different now, though, a hesitation out of sync with her normally put-it-out-there-and-it-will-happen approach to getting things done.

"Shoot," I said, my stomach tilting a little.

"I told you about it once. On Angel's Wings. Our program for older Russian orphans," she said. "We bring the children to Fairfax for a two-week stay with an American host family who then has the option of adopting them."

"Uh-huh," I said, running a hand around the back of my neck and sitting a little straighter in my chair.

"Here's the problem," Cathy said, exhaling as if she'd been holding her breath. "We have a group of kids arriving on Monday. One of the couples who agreed to host a nine-year-old girl has decided to back out at the last minute. The wife called to tell me this just a few hours ago, and now I have to find someone to take this child for two weeks."

"Um," I said, caught between what I hoped she would ask and what I knew would be impossible if she did.

"Forgive me if I'm out of line here, Rachel, but I wondered if you and Clay might be willing to let her stay with you."

I tried to respond, but failed, rendered speechless by a painful rush of enthusiasm, the flip side of which was my own certainty of Clay's reaction. "Cathy. I don't know. This is—"

"Sudden, I know. I tried two other families I thought might be interested first," she said. "Neither of them could take her right now. The thing is, this child came for the program last summer. The host family ended up not adopting her because they decided to divorce."

"Oh," I said, one hand to my mouth. It was like this with me. I kept my head low, got through my days with virtual blinders on, not wanting to hear about other people's pain, too focused on my own to have room for anyone else's. Until, in moments like this, I was reminded that I wasn't the only person in this world to know tragedy.

"We really wanted to bring her back this year, give

her another chance," Cathy said. "And then this second couple backs out. What are the odds?"

"That's terrible," I said, the words low and unsteady.

"It is," Cathy agreed. "She needs to be in a home where we could direct other families to visit her while she's here."

"With the goal that one will want to adopt her?" I asked.

"If it seems right for her," Cathy said. "Look, Rachel, I know you and Clay decided not to adopt last year, so please don't think I'm engineering this situation in the hope that you've changed your mind. We're really in a bind, though, and I know how good you'd be with her."

"When do you need an answer?"

"Tomorrow morning?"

"All right," I said, nothing in my voice to indicate the decimation taking place inside me. I'd perfected this skill, neutrality under the receipt of life's least kind blows.

"I'll e-mail a picture from last summer to you. Call me on the cell if you don't get me at the office," Cathy said. "And Rachel?"

"Yeah?"

"We would love to have you and Clay over for dinner one night. It's been too long."

"Yes, it has," I said, not adding that it was just too painful to sit at a table with a family who still had what we lost. To see how their daughter Amy, once Emma's constant playmate, had grown these past three years. I didn't say any of this because Cathy already knew it.

After I hung up, I sat with the phone in my hand,

not sure what to think. My laptop beeped. New
e-mail. I put my hand on the mouse, clicked on Read.
From Cathy.

Here's the photo. She's darling.

I clicked on the attachment, downloaded the file.
During the few seconds it took to come through, a rush
of anxiety flooded through me.

When the computer beeped, I clicked on Open File
and sat back in my chair. The picture filled the screen.

Above it was the name Sasha Ivanovicha. The girl
looked younger than nine. She stood beside a piece of
faded playground equipment, a tired old building in the
background. She was thin, and her hands were clasped
in front of her, plaited braids hanging to her shoulders.
Her posture was one of sad resignation, but her blue
eyes were hopeful, and it was this that snagged my
heart. Made me wonder if it might be a mistake to bring
this child into our home.

I stared at the photo for a long time, unable to make
myself close the file. It was one thing to be told of a child
in need. Putting a face to the words another thing entirely.

Clay would be against it. I knew this, and yet, staring
at the picture of this little girl—Sasha—I also knew I
could not say no.

Twenty minutes later, I took I-66 to Fairfax, the
traffic light at this time of evening. I felt anxious to get
there now, eager to put this in front of my husband.

The thought of him stirred a well of sadness deep
inside me. Our marriage had become something I never
imagined it would be. Clay and I lived in the same house,
shared the same bed. But we were like two strangers, our

conversations polite, forced. For so long now, we'd been treading water, still afloat, little more than existing, really. I'd told myself a thousand times that eventually we would get back to where we used to be, but the reality of that had become a pinpoint in the distance. As if the tide kept pushing us farther and farther out, and neither of us had the strength to get ourselves back to shore. It hit me with a sudden flutter of hope now that maybe Sasha was exactly what we needed, a reason other than work to get up in the morning.

At forty-two, I had a life that was in most ways ful-filling. A rewarding career as a pediatrician. Still married to the same guy I fell in love with at seventeen. Clay, an attorney who practiced by the principle of not making a living off the misery of others, was actually one of the good guys. And most days, I still couldn't believe my luck in being the woman he chose.

Except that lately I wondered if he now regretted that choice.

We lived in a big house that somehow made a mockery of the future I had once dreamed we would have. We bought it when Emma was two, and I had every reason to believe that we would fill the three extra bedrooms with brothers and sisters for her.

But I'd learned that life didn't always take the path we were so sure it would take, and now I walked through the waiting room of my office each morning, imagin-ing the whispers of the mothers sitting there. Poor Dr. Foster. Such a tragedy. Such a waste. To lose a child like that Emma.

That was when the anger hit me, the force of it so great that I could barely get through the door and down the hall to my office without collapsing beneath the weight of it. How could this be my destiny? On a good day, I asked myself what I did to deserve it. On a bad day, I did not want to know.

From the moment I met Clay Foster, I wanted to be his wife and have his children. I wanted the walls of our home to echo with laughter and silliness, unlike the houses we'd both grown up in as only children.

For a while, we had exactly that. Seven years of exactly that. Emma was like this incredible gift, this streak of sunlight that made us both wonder how we could have been so blessed.

When we lost her, I wanted to die, too. And if it hadn't been for Clay, I think I would have done whatever it took to go with my daughter.

Other people lost children and somehow managed to make their lives work again. That's what the therapist we saw for the first year after Emma's death told us. But it had been three years now. And Clay and I were still trapped in a maze of grief, neither of us able to find our way out.

I had tried to go on. Not because I wanted to. But because I knew I had to. I knew *we* had to, Clay and I. That if we didn't, the black hole that had been sucking at our marriage since Emma died would obliterate any love that had managed to survive.

I pulled into our driveway, pushed the garage remote, and stared at the brick house in front of me. I had once loved coming home to it, loved its warmth and the fact that Clay and I took refuge from the world here together. Now it felt more like a prison.

We'd lost so much. I knew we could never replace

any of it. But I didn't think I could go on the way we'd been. I didn't want to anymore. It was like standing behind some bizarre two-way mirror and watching us morph into some unrecognizable version of ourselves.

Melodramatic, maybe. But Cathy's call felt like a crossroads. Left turn, there was nowhere for us to go. Right turn, a road that might lead us back to something we once were. At this, I felt a lightness inside, recognized it as possibility.

I parked the car inside the garage and cut the engine. I sat for a long time, not moving. I would tell my husband how much I wanted this chance. How much I thought we needed this chance. And if he said no, I'd have no choice but to face where we were. No choice but to finally admit that our marriage was over.

CHAPTER TWO

VOICE MAIL PLAYED a message from Clay. He was working on a case and wouldn't be home until late. Nothing surprising in this, and yet disappointment sat like a rock in my stomach.

Not for the first time, I wondered if he was really working. I wondered if he'd found someone who had managed to take him out of his pain, someone who was not me, who did not remind him of what he no longer had.

I tidied a kitchen that did not need tidying, restacked a set of books on the coffee table in the living room. Clay and I were rarely here, our house too perfect in its un-lived-in state. I felt overwhelmed suddenly by memories of a very different house, a house made a home with its imperfections, toys strewn across the living room floor, Mickey Mouse pajamas thrown just short of the laundry chute, blueberry juice stains on the Oriental rug.

I sank onto the sofa, not bothering to wipe away the tears streaming from my eyes.

I finally went up to bed, lay there staring at the ceiling, rehearsing how I would bring up Cathy's call. I thought about the girl Cathy had asked us to invite into our home, recalled the sadness in her eyes, my heart aching with the unfairness of it.

The last time I looked at the clock, it blinked 2:00 a.m. Clay still wasn't home.

At five-thirty, after a few hours of tossing and turning, I finally got up and went downstairs to make coffee. This wasn't the first time Clay had worked through the night, but I was deeply bothered by it this morning. It felt like a glaring indication of how unbalanced our lives had become, how unsuitable for a child our home was now.

I'd just poured my first cup when I heard him come through the front door, the familiar clunk of his brief-case as he set it on the hardwood floor of the foyer.

I stood at the window facing the backyard, sipping from the pink-and-yellow cup Emma had made me in a mother-daughter pottery class. My hands tightened around it. Clay came into the kitchen and said good-morning.

"Good morning," I replied, taking in his short, dark hair, the lines of fatigue bracketing his blue eyes. He was a fine-looking man, the kind of man women automatically turned their heads to stare at when he entered a room. He continued to look better as he got older, something I could not say about myself.

"Where have you been?" I asked now.

He looked at me, startled, as if I had opened a door we both agreed to keep closed. "Working, Rachel."

"Must be a big case."

"It is," he agreed, cautious, as if he wasn't sure where I was headed with this.

Accusation was the subtext here. We both knew it. And I realized suddenly how much I wanted to doubt him. That I wished he were having an affair. Maybe if it were something as simple as another woman, I would have a fighting chance.

A painful yearning for what we once had nearly overwhelmed me. Clay got himself some coffee, said he was going upstairs to take a shower.

I whirled around and blurted out the whole thing. How Cathy had called. How her agency had a nine-year-old Russian girl whose host family fell through for the summer camp program.

"I want her to stay with us," I added at the end, my voice as firm as I could make it even though my hands were shaking.

Clay blinked, looked shocked, as if he'd been attacked. "We're hardly here, Rachel," he said carefully. "How could we have a child stay with us?"

It was on the tip of my tongue to say we once had a child that fit perfectly well into our lives, but I pressed my lips together and reached for a calm note. "I thought I might take two weeks off," I said.

His eyes widened. This really surprised him. Neither of us had taken any vacation time in three years. I thought how haggard he looked now, how tired, how in need he was of something other than work. He shook his head, retreated a step, said he was going to get that shower, and he'd be back down.

I decided to make him breakfast. I could not remember the last time I did so. Judging by the look on his face when he returned twenty minutes later, neither could he. Clean shaven now, he smelled of soap and shaving cream, his dark hair still wet. He wore his Saturday running clothes.

I made his favorite breakfast, consciously or not I didn't know. He sat down at the table, took a sip of the orange juice, a bite of the scrambled eggs, then put his fork down as if by showing too much enthusiasm he would be giving me the answer I wanted.

"Rachel," he said. "I don't see how we can do this."

I waited a moment, struggled to keep my voice level. "We both have plenty of vacation time we haven't taken."

"When are we talking about?" he asked.

"The children arrive on Monday."

"Monday? Rachel, that's crazy. I'm in the middle of a case. You have appointments booked three months out. We can't just not show up for work."

"I'm not asking you to do that."

Clay hesitated. "What are you asking me to do?" he asked finally.

From my pocket, I pulled the picture Cathy had e-mailed me. I unfolded it and slid it to the center of the table. "Let an orphaned girl live here for two weeks."

He glanced at the photo, stared at me for a moment, his expression weary. "And she just goes back to Russia at the end of it?"

"Yes," I said. "All the children go back at the end."

"Am I wrong, or isn't it the hope that the families will adopt these children?"

I started to answer, stopped, then looked away.

"Rachel," he said quietly. "I thought we had been through this before."

Suddenly, a fierce anger swept through me, out of control. "No, *you've* been through it, Clay. *You* made a decision about the rest of our lives, and I've had no choice but to go along with it."

"I thought we agreed," he said, his voice level with the control that made him such a success in the courtroom.

Somehow, this infuriated me, that he had put me in

the same category as a jury he must somehow convince, and I barely kept myself from screaming. "What choice did you give me? You are the one who changed your mind about adopting. We will never replace Emma. Don't you think I know that? But we are drowning in this, Clay. Both of us."

With that, I ran out of the kitchen, grabbed my purse from the table by the front door and left the house.

I DROVE AROUND for an hour or so, my mind racing in circles. I pulled into the parking lot of the health club where I was a member, grabbed my workout bag from the back of the car, went inside and got on a treadmill. I ran for an hour, shoes pounding, pushing the limits of my endurance. The exertion felt good, as if I could burn away the frustration inside me. When I finished, I took a shower in the women's locker room. Standing under the streaming water, I closed my eyes, Emma's sweet face an instant image in my mind.

I turned my face up to the nozzle, let the spray blend with my tears, my shoulders shaking with silent weeping.

Here, I allowed myself this indulgence without worrying that Clay would see me. That I would deepen his sorrow with a glimpse of mine. It was just one of the awful things about what had happened to us. The way the love for our daughter was no longer something we shared, but had to exist in its own lonely place inside each of us. She had been the most wonderful expression of our love, as if her birth gave it new and redefined life. But she was gone now. And with her, nearly everything of who we were.

I turned off the shower, limp now with resignation

for this place from which Clay and I could not manage to extricate ourselves.

Less than a year ago, I had told him I wanted to adopt. It felt to me like something we could do together, something that would not only allow the two of us to live again, but give a child without a family all the love we had. And at first, he had gone along, our home study complete before he told me he couldn't go through with it. And that was that. Door closed.

I left the club and drove home, letting myself into the house with a quiet defeat that was in direct contrast to the fury marking my earlier departure. In the kitchen, I found Clay sitting at the table exactly where I left him, his coffee cup full in front of him, as if he had not touched it.

But the picture of Sasha now lay in front of him, his thumb resting at the edge.

He glanced up at me, silent for a few moments, and then said, "If this is something you have to do, I'll go along. But don't expect me to be here 24-7. There's no way I can do that."

He got up, put his cup in the sink and left the kitchen. I stood there long after he went upstairs, not sure if I had won or lost.

AT JUST AFTER NINE, I called Cathy and told her we would host Sasha. Sounding both relieved and thrilled, she said, "Thank you, Rachel. This is wonderful. We'll need to update your paperwork, of course. Everything is pretty much the same, isn't it?"

"I guess so, except for an increase in income."

"Great. Fax me your W-2s, and I'll get our social worker to take care of it."

"Sure," I said.

"We'll be meeting the children at Dulles Monday at 1:00 p.m. I'll e-mail you the gate information."

"Okay."

"Oh, and I forgot to mention that Sasha speaks some English from being here last summer."

"That's great," I said, surprised by this and at the same time realizing I hadn't thought about the language barrier being a problem. I wondered if there were other potential issues I hadn't thought through and felt a pang of doubt for my haste in this decision. "Will she know we're not in a position to adopt?"

"The children are here for a summer camp experience," Cathy said. "Because of what happened last year, Sasha knows adoption is a possibility, but we will make sure she knows you are only helping us out because the original family could not participate. And that way, hopefully, we will have done our best not to raise expectations."

"I see," I said, suddenly subdued.

"The first week, just do whatever you think will be fun for her. The second week, she'll need to attend a camp of your choice."

"Okay."

"I'll see you then," Cathy said. "And, Rachel?"

"Yeah?"

"I'm hoping this will be good for all of you."

"Me, too," I said.

I spent the rest of the weekend arranging to take the next two weeks off. The other doctors in my practice seemed shocked at first, but then each offered to take some of my patients when I explained why. Their compassionate understanding reduced me to tears more than once for it was clear that they had made the connection between my desire to do this and the loss of my daughter.

I got the house ready, changed the bed in the guest room, ran out to Target for a couple of age-appropriate videos and a portable CD player.

Through it all, Clay was noticeably absent, working the rest of Saturday and all of Sunday. But I couldn't say anything, knowing I had forced his hand.

CHAPTER THREE

On Monday morning, Clay got ready for work, drank his orange juice at the sink as he always did. I asked him if he would meet me at the airport for Sasha's arrival. He would try, he said, but he had a full day.

At the airport, the host families, all couples except for me and two single mothers, along with representatives from the adoption agency, gathered outside the scheduled arrival terminal. The air nearly crackled with excitement and anticipation. Many of the parents held balloons and stuffed animals. I wished I had thought of this and already felt somehow lacking in this role I'd agreed to take on, as if I had failed Sasha before ever meeting her.

Cathy arrived late, running up to greet me, breathless and glowing in a linen sundress the color of kiwi. "I'm sorry I'm just getting here," she said, pulling me into a quick hug. "Tyler lost his pet rabbit. After we combed the neighborhood, we found her under his bed."

"That's all right," I said, my smile stiff under a pang of envy for the absence of such upsets in my own life.

Cathy spoke to the other parents and representatives from her agency, her manner warm and welcoming. She came back over to stand beside me. "Is Clay coming?" she asked.

I put my gaze just to the left of hers. "He said he would try."

I caught the flash of sympathy on Cathy's face which she quickly erased with a smile. "I met Sasha last year during the program," she said. "I think you're going to like her very much."

"Can you tell me anything else about her?" I asked, realizing suddenly how little I knew.

"She's lived in an orphanage in Siberia since she was four. Her mother died of cancer, and apparently, she had no relatives who were able to take care of her."

"Oh," I said, my heart dropping with the bleakness of the child's situation. It was hard for me to imagine it, and I thought again about those blinders I had been wearing these past three years, refusing to let myself see anyone else's pain, too focused on my own.

I checked my watch every few minutes, and then finally stopped looking. Clay wasn't coming. Why had I let myself pretend he might?

When the gate door opened, and passengers began to stream through, I stood with a knot in my throat, my arms crossed tightly against my chest. Cathy stepped forward to direct the host families to the appropriate child.

Sasha was the last of the children to come through, and I recognized her instantly. She stopped at the edge of the happy throng, looking completely lost. Her blond hair hung in the same braids she had worn in the picture, and she was much smaller than I expected. Shockingly so, as if her body had not had everything it needed to grow. Her clothes looked worn, but clean, and for a moment, I couldn't move. I finally forced myself to step forward, stuck out my hand and said, "I'm Rachel Foster. You're Sasha?"

The girl nodded, glanced at the other families and then back at me. "Oh," I said, "my husband, he's working. You'll meet him later."

Disappointment clouded her eyes. Acceptance quickly replaced it.

Cathy came over, hugged Sasha and said, "You've met my friend Rachel. You two are going to have such fun together."

The children were clearly exhausted, and the agency representatives encouraged everyone to get them home. Cathy explained to Sasha where she would be going. Sasha asked some questions in very accurate English, her accent lovely. Cathy promised to call me later. I led Sasha out to the parking garage, and we drove for a while without talking, the quiet roar of the Volvo taking up the space between us.

"You speak English amazingly well," I said.

Sasha looked out the window. "When they tell me I have chance to come back this summer, I study every day after school with my teacher who speaks English. She help me to learn."

"That's wonderful," I said, hearing the underlying note of determination in the girl's voice. I admired her diligence.

"You speak Russian?" Sasha asked.

"No," I said, wishing suddenly that I did or had at least tried to learn a few words.

At the house, we went inside, and I showed Sasha the kitchen, the rarely used pool out back, the room upstairs I had prepared for her. Sasha's eyes lit up at the

Walkman on the bed, and when I explained that it was for her, she thanked me in a shy voice. I asked her if she would like to take a shower and then come downstairs for a snack.

She appeared relieved at the suggestion, walking into the kitchen a little later smelling of the lemon-scented shampoo and conditioner I had put in the bathroom for her. She ate the grilled cheese sandwich I made her and drank her milk with an appreciation that put a knot in my throat.

We talked a bit. I told her I was a doctor for children. I could see she was visibly intrigued by this. She wanted to be a doctor, too, when she grew up, but for animals. I asked about the place where she lived, and she answered directly.

"It is not a bad place," she said. "The women who take care of me, they are nice, but not my mother."

I blinked hard, my throat tight. "Do you remember her? Your mother?"

"Yes," she said, solemn. "But the memories, they fade. I am afraid they will go for good. I am sad because it is all I have of her."

She sounded much older than her age, and I wondered if her life experience had honed this maturity in her before its natural time. In my practice, I had seen it before, children forced to face incredibly hard things too young. I wanted to say I understood, tell her that I worried my own memories of Emma would eventually fade altogether, but just the thought left me unable to speak. I left the table, carrying some of our dishes to the sink. Sasha helped me, rinsing the plates and stacking them neatly on the counter.

"Thank you," I said when we were done.

"You are welcome," she said, her eyes heavy with fatigue.

"Why don't you go upstairs and take a nap?" I suggested.

She nodded, again looking relieved.

Once she left, I wasn't sure what to do with myself. For so long, this house had been nothing more than a place to sleep. Even though my cooking skills were rusty at best, I decided to fix a special dinner and searched through some recipes, settling on Chicken Cordon Bleu with mashed potatoes and a chocolate torte.

I called Clay and left a message on his voice mail asking if he could be home at six-thirty.

It was six forty-five before Sasha came back down-stairs, pink-cheeked and refreshed. I put the dinner on the table, and at seven when Clay still wasn't home, the two of us sat down to eat. I apologized, unable to make an excuse for him since I could think of none that would begin to justify his not being here.

Sasha's disappointment played clear across her face. She again ate her food with an appreciation I had never before witnessed in a child. Her compliments were sincere, and I heard Emma's voice in my memory, "Mommy, will you make this again tomorrow night, please? It's my favorite."

Clay arrived home around eight o'clock, just as we finished up the dishes in the kitchen. I turned to find him standing in the doorway, staring at Sasha as if he had seen a ghost.

"Clay, this is Sasha. Sasha, this is my husband, Clay."

Sasha stayed close to my side and said hello in a mild

voice. Clay's greeting was short and cool, and the child visibly wilted beneath it.

When he went upstairs to change clothes, I took her to her room to get ready for bed. Quiet, she slipped on the mermaid pajamas I had bought her, brushing her teeth in the bathroom, then getting under the covers. She turned onto her side, facing the wall, away from me. I touched her shoulder briefly, then left the room.

Downstairs in the kitchen, Clay stood by the sink with a glass of water. A hard knot of fury sat in the center of my chest. Not only for his behavior this evening, but for how clearly unreachable he had become to me. "Would it have been so difficult to be kind to her?" I asked in a low, barely controlled voice.

He remained silent for a long moment, and then said evenly, "This is what you wanted, Rachel. I tried to make it clear that I didn't want any part of it."

Stunned by his bluntness, I reached for words. "I have no idea who you are anymore. You are so determined to shut out everyone and everything in your life. Is that what you want? To be alone?" The questions were out before I could stop them, harsh, angry.

Clay held my gaze for a long time, then said, "Sometimes I think it would be the best thing for us both."

There.

How long had I been waiting for him to say exactly this? We had once been inseparable, two halves of the same whole. He started a sentence, I completed it. But the loss of Emma had left a hole in our lives, and through it drained the connection we once shared.

"Maybe you're right," I said, lead in my voice. "Maybe there's just nothing left here for us."

He shook his head, a wrenching pain in his eyes. He started to say something, then stopped.

My heart dropped when he failed to deny what I had said. "Can you stay until Sasha leaves, Clay? Can you at least do that?"

I heard a sound and glanced up to find the child standing in the doorway. She looked at us both, then turned and ran back down the hall and up the stairs.

I lay in bed that night, Clay on the other side, completely lost to me even though mere inches separated us.

Over the past three years, I had existed in a state of quiet despair. Losing Emma, realizing once and for all that she was never coming back, that nothing I did would change that, I had thought I would as soon give up my hold on reality as accept it. The only thing that had gotten me through it all was Clay. He had always been my rock, the one consistent thing in my life.

In the beginning, we had stood together in our grief, hands entwined against the awful blackness of it. But somewhere along the way, our grip on each other had loosened, until we stood apart, alone in our sadness. The gulf between us had widened to the point that we could no longer reach each other. And worst of all, I knew deep down that Clay did not want to be reached. By me or anyone else.

I LAY AWAKE a long time, listening to his even breathing beside me. It seemed like I had just fallen asleep when something woke me. I tried to put definition to the sound, and then bolted from the bed, running as fast as I could down the hall to Sasha's room.

The door was cracked, and I stood with my forehead pressed against the frame.

It was a terrifying sound, her crying. Bottomless. No beginning, no end.

I walked into the room, some part of me reluctant now, my heart thudding hard. How could I even begin to address this little girl's pain?

I eased onto the edge of the bed, flicking on the lamp. She lay on her side, facing the wall, her slim shoulders shaking, deep, heart-wrenching sobs the only break in the silence. I put a hand on her arm. "Sasha?"

She didn't answer. The weeping continued, and it took me a moment to realize that she was asleep. "Sasha?" I said again, this time turning her toward me. She came awake with a start, sat up, her face wet with tears.

"Shh," I said. "You must have been having a bad dream."

She stared at me, confusion narrowing her eyes as if she couldn't place me. Her shoulders collapsed suddenly, the sobs pouring out of her nearly unbearable to hear.

I pulled her into my arms, rubbed her back in awkward reassurance, any mothering skills I might have once possessed long unused. "Can you tell me what's wrong?" I asked.

She said something in Russian then that I didn't understand, except for a single word. Mama.

Something inside me contracted at the sound of it, and I tightened my arms about her. I was not her mother, but I wished in the deepest part of myself for the ability to take away her grief.

We sat this way for a long, long time. The alarm

clock on the nightstand ticked, loud and insistent. After a while, she began to speak again, English with a few Russian words here and there, but not so much that I couldn't understand her. And as the snapshot of her life came into focus, I almost wished that I did not understand at all.

"After Mama become sick," she said, "we never have enough food. Neighbors bring what they can, but they have little. Mama cannot take care of me. I am four. I do not remember everything. But I remember the day she die. She cannot get out of bed. I am scared to leave her. It is many days before someone comes."

For moments, I could not find a single word to respond. "You waited with her that whole time?" I finally asked, the words like gravel in my throat, my voice barely audible.

"I keep thinking she will wake. And I do not want her to be alone."

I pictured this child as she must have been at age four, saw her sitting at the side of a sleeping woman who would never wake again. If anyone had asked me before, I would have said I understood every possible facet there could be to grief. I had lived it inside out. But I realized now that I had no idea what it would be like to lose my mother as Sasha had lost hers, to be taken away from everything I knew, to no longer have a home or family.

And at age nine…even this…being brought to a strange country, introduced to people she did not know.

"Is everything all right?"

I looked up. Clay stood in the doorway, his hair sleep-tousled, concern in his eyes. "She had a bad dream," I said, wondering how to explain everything I had just realized about this young girl. Looking at my husband, I knew I had done an awful thing. This child, this precious, broken child had come here looking for hope.

And I had brought her to a place where there was none.

CHAPTER FOUR

THE NEXT DAY was one of those perfect June days you wish you could shove inside a time capsule and pull out for your own personal pleasure in the middle of a bitter January.

I was determined that Sasha and I would make the most of it, just as we would make the most of her visit here. We ate our breakfast next to the pool—orange juice, English muffins with almond butter and blueberry jam, scrambled eggs with crumbled goat cheese and julienned basil.

"You are good cook," Sasha said, spearing another bite of egg with her fork.

"Thanks," I said, pleased by the compliment as well as the enthusiasm with which she had all but cleaned her plate. "I like trying new things. Although I don't cook very much anymore."

"Why?" she asked.

"Work," I said, shrugging. "I usually get home pretty late."

"You have important job."

"It's important to me."

She considered this, and then said, "It is nice to be able to help people."

"Yes," I said. "It is."

She studied me for a moment. "Your husband. He has important work?"

"He's an attorney." When she looked puzzled, I added, "A lawyer."

"He helps with trouble?"

I smiled. "Sort of."

She toyed with a last bite of English muffin, looked down at her plate, then out at the still surface of the pool. "He does not want me here."

It was a statement, not a question. As if this was not the first time she had perceived this fact about herself. I struggled with how to answer. "It's not about you," I said.

She nodded once, but I could see she didn't believe me. I wanted badly to explain, but found no words.

Instead, I cleared the table, and we both carried the dishes into the kitchen. I rinsed and began putting them in the dishwasher. Sasha watched for a moment, then took a plate from my hand and said, "Please. I help." She stood each one on end in the rack, as careful as if they were precious jewels.

I watched with a lump in my throat, and when she caught me staring, I picked up a dishcloth and began wiping down the counter.

In a few minutes, we were done, and it was nice, working quietly together that way. I felt a keen yearning for something I'd once had and pressed a hand to my middle, closing my eyes for a brief second. In a bright voice, I suggested we go for a swim. I already had on my bathing suit beneath a blue cover-up. Sasha ran upstairs to change, back in a few minutes in the adorable two-piece I had grabbed on my Target run, the boy-cut kind that only girls with no hips could wear. We went outside, and she lingered by the edge of the pool, casting worried glances at the water and then back at me again.

"Is something wrong?" I asked, unzipping my cover-up.

She looked embarrassed, not quite meeting my gaze. "I do not know how to swim," she said.

"Oh." This never occurred to me. "I'm sorry. I assumed…I shouldn't have assumed. It just so happens I taught swimming classes to help put myself through college. Would you like to learn?"

Her face brightened, the half smile I was starting to enjoy coaxing to life appearing at the edges of her mouth.

We began at the shallow end of the pool, wading in and getting comfortable. The water delighted her; her eyes were lit with the pleasure of it. "I never go in pool before," she said.

"Well," I said, clearing my throat, "we can stay in all day if you like."

She smiled and settled lower in the water until it was above her shoulders, her chin resting on its smooth, blue surface.

I started with the basics, getting her comfortable with putting her face under, blowing bubbles, holding her middle while she practiced kicking her feet. She learned quickly, determination clearly etched in her forehead, the set of her jaw.

After an hour, I suggested we rest, but she wasn't ready to stop. Another twenty minutes, and I insisted we relax a bit, afraid she might end up with cramps.

At the far end of the pool sat a small storage house for things Clay and I never used anymore. I hadn't been inside it in years. Dripping water onto the tile floor, I hesitated at the door, then turned the knob quickly and stepped inside. It was exactly as I remembered it, except for the addition of a few large cobwebs. An oversize inflatable whale stood propped in one corner of the room. I stared at it, tears springing to my eyes, sliding down my cheeks. I wiped them away with the back of my hand, then forced my feet to move. I picked up the whale and an electric pump, carried both back to the side of the pool where Sasha stood with her hands clasped in front of her, lips pressed together, eyes dancing.

And I thought then that this was another of life's cruel ironies. That the same thing that could bring one person such simple and complete happiness could bring another nearly intolerable pain.

But then maybe it was the merging of the two that would lead somewhere other than where I had been these past three years.

It was something to hope for.

WHEN CLAY GOT HOME around seven, Sasha and I were back in the pool. With breaks for lunch and dinner and a few snacks in between, we had basically spent the day there. Each time I had suggested changing the activity, her disappointment was so tangible I could not bring myself to insist, although I was beginning to look like an albino prune.

We were, in fact, laughing about our shriveled fingers when Clay appeared by the side of the pool. Our laughter ended abruptly as though an invisible mute button had been pressed. He stared at me as though I was someone he didn't quite recognize, a face from the past he couldn't place. It hit me then that I could not remember the last time I laughed in front of Clay. It felt wrong, as if I had been caught doing something entirely inappropriate.

"Sasha is learning how to swim," I said, sinking into the water until I was up to my chin.

Clay glanced at the plastic whale now bobbing at the other end of the pool. He looked at Sasha and then me. In his eyes, I saw a dark pain that filled me with instant guilt and regret.

Dripping water, Sasha got out of the pool, murmured, "Toilet," and headed for the house.

"Clay," I began, once she was out of sight.

"That was Emma's," he said, his jaw set.

I dropped my gaze. "I know."

He was quiet, and then said, "Are you trying to replace her? Is that what this is about? Is that why you brought her here?"

"No," I shot back, anger rocketing up from some deep place inside me. "How can you say that?"

He stared at me for a long moment, shook his head, before saying, "Is it really that far-fetched?"

And before I could answer, he turned and walked away.

OUR HOUSE WAS QUIET and awkward for the rest of the night. I fixed spaghetti, which Sasha ate with subdued relish, as if she loved it but was afraid to show too much enthusiasm. I wanted to tell her it was all right, that she'd done nothing wrong, but a glance at Clay's clenched jaw sealed the words in my throat.

We sat at our too-formal dining-room table, the three of us, twirling noodles onto listless forks until our plates were empty enough to declare the meal finished.

Clay disappeared in his office off the living room, closing the door. Sasha again helped me in the kitchen, and then gave in when we got to the pots, asking if she could go to bed, her small face etched with weariness. I yearned to scoop her up and carry her to her room myself. But I remembered Clay's face at the pool. And so I folded my arms across my chest instead and said, "Go on up. I'll come tuck you in as soon as I finish here."

"Thank you," she said, stepping forward to give me a quick hug around the waist. I pressed a hand to her back and then watched with a knot in my throat as she left the kitchen on silent feet.

Nearly an hour later, I finally made my way upstairs to check on her. Her room was dark except for the closet light. I stood beside the bed, watching her as she slept, her arms thrown out from her sides in that vulnerable way children sleep. Emma had slept just like that, all the defense mechanisms the world taught her during the day dissolving into the dark.

I turned away, stepping on the sandals Sasha had worn today. I bent down, picked them up and set them inside the closet, another pang of memory for the daily tasks of motherhood hitting me hard. Her Cinderella backpack sat at an angle in the corner. I straightened it, spotting the edge of a paper towel sticking out behind it. I picked it up. Three Oreo cookies and a half-eaten granola bar were tucked neatly inside. I lifted the backpack, found an apple and two browning bananas in the corner.

I stood for a moment staring at the small stash of food, then folded the paper towel, put it all back as it had been and quietly left the room.

DOWNSTAIRS, I MADE COFFEE and sat at the kitchen table, my hands embracing the warm cup even as the thought of drinking it made me nauseous. I considered calling Cathy, but it was after eleven, and I didn't want to wake her.

The coffee had long cooled when Clay walked into the kitchen and set a glass in the sink. He stood for a moment, his shoulders slightly hunched. He turned then, said my name, apology in his voice.

It took this and nothing more to break the dam inside me. I leaned forward, elbows on the table, my face in my hands, the sobs pouring out of me anything but delicate.

"Hey," he said, beside me, his voice soft in a way I hadn't heard it in a long time. It was the one thing he'd never been able to stand, hearing me cry.

I tried to stop, but it was like being caught in the ocean's undertow, impossible to fight.

He sat in the chair beside me, put a hand on my arm, his touch light as if he were afraid I would push him away. At the thought, my tears increased, even though I was the one who had conditioned this response in him.

We sat for a long time, just like that, until my tears were spent.

"What is it, Rach?" he asked.

I shook my head, trying to find the words. "She told me about her mother. She was sick for a long time. They had very little food. When she died, Sasha stayed with her for days, until neighbors found—" I ended it there, my voice breaking.

He studied the tabletop as if there were something there that would tell him what to say. "Rachel, you had to know when you said yes to this that it wouldn't involve a child who'd had a perfect life."

I slid my chair back, stood, a fresh stream of tears making tracks down my face. "Sometimes I'm not sure I even know who you are anymore. You used to be a man with a heart, a man who could feel someone else's pain even through his own. What happened to him, Clay? Where did he go?" And with that, I ran from the room.

CHAPTER FIVE

THE NEXT MORNING, Clay left before I woke. We'd perfected this dance of avoidance, me going to bed first, he
getting up first. I wondered how much longer we could
keep it up.

I said nothing to Sasha about the food in her closet.
But after breakfast, we drove to Whole Foods where I
intended to let her pick out some things she liked. Just
inside the door, I reached for a cart, then asked her if
she'd like to push it. She said yes, smiled a really big
smile and gave it a test circle around a display of potted
herbs. I headed for the produce department, turned to
ask what kind of fruit she wanted. But she had stopped
beside an enormous bin of white peaches, reaching out
to touch one as if she couldn't quite believe it was real.
I walked back. "Do you like peaches?" I asked.

"I never have one," she replied.

"White ones are my favorite," I said, picking up a
plastic bag and beginning to put some in. I held it out
then, so she could add a few. She did so, shyly at first,
as if she wasn't sure how many were acceptable. When
the bag was full, I closed it with a twist tie, and we
wheeled down the aisle, adding Gala apples, plums and
white grapes to our assortment.

We had reached the cereal aisle when she looked at the array of boxes, and said, "Where I am from in Russia, people see this and think it is museum."

"What do you mean?" I asked.

"So much food," she said. "It is like art. No one can afford to buy. Only look."

The starkness of her assessment was striking, and I looked around at the other shoppers, people who, like me, took it all for granted. I wondered how we must look to Sasha. I did not have the courage to ask.

WE SPENT THE AFTERNOON in the pool, and I was amazed by Sasha's progress. She now floated on her back and swam short stretches completely by herself. She soaked up my praise like a child who had been starved of it.

Just before five, the French doors at the back of the house opened, and Clay stepped out, a brown bag in each arm. I was so surprised to see him, I couldn't speak, and when I did, my, "You're home early," came out sounding more accusatory than pleased.

He glanced down at the terra-cotta tile beneath his feet, then met my gaze, apology in his eyes. "I stopped on the way home and bought a few things. Hot dogs, marshmallows and stuff. I thought we could cook out on the grill."

"I— well, yes, that would be good," I said, glancing at Sasha, who looked as startled as I had been by the suggestion.

"Maybe Sasha could give me a hand," Clay said.

"I would like to help," she said.

He nodded once. "Just let me change out of these clothes, and we'll get started."

WHEN YOU'D KNOWN someone as long as I'd known Clay, it was easy to think there were no surprises left. Maybe married people got arrogant that way, or maybe it was just that we simply didn't give each other enough credit.

Sitting at the table by the edge of the pool with my laptop, I thought it more likely the latter. At some point during these past three years, I'd given up on my husband. Accepted that he was no longer the man I'd married. That he was gone to me forever.

But I watched now as he showed Sasha how to turn the hot dogs so they didn't fall through the spaces in the grill, listened to her soft giggle when one slipped through anyway, noted the patience in his smile when he pulled another from the pack and plopped it on. Captured by the frame, I wished I could pause the movie in this exact spot. Because here, I saw a glimpse of the man I married, and a tiny ember of something that once was began to burn in an empty corner of my heart.

ON THURSDAY MORNING, I took Sasha into the city to register for the day camp she was to attend next week as part of the On Angel's Wings program. Once we finished, I called Clay at the office and asked if he would like to meet us at the National Zoo.

A stretch of silence followed the question, and then he said, "Sorry, Rachel. I've got a killer day."

"Oh. Okay," I said, keeping my voice neutral. "I just thought I'd check."

He kept quiet for another moment, as if he were re-considering. I held the cell phone tight against my ear and pressed my lips together, waiting.

"Okay, then," he said. "See you tonight."

"See you tonight," I said. I clicked off, tossed the cell phone back in my purse and glanced at Sasha who had been standing with her arms folded across her chest, staring at the city streets as if she hadn't been listening to the conversation.

But I only had to look at her face to know that she'd heard every word, and felt the same disappointment that I felt at its outcome.

THE ELEPHANTS WERE Sasha's favorite.

We stood outside their fenced area for almost forty-five minutes. They were fascinating, and I tried not to think of the times I stood in this exact spot with Emma, one hand on her shoulder, her excitement tangible beneath my fingers. The elephants had been her favorite, too.

A young woman in a khaki uniform put out hay for the four large creatures who waited patiently for her cue to eat. The caretaker told us one of the elephants had been at the zoo since 1964.

"I never know they live so long," Sasha said, her face lit with wonder. "Do you think they have good life here?"

I considered her question for a few moments, before saying, "Certain parts of it might be better than if they lived in the wild."

"They have food," she agreed. "People who take care of them. Even if they miss their other life, it is good to have place where you are wanted."

I tightened my arm around her shoulder, pulled her closer, giving in to a sudden protective instinct. We stood that way while the elephants ate the rest of their hay, then lumbered to the large sliding door at the back of their building where they waited to be let inside.

WE HAD JUST STOPPED to admire the giraffes when I heard my name and looked around to see Clay walking toward us carrying two mounds of cotton candy, one pink, one blue.

I was so surprised to see him I couldn't speak.

"Hey," he said, lifting both shoulders the way he did when he knew he'd just done something completely out of left field.

"Hey," I said.

"Zoo's not really the same without the junk food."

"No," I agreed.

He held both colors out to Sasha, told her to pick one. She chose pink, her face breaking into a smile of shy delight.

"What is called?" she asked.

"Cotton candy," Clay said. "Try it."

Sasha touched her tongue to it, then took a small bite, her eyes closing. "Mmm," she said. "Good."

Clay smiled, and I could see in his eyes that he was glad to have introduced her to something she'd never had, something capable of bringing such simple happiness.

He glanced at me then, held my gaze, and I felt the memory between us. We were seventeen, and he'd taken me to my first circus, bought me my first taste of cotton candy. It was also the first night he ever kissed me, and I remembered lying awake after he brought me home, not sure which had been sweeter.

In that moment, I missed us with a keen sense of

loss, of who we had been, what we'd once had. I wanted to scream at the unfairness of it, beg for just a single chance to go back. But the words were locked up inside me.

We walked on in silence, the sun high and bright above us. Sasha wanted to see the seals. Clay, the wolves. She ran on ahead. We followed, side by side, our elbows brushing, the cotton candy sweet against my tongue.

THE NEXT MORNING, I decided to make breakfast. The works. Pancakes, bacon, maple syrup with butter. Sasha helped me pour the batter, and I showed her how to wait for the bubbles to appear on the top half before flipping it to the other side. Three slightly burned first efforts, and she was an expert, the next half dozen golden and perfect.

"Something sure smells good."

Clay stood at the kitchen door, a folded newspaper in one hand. He looked unsure of his welcome, as if he had intruded on something to which he hadn't been invited.

"I am learning how to make pancakes," Sasha said. "I may fix you one?"

"I'd love one," Clay said, and I silently thanked him for not mentioning the many lectures I'd given him on artery-clogging breakfasts. Instead, he sat down at the table, unfolded the paper and waited patiently for Sasha to set the plate in front of him. She got one for herself, took the chair next to his, handed him the syrup, then waited for him to pour and pass it back.

He took a bite, chewed for a moment and said, "Mmm. I can't remember the last time I had pancakes. These are really good."

Sasha all but beamed. She sampled her own, then smiled a smile of agreement.

I watched the exchange from the corner of my eye, busying myself at the sink.

"You are having some?" Sasha called out to me.

"In a bit," I said.

The kitchen was silent for a few minutes, except for the sound of knives and forks clinking against plates.

"I notice a spot near the pool where there is no grass," Sasha said once she finished the last bite. "It was once garden?"

I turned from the sink, started to answer, when Clay said, "A long time ago, yes."

"It was your garden?" Sasha asked.

He put down his fork, glanced out the window, took a sip of orange juice. "Yes," he said.

"Mama had summer garden. I help her plant things. Potatoes, carrots. I help you."

I watched with a lump in my throat as Clay struggled to answer. Finally, he got up, dropped his napkin on the table and said, "Thank you, but I don't think anything will grow there anymore."

She hesitated as if she knew she'd said something wrong. "We try," she said, hopeful.

Clay didn't answer, just stood with a sort of stunned look in his eyes, then walked past me and out the front door. A few seconds later, I heard his car start and back out of the driveway.

I forced myself then to look at Sasha. But she avoided my gaze, got up from the table and began clearing away the breakfast things. I wanted to explain, throw light on

Clay's behavior, but I couldn't and we finished tidying the kitchen in an awful, awkward silence.

She spent the rest of the morning watching *Finding Nemo* in the living room while I checked voice mail from the office and returned some phone calls.

Later in the day, we went shopping at Tyson's Corner. In Bloomingdale's, I bought her another swimsuit, two sundresses, shorts, sandals and a pair of Nike running shoes. I had looked forward to bringing her here, but I wondered now if I were somehow trying to make up for Clay's rejection earlier. I wanted to be angry with him. Part of me was. And yet, another part of me understood.

The reminders of Emma were constant. Each one its own needle of pain. None of it was Sasha's fault, and yet the reality was that she brought so much of it back, fresh as yesterday. Had Clay been right all along? Was I wrong to bring her into our home? A sudden, unyielding sense of the irreversible overcame me, on its heels a too-real fear that none of us would escape permanent hurt.

We ate a late lunch at Maggiano's, Sasha picking at her panini sandwich. I did little justice to my own chopped salad, mostly moved it around on the plate. "Sasha," I finally said, "about this morning—"

"It is okay," she interrupted, meeting my gaze with knowing eyes. "You do not have to explain. Thank you for the clothes. I like them very much. But you do not have to spend so much for me. I understand. Even without them."

Something different colored her voice now, and I wasn't sure how to respond to it. "I thought you would enjoy them," I said.

"They are very nice," she said quickly, looking down at her hands.

"What is it, Sasha?" I asked after a bit, sure there was something she had not said.

She remained silent for a few moments, then said, "Last summer, the family I am with...the mama bought me many presents at the end. It is how I know they do not want me. Cathy already tell me you are not able to adopt me. Maybe I hope, anyway."

The words were like a knife to the center of my chest. I stared at this young girl, my fork suspended in midair, my own selfishness sickeningly clear to me. From the moment Cathy called me, I'd had nothing in mind except my own needs. I could not imagine what it must feel like to be Sasha. "Oh, Sasha," I said. "You are a wonderful little girl. Clay and I...what's wrong between us has nothing to do with you." I stopped, struggled for words. "There's something broken inside both of us, and I'm not sure we can ever fix it. I'm sorry. I'm so very sorry."

She studied me with a kind of sad acceptance in her eyes. "Do not worry," she said, and I no longer felt like the adult between us.

A waitress appeared, her smile like a sudden flare of light in the dark, causing me to look away. "Can I get you anything else?"

I asked Sasha if she would like dessert. She shook her head.

"Just the check," I told the waitress. Once I finished paying, we gathered our things and left, most of our food still on the table.

CHAPTER SIX

SASHA WENT TO BED early that night.

Exhausted, I determined to wait up for Clay, but fell asleep in the leather chair where I read at nights in our bedroom.

I came awake with a start, the hardcover novel on my lap sliding to the floor with a thump. I ran a hand through my hair, disoriented at first.

I glanced at the bed, still made, saw that Clay hadn't come home. I heard something then, strained to listen. Realized it was Sasha, crying.

My bare feet pounded the hardwood floor to her room. She wasn't there. In the hallway, I followed the sound and stopped just short of the room at the end.

Emma's room.

I froze, my feet suddenly unwilling to move.

The light was on. I stood in the doorway, one hand to my mouth. Sasha sat at the end of the bed. Clay stood by the window, his hands shoved deep in his pockets, his jaw tight.

"What's wrong?" I asked, even as I realized the ridiculousness of the question when obviously everything that could possibly be wrong was wrong.

"I don't mean to hurt anything," Sasha said. "I see

pictures of little girl in your room. You are so sad. I know she must die."

I looked at Clay, wincing at the stricken look in his eyes. We'd left Emma's room exactly as it was. Her toys stacked neatly on shelves by the window. Books on the nightstand by her bed. A stuffed rabbit propped on her pillows. I came in here when I needed to feel something of her, to see visual evidence that she had actually been here, that I hadn't imagined her. But Clay had not been in Emma's room once since her death. His face was etched now with every ounce of the grief I knew he carried inside him. And I saw what it cost him to be here.

"When I got home, I heard her crying," he said, his voice far-off. "She shouldn't have come in here." With this, he got up and left the room.

I glanced at Sasha who was still quietly weeping, her small shoulders hunched forward.

"Clay—" I called out. But he didn't stop, and I knew he wouldn't. Or couldn't.

I sat next to Sasha on the side of the bed, put my arm around her shoulder. She tucked her face against me, and something near my heart gave.

Her tears made tiny tracks on my khaki pants, and it was like this that I told her about Emma. Sweet Emma. Our only child. How we had lost her in a skiing accident where she had fallen backward on a patch of ice and hit her head. How our world went from bright sunshine to the darkest night either of us could imagine. How Clay and I were no longer the people we used to be. I told her all of this, and when I finished, I sat quiet.

"I am sorry," Sasha said, her eyes brimming with

fresh tears. "For her. For you. I should not come in here tonight. I ruin everything."

"No," I said, smoothing my palm across the back of her hair. "No, sweetie. You've ruined nothing." I thought of Clay then, of how he had closed this room off as if it never existed, the same way he had closed himself off to me. And I added quietly then, "You opened a door tonight, Sasha. Maybe to more than you can know."

WHEN I GOT UP the next morning, I heard the hum of Clay's electric razor coming from his bathroom. I slipped on a robe and walked to Sasha's room, only to find the bed empty.

Downstairs, I called her name, but she didn't answer. Heart pounding now, I walked quickly into the kitchen, spotted an empty juice glass in the sink. The French doors that led to the pool were slightly ajar. I stepped outside. She sat on her knees in the middle of the overrun patch of weeds that had once been Clay's garden. She pulled furiously, tossing each handful onto the growing pile at the edge of the rectangle, purpose in every motion.

The kitchen door opened, and Clay came out. He wore a white T-shirt and the Calvin Klein pajama bottoms I gave him for Christmas last year.

He stood beside me, both of us quiet. This used to be our favorite time of day, early, but light outside. We would sit out here, drinking coffee, talking about our day, what to have for dinner that night.

I felt his gaze on me, glanced up to see the same awareness in his eyes. For the first time in longer than I could remember, neither of us looked away.

"Maybe it's not too late to try some tomatoes," he said, his voice threaded with a subtle uncertainty, as if afraid I might criticize the suggestion. Again, I felt a pang of shame for the pattern of expectation I had set in our relationship.

"I love the yellow ones you used to plant," I said, my voice soft.

"Hargraves may still have a few."

"Mmm. That would be nice."

No words then. Just the two of us staring at each other, maybe seeing each other as we hadn't allowed ourselves to for so long.

He touched my elbow, then walked across the yard where he dropped onto his knees next to Sasha. She looked up at him and smiled. I watched as they pulled and tossed, pulled and tossed, working together until the pile of weeds grew higher and higher, and the rich, dark earth beneath began to show signs of resembling what it once was.

WE WENT TO the eleven o'clock church service, Clay in a suit, me in an ivory dress, Sasha wearing the pink sundress we bought the day before.

We had let this ritual lapse since losing Emma, those times we had been here, present in body, but not heart.

Emma had loved going to church, made her profession of faith when she was six years old. She sang in the children's choir, and on the Sundays when they took part in the service, Clay and I would sit in our pew, hands joined, beaming with parental pride.

Today, we sat with Sasha between us. I felt the gazes of the people around us, curiosity blended with sympathy.

I closed my eyes against the intrusion, forced my focus to the beauty of the music filling the sanctuary.

When the service ended, we made our way down the aisle to the door where Pastor Norman thanked us for coming. He greeted Sasha with a warm welcome, told her how glad he was to have her visiting. A good man, he had been there for Clay and me in some of our blackest hours, but I found it hard to meet his concerned gaze now.

Outside, the Thompsons stopped us with a friendly greeting. They were both close to seventy with a dozen or more grandchildren who rotated shifts at their farm off I-66. Emma had spent a couple of weekends there with one of the younger girls who had been a classmate, coming home with heartfelt pleadings for kittens, puppies and ponies.

"It's so good to see you here, Rachel," Mrs. Thompson said as Clay and Mr. Thompson started a thread of conversation. Her hand touched my arm, her warm gaze shifting to Sasha. "And who is this young beauty?"

"This is Sasha Ivanovicha," I said, my palm resting lightly on her back. "Sasha, this is Mrs. Thompson."

"Hello," Sasha said shyness in her voice.

"Oh," Mrs. Thompson said, as if she had just made a connection. "You must be with the Angel's Wings program I read about in the paper last week."

Sasha nodded once, but before she could answer, Mrs. Thompson looked at me and said, "What a wonderful thing you're doing, Rachel. It must be incredibly hard for you, though."

Sasha looked down at her white sandals. The older woman's insensitivity struck me mute, even though I knew hurting me or this child was the last thing she would ever intend to do. I put my arm around Sasha's shoulders. She looked up at me, as if she, too, were waiting for the answer. I glanced back at Mrs. Thompson, injecting sunshine in the words when I said, "We'd better be going. It was really nice to see you."

Mrs. Thompson answered in a fluster. "Well, of course. I didn't mean to keep you. Take care, dear."

Sasha and I headed for the car then, sat inside until Clay came out. We drove away from the parking lot in silence. I could feel the young girl's disappointment as acutely as I felt Mrs. Thompson's minutes before. She wondered why I didn't answer. I wondered myself.

WHEN WE GOT HOME, I fixed a salad for lunch. None of us appeared to be in the mood for eating.

Once we were done, most of it still on our plates, Clay surprised me by saying, "Maybe I'll take Sasha over to Hargraves with me. I called, and they have a few plants left."

"Oh," I said, unable to hide my shock. "Okay."

"Do you want to go?" he asked, his expression neutral.

"No," I said. "You two go ahead. I have a few things to do around here."

I stood at the living-room window, watching as Clay backed the Tahoe out of the driveway, Sasha's blond head barely visible above the passenger seat window. Déjà vu echoed through me, other Sunday afternoons when Clay had taken Emma out for ice cream, and I'd stayed behind with paperwork as a pretense. The truth was I knew how much Emma loved time alone with her Daddy, and it seemed right to let them have it. I wondered what Clay was thinking now, driving down the same roads he'd driven with Emma, Sasha next to him.

I thought about Mrs. Thompson's remark earlier. Tears welled in my eyes. And it seemed to me that I'd put this little girl in an impossible position, a constant state of comparison with a child for whom we still grieved, would always grieve.

I WAS UPSTAIRS folding laundry when I heard the Tahoe in the driveway, then Clay and Sasha as they walked through the foyer and out the back of the house.

I forced myself to finish the basket, putting everything away before going outside. Both Clay and Sasha knelt along a freshly dug row, several black plastic trays of plants next to them. I listened as he showed her how to remove one from its cup without damaging the roots, then gently break the bottom of the plant apart before setting it down in the ground and covering it with dirt. Sasha watched intently, then repeated the process with the one in her hand.

Clay glanced over his shoulder and sat back as if I'd startled him. "Hey," he said. "I didn't hear you."

"Sorry," I said, folding my arms across my chest. "Found some, huh?"

"Yeah. Some of the leaves are a little yellow, but they should make it."

Sasha looked up at me and smiled. "You will help, Rachel?"

"You two look as if you have it under control," I said.

"Under control?" she repeated.

"Don't need help," I clarified.

"Actually, we could use some help," Clay said,

working another plant free of the plastic. He looked up at me. "That is, if you don't mind getting your hands dirty, Doc."

I stared at him for a moment, too surprised to respond. He was teasing, and I realized it had been so long that I barely recognized it as anything familiar between us. I actually felt myself flush. I glanced away, then back again. "I guess it couldn't hurt my manicure," I said, holding up one hand with its clipped-short nails.

He passed a tray to me. I took it from him and moved around to the row parallel to them. I dropped down on my knees, the moist soil making instant circles on my jeans.

We worked, the three of us, in silence, taking turns with the trowel and spade, passing the watering jug up and down the row. The late-afternoon sun hovered warm on our shoulders. Sweat beads broke across my upper lip. It was good work, hands in the soil, planting something that might eventually thrive beneath a generous touch. I looked up here and there, saw a glimmer of the same conclusion on Clay's face.

At one point, our eyes met, and we were simply in the moment, no past, no future, just the here and now. And it was a good moment. Really, really good.

CHAPTER SEVEN

WHEN WE FINISHED the three rows, we stood back and admired our efforts. The plants were spaced evenly apart, a small stake giving each one the support it needed to grow straight and tall.

"How long before they will have tomatoes?" Sasha asked.

"Maybe the end of August," Clay said.

Sasha was quiet for a moment, and then said, "Maybe you will send me picture of them?"

Clay and I looked at each other, then glanced away, instantly sobered. The realization that she would not be here to see the results of our efforts was like a pin to a helium balloon, deflating us all.

Clay's cell phone rang. He pulled it from his pocket, then turned and walked toward the house, his voice low and serious.

Sasha and I began picking up our tools, stacking the empty containers. We'd just finished cleaning up when Clay rejoined us. He looked at me, dropping the phone in the pocket of his T-shirt. "Mark Evans was in a car wreck last night," he said. "He's okay, but he'll be in the hospital a couple of days. He had a meeting with a client in Manhattan tomorrow morning. I've been asked to stand in for him."

"When do you have to leave?" I asked, pushing away the suspicions I had grown to hate. How could I have thought for even a moment that my husband would lie about such a thing?

"The flight's at six out of Dulles," he said.

"Oh," I said, nodding.

He glanced at Sasha, backed up a step. "I'd better shower and pack."

Sasha and I both stood in the same spot, watching him walk away.

THE NEXT MORNING I drove Sasha to the YMCA in downtown D.C. We went inside, and I got her checked in. We walked to the room where a group of children sat in a circle, chattering happily and hurling paper airplanes at each other.

Sasha reached for my hand, and I was hit with a memory of Emma, first day of school and a wash of tears for the prospect of my leaving her. I glanced at Sasha, noted the stoic set to her small face. Holding on to her hand, I led her away from the room to a quieter spot where I squatted down in front of her. "Would you like me to stay with you today?" I asked.

She bit her lip, struggling with the answer. "I will be fine," she said after a moment.

From my purse, I pulled a piece of notepaper and pen, jotted down my cell number, folded it up and stuck it inside her lunch box. "If you need me for anything at all, ask the instructor to call this number."

She nodded a little too vigorously, her eyes bright.

"I'll be back at one o'clock, okay?"

"Okay."

We walked back to the room. This time, she went inside and found a spot in the circle. I watched for a moment, unable to imagine how much courage it took to do everything she had done these past few days. She looked back at me and waved slightly. I waved back, then turned quickly and walked out of the building, a knot in my throat.

Inside my car, I sat for ten minutes or more, at a complete loss for how to spend the next four hours. Amazing, this, in a life that a week ago spun at a pace so dizzying I never stopped to think about what came next. Loneliness washed over me in a great swamping rush, and I realized with total clarity that this was why I never stopped before. As long as I kept spinning, it was easy enough to keep my aloneness at arm's length. There, I could tell myself I didn't need anyone.

The complete farce of this now seeped up from somewhere deep inside me. I closed my eyes for a moment, then grabbed my cell phone from my purse before letting myself think too long about what I was doing.

Half a minute later, Cathy answered on the other end, concern in her voice. "Is something wrong, Rachel?"

"No," I said. "I just dropped Sasha off at her day camp. Would you...do you have time for a cup of coffee?"

Her silence did not surprise me. I wouldn't have been shocked if she said no. In fact, I wouldn't even blame her. But that wasn't Cathy. "Absolutely," she said. "Name the place."

Her voice carried not a speck of resentment for my lapse these past three years. She was just there, as she always was before, waiting to pick up the threads of our friendship. I felt humbled. And grateful.

WE MET AT A STARBUCKS on Pennsylvania Avenue, arriving at the door at nearly the same moment. She gave me a hug, squeezing tight, as if she had already figured out how much I needed it.

We each ordered a latte from a smiling young woman in smart black frame glasses, then grabbed a corner table by the window.

"I'm so glad you called, Rachel," Cathy said, both hands anchored around her cup.

"Thanks for coming, Cath," I said, meeting her direct gaze. "I've been such a lousy friend."

Cathy shook her head, raised one hand. "Don't, okay. There's no need. I can only imagine where you've been these past three years. And besides, I knew you'd come back eventually."

My eyes welled up at her generosity. But then that was what separated the real friends from the fair-weather ones. They took you back even when you'd shown them your worst. Even when you didn't deserve it.

We talked for a while about inconsequential stuff, before she asked me how things were going with Sasha.

"She's wonderful," I said, hearing the instant warmth in my voice. "An incredible little girl." I told her then about our swimming lessons, how she and Clay started a garden and I ended up helping them.

"That's great, Rachel," Cathy said, her smile warm. "I worried that Clay might not—" She broke off there, as if what she was about to say might offend me.

"He was against having her stay with us," I said, rubbing a thumb around the rim of my cup. "I all but pushed him into it."

She was quiet for a moment before saying, "And now?"

"It was amazing to watch him with her yesterday afternoon. It was like seeing a part of him come alive again."

"I'm so glad," she said. "I think we may have a family interested in meeting Sasha. I expected to have someone sooner, but you just never know."

My heart dropped. I blinked hard and struggled for a response. The words shouldn't have come as a shock. Cathy had told me up-front they hoped to find a home for her. But already, the thought of letting her go felt like a cord that would be painful to sever.

"What about you and Clay?" Cathy asked. "How are you?"

I bit my lower lip, willing my voice to remain even when I said, "I think it may be too late for us."

"What do you mean?" she asked softly.

"We've just closed each other out so completely." I looked away for a moment, and then, almost afraid to say it out loud, added, "I've even wondered if he's having an affair."

"Oh, Rachel," Cathy said. "That doesn't sound like Clay."

"No. But I wouldn't blame him. I haven't exactly been there for him."

"And has he been there for you?"

"He tried, at first. I pushed him away," I said, shaking my head.

"Do you still love him?"

"I don't know," I said, hearing the pain of honesty beneath the words. "I've just been numb. Not wanting to feel anything."

"Rachel," she said, "what you went through…what could be worse? I don't know how you even survived it. But you did. And I have to believe we're meant to go on, do the best we can. You and Clay…I always admired what the two of you had. I've never known a couple who completed each other the way you two did."

I pressed my lips together, unable to meet her gaze. "I guess the truth of it is that we failed each other."

Cathy reached across the table, covered my hand with hers. "That said, there's a place to go from here. You don't have to throw it all away."

I looked at her then, saw the caring in her eyes, realized that we could be talking about our friendship as well as my marriage. I put my other hand on top of hers, squeezed hard. It was a beginning.

THAT AFTERNOON, I picked Sasha up from camp. She jumped in the car, a different child from the subdued girl I dropped off that morning. She chattered happily all the way home, telling me about the swimming class and how they had a contest to see who could collect the most plastic rings from the bottom of the pool. She made a new friend, Suzanne, who shared her jelly sandwich with her and took up for her when a boy made fun of her accent.

When we got home, she admitted to exhaustion. We had an early dinner, and she was in bed by seven-thirty. Clay wouldn't be home until tomorrow night, and so I turned in early, as well, sitting in bed with a book propped in front of me, my thoughts refusing to focus on the words. Instead, I wondered about this family who would like to meet Sasha, but couldn't quite imagine what it would be like to invite them into our house and step aside.

At the same time, I knew this might be Sasha's single

opportunity for finding a permanent home. As much as I wished Clay and I were in a position to offer her that, I knew we were not. Our entire life together was mired in uncertainty, and once she left, I didn't know what would happen between us.

The next morning, Sasha was already up when I came downstairs. Out back, she was on her knees, watering Clay's tomato plants, gently spraying the base of each one with the hose. The expression on her face was one of intense concern, small white teeth tugging at her lower lip.

I scrambled eggs, and she came in a few minutes later, joyfully reporting that each of the plants appeared to be thriving. She couldn't wait to show Clay.

In fact, she stood waiting at the door for him when he got home that evening. I'd just finished fixing dinner when I heard the thump of his briefcase on the foyer floor, the low pitch of his voice against the high enthusiasm of hers.

A minute later, she tugboated him through the kitchen, exclaiming, "You must see! You must see!"

I stood by the stove, arms folded across my chest, a pot holder in one hand. Clay raised his eyebrows at me, a smile at the corners of his mouth. "Hey," he said.

"Hey," I answered back, surprised when he held my gaze and did not look away. "'Jack and the Beanstalk,' huh?"

I followed the two of them outside. Sasha showed Clay the plants, indicating how she made little mounds of dirt around each one to give it support. "I think they will grow well here, yes?" she asked, beaming.

He studied her for a moment, then looked at me and said, "Yes, I think they will."

CHAPTER EIGHT

WHEN WE FINISHED with dinner, Sasha and I loaded the dishwasher. Clay came into the kitchen with a photo album. My stomach dropped at the sight of it, my mouth suddenly so dry I couldn't swallow.

Clay sat down at the table and asked Sasha if she would like to take a look. She wiped her hands on a towel, then took the chair next to him, cautious.

Clay opened the album, and there was Emma as a newborn in my arms. Unlike all the times before, memories flooded me, good and comforting memories.

Clay turned the page, and I walked over to stand behind his chair. Emma. Crawling, walking, riding on her Daddy's shoulders. Sasha studied each photo as if she wanted to know everything there was to know about Emma.

And when he reached the last page, I felt tears sting the back of my eyes. Sasha looked at Clay and said, "Thank you for showing me."

He nodded once, closing the album. "Thank you for looking," he said.

THE NEXT MORNING, I'd just dropped Sasha off at camp when my cell phone rang. Caller ID showed Clay's office number, and I picked it up, a flutter in my stomach at the sound of his voice.

"Do you have anything planned for tonight?" he asked.

"No," I said.

"There's a Disney on Ice show at the coliseum." A pause, as if he weren't sure of my response. "I thought Sasha might like it."

"Oh," I said.

"Yeah, whatever you think."

"I think it would be good."

"Okay," he said.

"Okay." And I hung up, something warm unraveling inside me.

We met him at the main door of the coliseum just before seven that night. Sasha could barely contain her excitement. At the concession stand, we loaded up with popcorn and sno-cones that came in an unnatural shade of blue.

The lights had already dimmed when we got to our seats. Clay and I sat on either side of Sasha, and for the next hour and a half we watched brought-to-life cartoon characters skate across the ice in a series of slapstick high jinks that had her giggling nearly nonstop.

Every so often, I glanced at Clay out of the corner of my eye and found him looking back. A softness floated between us that was new, and yet not, but familiar, as it used to be. My heart actually ached with recognition of it and a yearning for something I knew we were so close to letting go.

When the show was over, we followed the throng outside. Clay walked us to my car. He'd see us at home, he said, then turned to go.

"Wait!" Sasha jumped forward to throw her arms

around his waist. She hugged him hard, her cheek pressed to his midsection. Clay's hands hovered at her shoulders for a moment, and then settled there. When she pulled back to look up at him, there was Christmas in her eyes. "Thank you. I will never forget."

Clay started to say something, stopped, then dropped a sharp nod, before turning and threading his way through the sea of cars.

AFTER GETTING SASHA into bed, I brushed my teeth and put on my pajamas. I heard Clay come in downstairs, but when I came out of the bathroom, he wasn't in the bedroom.

I glanced down the hall and saw the light on in Emma's room. My heart tripped, and I stood for a moment, not sure what to do. My feet moved of their own will, and I stopped just inside the door.

Clay sat on the bed, his back to me, his shoulders bent forward. "Are you all right?" I asked, my voice barely audible.

He nodded, not speaking. I walked over to the bed, spotted the scrapbook on his lap. A hard lump formed in my throat. I pressed my lips together, fighting back tears.

I sat on the bed beside him, several inches of space between us. The drawings were so familiar, preschool, kindergarten, then first grade. It seemed as if it were all just yesterday. Yesterday, and another lifetime.

On the last page of the book was a cutout of an angel. White on a light blue background with clouds drawn like big puffy circles. Emma made this one at summer Bible school. At the bottom, in her childish scrawl were the words:

Angels have wings. My teacher said people go to Heaven at different times. Someday when I go, I want to have wings so I can fly back to see Mama and Daddy if they aren't there yet.

We sat for a long time, a pounding cascade of grief between us.

At some point, Clay reached for my hand, tentative at first, as if sure I would pull away. But I didn't, and instead, linked my fingers through his.

"I don't know if I can ever forgive myself," he said.

The pain in his voice, jagged and raw, took the breath from my lungs. I squeezed his hand hard. "Oh, Clay. What happened to Emma wasn't your fault."

"You didn't want her to go," he said. "I should have listened to you."

"It could just as easily have been something I wanted her to do." It was true, and yet I realized suddenly that somewhere in a hidden spot inside me, I had blamed him. The admission washed over me in a rush, and an unrelenting sense of shame filled me. I had pushed my husband away. And even though I never once said the words out loud, I knew I had let him take responsibility for Emma's death.

Tears fell from my eyes onto our joined hands. I slipped off the bed, onto my knees in front of him. I took his other hand in mine and held on as if it were the only thing keeping me from falling off the edge of the earth. "Oh, Clay. I failed you. Instead of being there for you, I put blame on you. Blame you didn't deserve. My God, I'm so sorry."

I dropped my head onto his knees and wept as if I

would die from it. I longed for his forgiveness, and I didn't think I could go on without it. Clay put his hand to the back of my head, and in his touch, I felt absolution. The kind that can only come from unconditional love.

I looked up, my face wet with tears. He took my hand again. The connection between us had frayed, but the current was still there, a trickle of feeling that recharged within me something I had thought long gone.

Clay closed the book, put it back on the nightstand shelf, all without letting go. He led me out of the room, turned off the light and closed the door.

Without words, we walked down the hall to our own room, stepped into its darkened interior. He closed this door behind us, as well, and we stood facing each other, our gazes direct and searching. And for the first time in so long, I saw my husband before me, this man I had once desired and adored. He was the same, and yet different. Still beautiful to look at, his dark hair falling across his forehead in its haphazard way. His blue eyes no longer certain of what life had ahead for him. There was vulnerability there now, and it was this which filled me with a deep yearning to be the wall between him and any more crashing waves.

With his eyes on mine, he pulled me toward him, until we were almost touching, our joined hands the only thing separating us. We let go then, apart for only a second, before we fell into each other, my arms locking tight around his neck, his around my waist. We held on as if our very existence depended on it.

And, oh, it was so wonderful to be here, locked in my husband's sweet embrace, this place where I used to take refuge from all hurts, large or small. To have deprived myself of this these past three years now seemed beyond the watermark of sanity.

For a long time, we simply held each other, refilling the well of what we had both thought lost to us. After a while, Clay drew back, cupped my face with his hand.

"Rachel," he said. That was all, and yet there were a thousand layers within his voice. I leaned in, kissed one side of his mouth, then the other. He made a low sound of longing, and then sank his lips onto mine, pulling me tight against him.

And it was sweet. So sweet. How could I have forgotten this? But then the truth was I didn't forget. I just didn't want to remember. The truth was I let our marriage die because it was what I thought I deserved.

Tears welled in my eyes now, fell down my face unchecked. Clay wiped them away with his thumb, then kissed my forehead, one hand at either side of my neck. "Thank God," he said. "I thought I had lost you, too."

The words were bracketed in anguish, and I wanted so badly to take that away from him. I unbuttoned his shirt, ran my hands across his chest. I took off my own sweater then. He studied me with a hunger that made me feel things I had not felt in such a long time.

The rest of our clothes found their way to the floor, and at first, I felt vulnerable beneath his gaze. But Clay looked at me exactly the way he used to look at me, as if I were the most beautiful woman he had ever seen. And I remembered how this felt, how amazing it was in this world of disappointments not to be found wanting.

He kissed me then, a kiss filled with such desire, such need. I felt weakened with gratitude by it, and together, we fell onto the bed, entwining ourselves around each other, as if we could not get close enough. I thought of how we had continued to share this bed these past three years, sleeping side by side each night. But it was only now that we were really here together, one again, instead of two.

And when our bodies finally merged as one, I felt the reconnection of what had once been the most important thing in my life. This love between us had made Emma, given us for a brief time a wonderful gift.

Later, Clay held me while I cried, kissed my forehead, said, "Shh, baby, it's okay."

I wanted him to know how happy I felt, so I bit my lip hard to stop. But the kindness in his voice only increased the stream of my tears. Because I knew it was okay. It really was.

CHAPTER NINE

THE NEXT MORNING, I woke to the delicious smell of coffee. A tray sat on the bed beside me, two cups, a French press pot and a single white rose from the bush in our front yard.

I squinted at the alarm clock. Not quite six. I dropped back onto the pillow, closed my eyes, an exquisite sense of contentment coursing through me.

The bathroom door opened, and Clay came out, a towel wrapped around his waist. He stood for a moment, looking at me. "Good morning," he said.

"Good morning."

This was one of the things I had once loved about being married. The cloak of intimacy that followed a night of lovemaking. The way we were at the same time bold and shy with each other.

Clay came over, sat on the side of the bed, ran the backs of his fingers across my hair. There was love in his touch, and I savored its sweetness.

He leaned in, kissed me, tasting of toothpaste, his face now clean shaven. He moved the tray to the night-stand, then joined me beneath the sheet, the towel falling to the floor.

We made love again in the early-morning light, not

so hurried now, as if we finally believed we had time, that neither of us was going anywhere.

The coffee was lukewarm when we got around to pouring ourselves a cup, but I didn't mind. We sat with our backs against the headboard, me in the curve of his arm.

The world felt so much safer here, the two of us facing it side by side.

The phone rang. I sighed and Clay said, "We could ignore it."

"We could," I said, but I had never been one to let a phone go unanswered, so I reached for it, propped the cordless between us and murmured hello.

"Sorry to be calling so early," Cathy said, her voice apologetic. "But I wanted to give you as much notice as possible."

I gripped my cup a little tighter. "What is it, Cathy?"

"The family who would like to meet Sasha," she said. "They've had something come up and have to go out of town today. The only time they'll be able to see her is this morning."

I felt Clay stiffen beside me and realized he could hear the conversation. I put down my coffee cup and swung my legs over the side of the bed, my back to him. "Oh. Okay," I said. "What time?"

"Is nine too early?"

"Ah, no. That's…yes, that's fine."

Cathy hesitated, as if waiting for me to say something. I glanced over my shoulder at Clay, but he wasn't looking at me, his gaze set on something in the distance. I turned away and listened as she told me a little about the family. He was a surgeon. They had three other children. All boys. They'd always wanted a girl.

I murmured acknowledgments at the appropriate times and then hung up a minute or two later, convinced that they would be a wonderful family for Sasha. And yet, I felt as if a plug had been pulled inside me, the last few drops of hope draining away. Neither Clay nor I said anything, silence heavy in the room. Finally, I stood, reached for my robe at the bottom of the bed and shrugged into it.

"I think I'll take a shower," I said, going into the bathroom and closing the door. I flipped on the faucet, hung my robe on the back of the door, then stepped under the streaming water. And only there with the spray drowning out the sound, did I let my tears fall.

WHEN I CAME OUT, Clay was dressed in casual clothes, his hair still wet from his own shower.

"I think I'll work from home today," he said.

Not sure what to think of this, I simply nodded and went downstairs where I made Sasha blueberry pancakes because she loved them. She came down in her pajamas, her ponytail barely contained in its pink rubber band. She smiled at the sight of the pancakes, ate a stack of half a dozen with barely a pause. I refilled her juice glass and keeping my voice casual, said, "A very nice man and woman are coming by this morning to meet you."

She put down her fork, looked up at me, her face suddenly serious. I rushed on, telling her the specifics about them, laying it all out as Cathy had laid it out for me. "They sound like a wonderful family," I added at the end, my voice unnaturally bright.

"*Dah*," she said, nodding. "Yes." She pushed her

plate away then, wiped her mouth with her napkin. "I should dress."

I stood with the orange juice pitcher in my hand, not moving for a long time after the echo of her footsteps on the stairs disappeared. It seemed so wrong, all of this, and at the same time, I realized that I needed to think of what was best for Sasha. That there was every possibility last night would not repeat itself. That Clay and I were only at the brink of finding our way back. That our healing had just begun.

Sasha had an opportunity to be a part of a whole and complete family. How could I stand in the way of that?

I couldn't. I simply couldn't.

THE CRAWFORDS ARRIVED at exactly nine o'clock. Bill and Marion Crawford. Both tall and blond with warm smiles and eyes only for Sasha. Clay invited them into the living room where we all took a seat.

It was so stiff as to be comical, Clay and I sitting side by side on our leather sofa while the other couple asked Sasha so many questions that I finally intervened and suggested she might want to show them the garden we had planted. She did so with enthusiasm, and they stood at the edge of the rich, dark soil with its carefully staked tomato plants, their smiles indulgent.

Mrs. Crawford looked at me and shrugged. "I can't imagine any of our boys putting down their Game boys long enough to plant a garden."

I felt Sasha's gaze on me, as if she were waiting for my response. "This garden was pretty much a lost cause. I think it is one of Sasha's gifts," I said. "Bringing things to life again."

"That's wonderful," Mrs. Crawford said, touching a hand to Sasha's shoulder. "I can tell she's a special little girl."

"Yes," I said. "She is."

Sasha stepped closer and took my hand. I willed myself not to cry.

The Crawfords stayed for another hour or so, and I could not deny my own relief when I closed the door behind them at last.

In the kitchen, Clay and Sasha poured juice into skinny glasses. Awkwardness weighted the room, preventing us from meeting eyes.

"Do you think they liked me?" she asked.

I turned from my spot at the sink, saw that she had directed the question at Clay.

"I'm sure they did," Clay said. "How could they not?"

"Enough to make me their daughter?"

Clay didn't answer for a few moments and then said, "Would you like to be?"

She rubbed her thumb through the condensation on the side of her glass, looking out the kitchen window at our little garden. "I worry if I have a new mama and papa, my mama in Heaven will think I love her no more."

Clay studied the child, emotion playing across his face. "Sometimes, I feel the same way about Emma."

Sasha nodded. "This is why you do not want to be my papa. You are afraid Emma will think you do not love her anymore. I understand."

Unable to listen any longer, I left the kitchen and ran up the stairs, closing myself in the bedroom and sliding down the door onto the floor. I sat with my face in my hands until I heard the downstairs door open and shut,

Clay's car start and pull away. It was cowardly, I knew, hiding here this way, when everything that had happened was my own doing. I could not blame Clay. From the beginning, I knew how he felt. I couldn't pretend otherwise.

A knock startled me out of my misery. "Rachel?"

I jumped up, swiped my hand across my eyes and opened the door. Sasha stood in the hallway, looking uncertain. "Are you all right?" she asked.

"Oh. Yes," I said. "I'm fine. Did Clay—"

"He left just now."

"I guess it's too late for camp today," I said.

Sasha nodded and then said, "Please. Do not be sad. I have so much fun here."

I took her hands, pulled her over to the bed, where we both sat on the edge. "I wish things were different," I said, trying hard to hold back my tears. "I wish I could make them different. You are so special, Sasha."

She put her arms around my neck and squeezed tight. Neither of us said anything more. We didn't need to.

SASHA AND I SPENT the rest of the day at the pool. We ate Ben & Jerry's Phish Food ice cream until we were sure we would sink if we got back in. Sitting there in the late-afternoon sun, I thought about my old life, the one where I spent all my time working so I wouldn't have the energy to see the truth of it.

I didn't want that life back. Amazing how clearly I knew this.

The sun had lost its intensity when I heard the back door open and looked up to see Clay standing there. I saw the uncertainty on his face and realized that I wasn't angry with him.

He walked over and sat down on the lounge chair beside us. His eyes were red, and I could see that he had been crying. He stared at me, quiet. My heart started to pound hard.

"I took some flowers out to Emma's grave this morning," he said. "And I thought about what you said, Sasha. You're right. I have been afraid to let myself love anyone else. Afraid if I did, it would take away my love for Emma. But that's not how love works, is it?"

Sasha bit her lip, as if she weren't sure what to say.

Clay took my hand, then looked at Sasha and said, "Would you like to be our daughter?"

I stared at him, not sure if I had imagined what I thought he said.

"You would be my papa and Rachel would be my mama?" Sasha asked, her pretty face lighting up with hope.

Clay nodded, looking at me.

"I would like that very much," Sasha said.

Clay stood, pulling me up beside him and then lifting Sasha into his arms. And there we were, a family-to-be. Nothing less than a miracle, really. A family.

EPILOGUE

Sasha

THEY ARE COMING for me today.

I've wondered a thousand times if it could really be true. Five months have seemed like a lifetime. Many days, I did not believe it would happen.

I sit on my bed, fully dressed, even though it is not yet light outside. The four other girls in my room still sleep soundly. I feel guilty at the thought of leaving, that they still have no family. But I will not forget them. And I hope that there will be someone for them.

It seems as if the sun will never rise. When it finally does, I wait for the other girls to dress, and we go downstairs for breakfast. But I cannot eat for the butterflies in my stomach and return to the room where I stand by the window, staring out at the glittering snow, my backpack held tight at my side. Christmas will come soon. Mama said we will have a big tree and that I must help to decorate it. I've made something for it.

I unzip my bag and pull out the angel I've worked on after school each day. It is for the top of the Christmas tree. I rub my finger across the words stitched along her skirt.

Emma Foster. Much missed. Forever loved.

A car pulls into the drive at the front of the building. My new mama and papa get out, both looking up at the windows, looking for me. I wave from my room. They wave back, big smiles breaking across their faces. I touch the angel's face one more time and then put her back in my bag. I turn from the window and run down the stairs to meet them. Today, I am going home.

Everything you love about romance...
and more!

Please turn the page for Signature Select™
Bonus Features.

From Here to Maternity

**BONUS
FEATURES
INSIDE**

Pregnancy after Forty— the Risks and the Joy

by Tara Taylor Quinn

I wanted to share with you some of the facts I came across during the extensive research I did while writing *A Second Chance*. The writing of this book—and the research—has become deeply personal to me. Quite a while ago I was contracted to write a story about a woman who becomes a mother in her forties. My brother and I are both in our forties and had both had our families, but I was interested in exploring the topic. It was almost a year later that I actually started writing the book. About that time, I got a call from my brother. He and his wife had taken surgical means—permanent birth control—to have no more children, but somehow they were expecting a baby anyway. Suddenly everything I'd read—and everything I was to read over the next weeks—became very significant to me.

Here's the gist of it. (The same information is repeated in many sources.) In the past thirty-five years, birth rates among older women have increased steadily. According to the National Center for Health statistics, from 1978 to 2000 birth rates among women aged forty to forty-four doubled. The overall conclusion, found in most of the sources I used, is that it is quite common for women in this age bracket to have normal pregnancies and perfectly healthy babies. There *are* risks and I'll get to those, but there are also many things women can do to help lessen their chances of something going amiss. Overall, your chances of having a healthy baby after forty are much greater than not. So, on to the challenges:

- Decrease in fertility—it's just a fact. Women's fertility rates start decreasing in their thirties, so if you're working toward an over-forty pregnancy, be patient! It might take a little (or a lot) longer. But be careful! It happens often enough that being over forty doesn't mean you're safe from the need for birth control if you *don't* want a baby!

- Increase in pregnancy loss. The chance of miscarriage doubles in women over forty. Most sources attribute this increase to genetic abnormalities that the body disposes of naturally.

- Increase in the possibility of multiple births. Due to hormonal changes in a

woman's body as she gets older,
stimulation of the ovaries sometimes
occurs, which leads to multiple ovulations.

- High blood pressure. The chances of
developing high blood pressure during
pregnancy increases in women over forty.
This risk can be reduced with diligent
prenatal care, careful diet and exercise,
and need not pose a serious risk to
mother or baby.

- Gestational diabetes. It's always a
possibility, but the chances are greater
with older women. Again, being on top of
medical care, diet and exercise decreases
the risk of serious complications in
this area.

- Premature birth. The likelihood of early
delivery is only slightly higher in older
women.

- Longer labor, hemorrhaging, increased
chance of caesarean section. Studies show
that older women often experience a
longer second stage labor, which can
cause fetal distress. They also have more
chance of hemorrhaging, due in part to
premature separation of the placenta.
Both of these, and other less common
problems such as abnormal placement of

the placenta and breech positions,
contribute to the higher rate of caesarean
births (which usually alleviate the problem).

- Birth defects. There's no way around this
  one. As women age, their eggs don't
  divide as well and genetic problems can
  occur, but early detection is frequently
  possible through prenatal testing. Genetic
  counseling is available at most hospitals
  as part of prenatal care and is highly
  recommended. The most common birth
  defect, defined as a chromosomal
  abnormality, in women over forty is Down
  syndrome. Some statistics say a woman
  over forty has a six to eight percent chance
  of delivering a baby with a genetic defect.
  Others place women in their twenties
  with a 1 in 1250 chance of delivering a
  chromosomally abnormal child, women
  over forty with a 1 in 100 chance, and
  women at forty-five a 1 in 30 chance. There
  are fairly simple tests, most often
  amniocentesis and chorionic villus
  (usually called CVS), that can detect these
  abnormalities at an early stage of pregnancy.
  The American College of Obstetricians
  and Gynecologists recommends genetic
  testing for pregnant women aged thirty-
  five and older, and states that 95 percent

of the time the testing rules out abnormality. And in the event that a woman of any age delivers a baby with Down syndrome, the future can be a world filled with love. While this defect can cause various levels of mental retardation and sometimes other physical challenges, people with Down syndrome are universally known to be happy, loving individuals who contribute positively to the society in which they live.

A few other important points: Before you conceive, see your doctor to make sure you're in the best possible shape before you proceed. Quit smoking. Don't drink alcohol, and drink caffeine only in moderation, if at all. Start taking prenatal vitamins before you get pregnant. Exercise regularly, but moderately. Eat a lot of fruits and vegetables. After you conceive, be diligent about prenatal visits. Take your vitamins as prescribed. Get plenty of rest. Maintain your doctor-recommended diet. Reduce stress.

There are some advantages to later-in-life childbirth. Older parents often find themselves more realistic in coping with a new baby. In many cases, older parents appear to be more patient and more appreciative of the joy involved in raising a child. They've learned to take time to "smell the roses."

One last note: My little miracle nephew, William Wright Gumser, was born six weeks premature, in June 2005, after a very quick birth that allowed his mother to be up and around in less than twenty-four hours. He was the biggest baby in the neonatal nursery, weighing in at almost six pounds. He spent less time in the hospital than predicted, learning how to suck, swallow and breathe properly. And he is now the darling center of attention at home and the proud owner of his aunt Tara's heart. This is one pregnancy after forty that has thoroughly blessed every single person involved.

Sources:
University of Pennsylvania Health System
www.pennhealth.com/health_info/pregnancy

Parents Canada
www.parentscanada.com/340/
Pregnancy_Later_in_Life.htm

Very Best Baby
www.verybestbaby.com/content/article.asp?
section=pr&id=2002107112419632723

March of Dimes
www.marchofdimes.com/professionals/681_1155.asp

Emory Healthcare
www.emoryhealthcare.org/HealthGate/14711.htm

OBGYN.net
http://www.obgyn.net

University of Utah Health Sciences Center
www.uuhsc.utah.edu/healthinfo/adult/Pregnant/
stats.htm

Heartlink
10 www.family.org

U.S. Census Bureau, Statistical Abstract of the
United States: 2002

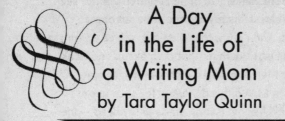

A Day
in the Life of
a Writing Mom
by Tara Taylor Quinn

The eyes open—sunrise is streaming through my bedroom windows, which look over a desert ravine and the mountain towering close behind. Various feelings linger, not quite meshing with the visual stimuli around me. Good or bad, it all depends on the particular dreams I've had— dreams that are always reluctant to be left behind. I ease the transition, silently greeting the fictional people with whom I will be sharing my day. Mark's having a crisis but refusing to see that. And Meredith is strong and determined and in trouble. I'll start chapter seven today. The beginning sentence reveals itself to me....

I stop. I can't write yet. And I don't want the writing that follows to be secondhand goods by the time I get to my computer. I roll out of bed, wake my teenage daughter, Rachel, for school, and climb into the shower. I dry myself and brush my hair and dress and nag my daughter— infusing enthusiasm into my voice for whatever chore she has ahead of her. I pretend not to see when she steals my favorite shirt out of my closet. And I know that Meredith will be wearing a blouse just like that. I put on makeup and think about Meredith's eyes. I choose my jewelry, hearing Meredith's disregard for such useless frivolity. A conversation starts in my head—one between Meredith and Mark. It's important, something I need to know. Even if I'm not ready to know it yet...

"Ma!" Rachel is standing next to me, ready to go. I have to drive her to Arizona State University, where she is the youngest sophomore in the school's history. And because of this, I have to stay on campus with her while she attends class.

She grabs her backpack full of books and notes and far too many pencils and pens. I grab my own backpack, weighted down by the lightest laptop computer I could find. With a quick goodbye to the man of the house, we're out the door. We make a stop at a drive-through for a fast-food breakfast that we eat on the way, listening to a *Phantom of the Opera* soundtrack—the original with Michael Crawford. We both think his voice is phenomenal. I tap in to the emotion, thinking about a love that is so compelling it drives all action. It occurs to me that Mark and Meredith feel that way about each other.

Of course, they don't know it yet. I have to be patient, let them discover this on their own or I could blow the whole thing.

I fight traffic as we get close to campus, and then have to bully my way into one of the few remaining parking spots. Rachel's concerned about her class. She might get a paper back and she doesn't want to know if she didn't do well. I talk to her about her worth as a person and how everything happens as it should. I remind her that she did her best and that is all she can ask of herself. I talk to her about a movie we're going to watch together when we get home.

And I stand with my heart halfway in my throat as she walks into class. I send up a prayer that she did well on the paper—not because I care about her grades at this point, but because I know how hard she'll take it if she didn't. And then I slide my back down the cold cement wall, settle on the floor, unzip my laptop and plug it into the wall socket close by, put on my headphones and become Mark Shepherd and Meredith Foster.

In what seems only a second later, the lecture hall door beside me opens and a flurry of college students spill out, always in a hurry to get someplace else. I bite back my frustration at the interruption right when I was getting to something crucial; I save my work, shut down and pack up, watching for Rachel the entire time. I know the minute I see her that she did well on her paper. I can't wait to get outside and hear what she has to say.

On the way to the next class we talk about the professor's comments. She's afraid of being bored in her next lecture. This professor tends to wander off subject. I tell her to do whatever she needs to do to stay awake—doodle with her colored pens or something—and watch as she walks through the door with a slew of young adults who are so far out of her innocent young league. I always hate that part.

And then I feel the cold brick wall at my back as I slide down, hook up and rejoin the people who are, right now, my closest friends.

Until I'm interrupted again. This time I lug my backpack over to the student union, trying not to pay attention to the pain that's slowly forming in my left hip, and stand in line for lunch. While Rach and I eat, I hear all about whatever topic her last professor got lost in. We discuss the homework she has to do that night. We also talk about the boy she instant-messaged with the night before. She wonders what he meant by certain things. I try to give her insights into kids her age.

And then we're off to dance. Rachel's a member of a professional company in town, and she has class followed by rehearsal. I'm helping with the costuming of the upcoming show and turn my mind to the ways I can make strange pieces of fabric stay in place during total-body gyrations. I've been doing this for years and know many tricks. I just have to figure out which one to pull out of the hat. I think about the dancers in this particular piece, the challenges, and I wonder if Mark and Meredith have ever seen a modern dance performance. Meredith has—once—with her sister. Mark has not. I'm not sure whether they ever will. Or if the information is even pertinent.

An hour later I'm sitting in a darkened theater, unable to write, as the technicians are working on lighting for the show and my laptop throws up a glare. I've seen these pieces performed more times than I've slid down that cold brick wall at ASU. I'm anxious to get to my life, my work. I have a deadline, and not one person there is aware of that—except my daughter. And she cares.

That's all that matters.

I see dancers on the stage. I know they're there, creating movement and shape that I recognize, but suddenly there's a woman in a car. She's rich, but posing as a low-income single woman. She's infiltrating small towns, getting jobs in fast-food places or school cafeterias, looking for her missing five-year-old son, who was abducted while on a ride at an amusement park. As I sit there I'm going from town to town, picking up clues about the whereabouts of this little boy—and then discover that what I thought was a clue wasn't, and I wonder if the whole thing is a figment of the woman's imagination.

Suddenly the lights pop up and I'm blinded for a moment while my eyes adjust to the brightness. Rach is beside me in the theater, her dance bag over her shoulder. I stand up slowly, dazed, call goodbye to everyone and head out into the night. A quick call home reassures me that my husband's had dinner, and it's another pass through a fast-food restaurant for Rachel and me. But this time we wait to eat until we get home.

I eat—not really tasting whatever I've brought home, listening while Rachel tells her father about her day. At least, I'm half listening. The other half of me is on my way into my office and the computer that's waiting there. I have another couple of hours before bed and I think longingly of uninterrupted time with the woman in the car—with me sitting in a comfortable chair.

Rach wanders to the other desk in our home office. I can hear her online, the beeps of her instant messages blending into the Pachelbel's Canon CD I have playing. At some point she laughs out loud. I stop to ask what was so funny and she shares an anecdote from a conversation she's having. It makes me laugh, too.

Hearing my voice, my husband comes in to ask how much longer I'll be. He's waiting up for me. Rach laughs again. I'm thinking Mark and Meredith might end up making love. I look at myself, sitting at my desk with things I love to look at scattered around me, my favorite music playing, the lights low, a lavender candle burning, my family close by, and know that I am very, very lucky.

This is my life. And I am happy.

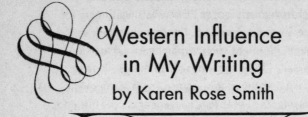

Western Influence in My Writing
by Karen Rose Smith

Exactly how does my love of the West influence my books? I vary settings for my readers—from small towns to ranches to cities. However, my heroes are always men of strong character with a passion for life and abiding values that give them integrity...like cowboys. My heroines are compassionate, independent women with a gift for nurturing...like pioneer women. Am I a cowgirl at heart? You bet. And I know how to recognize a cowboy even if he's wearing a suit!

When I wrote my first "cowboy" romance, I was intrigued by my hero. Something about the cowboy mystique took over and gave the romance a flavor I'd never used before. I was hooked. I'll admit I once had a crush on Roy Rogers, longed to own a horse like Trigger, and as a child was more comfortable in a barn with horses snuffling and kittens playing amidst the hay bales than almost anywhere else. I liked the peace and the animals and the "set apart from the world" feeling. Although I lived in Pennsylvania, I felt an affinity with all things Western and dreamed of someday visiting a "real" ranch out west. But over the course of my career I've also found I'm inspired not only by ranches but by a very special place in Oklahoma that draws me to it again and again.

Oklahoma is a long way from Pennsylvania, but our son lives there now and we visit at least twice a year. Each time we do, we plan an afternoon at the National Cowboy & Western Heritage Museum. The first time we toured it, I'm not sure what I expected. I'm not a museum fan. I'd rather be "experiencing" than "viewing." But the cowboy museum changed my outlook. This is why in my novella *Promoted to Mom* the cowboy museum is a favorite and even romantic dating venue in my couple's history.

Every time I visit this museum I'm uplifted by the architectural beauty of the building and the light pouring in the floor-to-ceiling windows in the lobby where the original plaster statue of Fraser's *The End of the Trail* stands. I usually follow the off-white tile to the galleries. There are sixteen points of interest, but I definitely have my favorites. Even before reaching particular galleries, I can view contemporary artists' work in the hall. I've become acquainted with newer artists—both photographers and oil painters.

Their works capture the West in all its facets—from children on a ranch to the magnificent scenery in Big Sky country.

One of my favorite rooms safeguards and displays the works of Reynolds, Russell and Remington—from bronzes of cowpokes at work to paintings with varying color palettes of the West. I usually want to linger there, absorbing history in a way I could never discover it in a book or on the Worldwide Web.

The Native American gallery is another favorite. The artifacts—clothing, tools and implements—show incomparable creative expertise, particularly in design motifs, from generation to generation. Weaving patterns passed down from mother to daughter and designs—whether abstract or geometrical—are intrinsic to the natural world. I am fascinated by their simplicity as well as their complexity.

For a different view of the ambience of the Old West, I time-travel to Prosperity Junction, the life-size replica of a cattle town with two-story structures, kerosene lamps and even sound effects that make the twenty-first century disappear. From there, as a Roy Rogers fan, I step into the Western performers' gallery—a presentation of how the West has been portrayed in film and books. Moving on, I can easily spend hours at the American Rodeo Gallery, which is interactive and a wonderful source of research for my "cowboy" books.

I can never leave the cowboy museum until I've visited the gardens, lovely with their waterfalls, larger-than-life sculptures and memorials to famous horses. There is one particular secluded spot with a bench and pond where I envisioned my hero proposing to my heroine. With the overhead sun bright, the Oklahoma breeze blowing, the splash of water dribbling over rock gardens, I find a peace that is rare and a contentment from doing the work I love—imbibing the history, struggles and beauty of the West to pour into my books.

I've taken several research trips to the West and each time I visit there, part of my heart remains. On my first trip I was sixteen and rode on a train with my grandparents to California. We stopped only briefly in Albuquerque, but I never forgot the flavor of it or the red bluffs and turquoise sky as we sped through New Mexico. After I wrote my first cowboy book, I decided I needed Western inspiration in Pennsylvania.

Just as writing has seemed to come naturally, I've always enjoyed mixing colors and textures. When our son was small, I was a decorator for Home Interiors and Gifts. I became an expert at coordinating styles, forming groupings and adding color with paint or material. I've always known what colors make me feel good, which fabrics feel formal or comfortable and what knickknacks lift my mood. After we sold our first fixer-upper house to move to a quieter neighborhood, we eventually decided to add a garage with an office above it for me. I wanted this space to reflect my love of the West and Southwest.

I began planning decor for the room with a beautiful Native American vase my son gave me for Christmas that was painted in turquoise, teal and tan. Those were my basic colors. When in doubt I added rust and off-white. I carefully collected decorations from catalogs and a Southwestern shop in Tennessee where our son went to grad school. Every time I walk into my office, the cream buttered-plastered walls, Native American motifs and trading post rugs welcome me and help me invoke my muse.

More recently, after research trips to Albuquerque and Santa Fe, we redecorated our living room. My husband decided he wanted to install a hardwood floor to replace worn carpet. I wanted more of the West in our home. Our living room is now a haven with a blue three-foot-long spirit horse on the wall, chunky oak furniture, Kokopellis and my favorite statues—*The Cowboy's Prayer* and *Welcome Home*—sitting in prominent spots. In Oklahoma I found a candle that actually smells like saddle leather! This year when we took a research trip to Wyoming, we came home with a throw pillow and cowhide mats that went beautifully with the rawhide shades on our handcrafted drum lamps.

When I do have the opportunity to set a book on a farm or west of the Mississippi, I embrace the setting and attempt to give my readers an accurate feel for the scenery, an iota of my love for furry creatures and the fulfilling grounding I feel every time I work in my office or relax in our living room. Whether I write about doctors, lawyers or CEOs, I think my readers will always find the cowboy spirit in each of them. Whether my heroines are stay-at-home moms or businesswomen climbing the ladder to success, they will possess a pioneer spirit. In whatever settings I choose, often my readers will see a horse or feel wide open spaces around them somewhere. My love of the West is part of me as much as my Pennsylvania roots and hopefully they will both always enrich my writing.

Bridge of Hope:
A Real-Life Hosting Program for Russian Orphans

by Inglath Cooper

Dear Readers,

On Angel's Wings is a work of fiction in which I employed full creative license. My story in no way represents the policies, opinions, guidelines or representatives of any such real-life program.

I have worked as a volunteer with a program called Bridge of Hope, a summer camp for older Russian orphans, ages six to eleven. The children in Bridge of Hope come to the United States for a one-month stay with a host family. Many of the children end up being adopted by these families.

Below is a conversation I had with Patrice Gancie, director of the Bridge of Hope program.

IC: Tell us about Bridge of Hope.

PG: Bridge of Hope was started in 1997 by families who'd adopted children from Russia but couldn't forget the kids they saw and left behind in the orphanages—especially the "older" ones, who have little chance of adoption. With this year's program, we'll reach about 380 children who have been hosted and adopted through BOH, and every year our families come home with the same haunted memories.

My own two sons were adopted through BOH in 1998, and my husband and I remember the tug between the happiness of our reunion with our boys at the orphanage and the sad feeling of all those other kids standing by, observing our joy. Our boys entered the orphanage when they were three and five (we adopted them at six and eight), and they still recall being the observers who wondered why families visited and chose only the younger children. Can you imagine such young boys feeling too old to be loved?

IC: What makes Bridge of Hope unique from other programs of this type?

PG: We are one of the oldest, most experienced Russian hosting programs, and we are very proud of our outstanding 90 percent adoption rate for our children. I often tell people that I work for BOH after adopting through this program because we and our children were taken care of so well throughout the hosting and adoption process. Our parent organization, Cradle of Hope Adoption Center, is an international adoption agency founded by adoptive parents and working year-round in Russia. We are committed to protecting our host children and giving host families the best support we can give them. We know that the road to international adoption is often a difficult one. We provide host parent training, social worker and other staff consultation and assistance, dedicated local volunteers (many of them adoptive parents themselves) and an extensive support network for traveling families in Russia.

IC: How did you become involved with the program?

PG: We, like many of our families, felt that fate played a hand. We were in our late forties with no children, but had never been able to agree on adoption. In spring of 1998 a friend forwarded a fund-raising letter for BOH, a program we'd never heard of before, and the idea of being able to host before making an adoption decision struck a chord. What better program for people like us? We decided we didn't want to give money—we wanted to host a child! Even though we called very late in the application process, we were told there were still two sibling groups who needed families. One was two brothers. My husband had always wanted a son, and I had always thought if we ever adopted one child, we should adopt two. That's how our boys came into our lives.

IC: Can you tell us about your sons' experience with Bridge of Hope and your hosting experience?

PG: I remember all of us feeling excitement, joy, panic, so much emotion and exhaustion in that first month! We were astounded at how brave and resilient these little guys were. They gave us courage to work through our own fears about our lack of experience as parents. We had great days of happiness, some of uncertainty, many tears, a few battles of wills. But when BOH asked us halfway through the program what we were thinking about adoption, there was no question—the answer was yes! These were our sons. We wanted to be a family.

IC: What are the age requirements for a couple or single woman hoping to host a child?

PG: BOH is not a host-only program, so we prefer hosts who have a serious interest in adoption. We consider applicants on a case-by-case basis, but generally our host families are married couples or single women between the ages of thirty and sixty. If families are at the older end of this spectrum, they should expect to host older children in our six-to-eleven age group.

IC: What do you see as some of the reasons a family might consider adopting an older child?

PG: Some of our families, like mine, apply at an age when adopting infants or toddlers just isn't feasible. Others have children at home, and the family wants to add an older or younger sibling. Some older families have grown children who have already left home, but the parents feel they have more love to share. Others have always planned that at some point in their lives, they would adopt a child who needs a family.

IC: What's it like when the children finally arrive each summer?

PG: My sons asked if they could give the answer to this question, so here it is. At first the children feel scared, nervous and anxious. They're coming to a new place, and they don't know if their families will be nice or what they are going to do. The children might be very, very shy. They're going to a new land with a new language and new food. When they come to your house, welcome them and show them every room, so they get used to it. But the children are excited, too, once they see how big their bedrooms are, compared to their little rooms or dormitories in the orphanages. Most of the kids will respond to you if you play with them. Have the days planned, so the kids are kept busy.

From mom: On the parents' side, there's a similar mix of feelings. For most families, the hosting experience is the answer to years of longing. At the same time, there's anxiety about language and communication, food, what the children will be like, how the adults will do as parents, whether the experience will live up to their expectations, how to make the adoption decision. But for most families, by the end of the month there's a wonderful sense of comfort, familiarity and belonging together.

IC: Is it difficult for the families when the children return to Russia?

PG: Yes. The children must go back to Russia at the end of the hosting program. This is a sad time for everyone—parents (especially those who plan to adopt their host children), the children and even our staff. We actually give advice to families very early in the process about this, since both parents and children must be prepared for departure. We assure everyone we take very good care of "their" children on the trip back to Russia. And for the children, once they get through the goodbyes, there's a certain excitement about their return to their country and their familiar lives. We encourage families to finish their adoption paperwork as quickly as possible so they can make their own trip to Russia to finalize adoption and bring the children home. And for most regions, we have methods for families to communicate with the children in the meantime.

IC: Tell us about the opportunity for communities to bring Bridge of Hope to their area.

PG: We are always interested in talking with volunteers willing to start a new BOH region. We have guidelines we can provide anyone thinking about starting a local organizing committee. Local volunteers are the heart of our program, but our staff works closely with them, providing guidance and sharing ideas that have worked in our more experienced regions. Some of the tasks include fund-raising, outreach to potential host families, media work and logistical support when the children are here. To bring children to a new region we need about eight to ten host families.

30

IC: How can a family find out more about the program?

PG: Families can check out our Web sites, www.cradlehope.org and www.bridgeofhope.cc, call our office (301/587-4400), or send me an e-mail at pgancie@cradlehope.org. I'm very happy to talk with families about BOH and my own family's experience, as well as put people in touch with other BOH adoptive families.

Where Children Wait

by Inglath Cooper

You've done it all
Stared at a wall
Thought of summer days
And other ways
While sterile hands practice science
Try to make life grow inside you

Nothing works
Still alone
Hope is gone
And then one day
On a warm morning in May
You arrive at a place
Where children wait

Where children wait
Born in a moment that is not theirs
No one to take them home
Call them their own
Call them their own

The building is small
With brightly colored walls
Women in modest clothes with modest smiles
Lead you to a room
Where a little girl waits
In a circle full of children

She smiles
Your heart is hers
If you had only known
Life does not have to be made
But already exists
Where children wait

Where children wait
Born in a moment that is not theirs
No one to take them home
Call them their own
Call them their own

Little hands clap and cheer
Voices raised in words only you can hear
What are they saying, you ask
Irina is going home
We're all going home
As soon as our mama and papa come

So sure, so certain they are
And then you're in the car
Trusting child tucked between you
Your daughter now
A glance back, children waving from a window
Waiting for their mama and papa to come

Where children wait
Born in a moment that is not theirs
No one to take them home
Call them their own
Call them their own

—Inglath Cooper

The much-anticipated conclusion to this gripping, powerful continuity!

THE FORTUNES OF TEXAS:™ *Reunion*

The Reckoning

by

national bestselling author

Christie Ridgway

Keeping a promise to Ryan Fortune,
FBI agent Emmett Jamison offers his help to
Linda Faraday, a former agent now rebuilding
her life. Attracted to him, yet reluctant to
complicate her life further, Linda must learn
that she is a stronger person than she realizes.

On sale May.

Silhouette®

Where love comes alive™

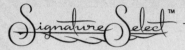

COMING NEXT MONTH

Signature Select Spotlight
ANGEL EYES by Myrna Mackenzie
Her special clairvoyant ability has led to painful betrayal for
Sarah Tucker, leading her far from home in search of peace and
normalcy. But an emergency brings her back, throwing her
headlong into her past—and into the passionate but wary arms
of police officer Luke Packard.

Signature Select Collection
PERFECT TIMING by Julie Kenner, Nancy Warren, Jo Leigh
What if the best sex you ever had was two hundred years ago...
or eighty years ago...or sixty years ago? Three bestselling authors
explore the question in this brand-new anthology in which three
heroines travel back in time to find love!

Signature Select Saga
KILLING ME SOFTLY by Jenna Mills
Brutally attacked and presumed dead, investigative reporter
Savannah Trahan assumes a new identity and a new life—but is
determined to investigate her own "murder." She soon learns how
deep deception can lie...and that a second chance at love should
not be denied.

Signature Select Miniseries
NEW ORLEANS NIGHTS by Julie Elizabeth Leto
The protector becomes the pursuer in two editorially connected
tales about finding forbidden love with the bodyguard amidst
murder and mystery in New Orleans.

Signature Select Showcase
ALINOR by Roberta Gellis
Ian de Vipont offers marriage to widow Alinor Lemagne as
protection from ruthless King John. His offer is sensible, but Alinor
cannot deny the passion that Ian arouses within her. Can their
newfound love weather the political unrest within England?

Fortunes of Texas Reunion, Book #12
THE RECKONING by Christie Ridgway
Keeping a promise to Ryan Fortune, FBI agent Emmett Jamison
offers his help to Linda Faraday, a former agent now rebuilding her
life. Attracted to him yet reluctant to complicate her life further,
Linda must learn that she is a stronger person than she realizes.

SIGCNM0406

Signature Select™

TARA TAYLOR QUINN

Though she wrote her first story at the age of six, Tara's professional writing career began ten years later when she was hired as a stringer with the *Dayton Daily News* in Dayton, Ohio. Tara's first book, *Yesterday's Secrets,* published in October 1993, was a finalist for the Romance Writers of America's prestigious RITA® Award. Her subsequent work has earned her finalist status for the National Readers' Choice Award and the Holt Medallion, plus another two RITA® Award nominations. A prolific writer, she has forty-two novels, three novellas and an Internet story published. Tara is a past president of the Romance Writers of America association. When she's not writing or fulfilling speaking engagements, she enjoys traveling and spending time with family and friends. Readers can contact Tara at P.O. Box 13584, Mesa, Arizona 85216, or visit her Web site at www.tarataylorquinn.com.

KAREN ROSE SMITH

Karen Rose Smith, award-winning author of over forty published novels, loves to write. She began putting pen to paper in high school when she discovered poetry as a creative outlet. Also writing for her high school newspaper, intending to teach someday, she never suspected crafting emotional and romantic stories would become her life's work! Married for thirty-four years, she and her husband reside in Pennsylvania with their two cats, Ebbie and London. Readers can e-mail Karen through her Web site at www.karenrosesmith.com, or write to her at P.O. Box 1545, Hanover, PA 17331.

INGLATH COOPER

Inglath Cooper is s RITA® Award-winning author of six published novels. Her books focus on the dynamics of relationships, those between a man and a woman, mother and daughter, sisters, friends. Her stories are often peopled with characters who reflect the values and traditions of the small Virginia town where she grew up.